# RUNAWAY

# RUNAWAY

a novel

## CLAIR M. POULSON

Covenant Communications, Inc.

Cover image by Don Farrall © Photodisc Green/Getty Images

Cover design copyrighted 2004 by Covenant Communications, Inc.

Published by Covenant Communications, Inc.
American Fork, Utah

Printed in Canada
First Printing: February 2004

11 10 09 08 07 06 05 04     10 9 8 7 6 5 4 3 2 1

ISBN 1-59156-396-8

# DEDICATION

To my wonderful family.
They are the ones who make my life full and rich.
The good times we enjoy together create
memories that will never fade.

# ACKNOWLEDGMENTS

I appreciate the wonderful, friendly people of Abaco. They are truly unique. Had I not gotten to know a number of them, this book would never have happened. I also wish to express appreciation to my high school geology teacher, Bill Lewis, who helped me understand what the black hole referred to in this book really is. No one on the island who knew of its existence—and many did not—could explain what it was. There were many theories, but Bill unraveled the mystery for me.

# PROLOGUE

Winning a case was not an everyday occurrence for the county's contract defense attorney. Meredith Marchant handled the cases the courts ordered her to take and did the best she could to ensure her clients a fair day in court. She enjoyed her work, and she felt like she was good at it. But winning with a clear finding of "not guilty" by a judge or jury—or even by persuading the prosecutor that his case was weak and he should move the court for a dismissal—just wasn't her fate very often. Most of her *victories* weren't victories at all, just plea bargains.

So why did she feel so empty now as she walked back into the courtroom to join her client? After all, she was about to win. The county attorney had just thrown in the towel on this one. And unlike most of her cases, the man sitting at the defense table waiting for her return was not a typical client. He'd contacted her at her office, dropped two thousand dollars on her desk in hundred dollar bills, and said smugly, "The cops ain't got a case, and it's your job to prove it for me."

She had agreed to defend him, but certainly not because he was a nice man, nor because she was convinced he had been framed by Detectives Osborne and Fauler. The money had been the deciding factor. Any case she took in addition to her court-appointed ones helped her save for the future.

"Well, is he going to drop it?" her client asked with a sneer.

"Of course," she said as brightly as she could muster.

Her client sat back with a satisfied grin on his face, not a word of thanks for her efforts. She glanced at him as she waited for the judge to enter the courtroom. Except for his eyes, her client looked the part of a successful businessman. She supposed he was, but she was almost certain that his business was anything but honest.

The client's eyes caught hers, and once again she was vaguely aware of the impression that there was an evil person within the facade of honesty and integrity he was trying to put on. But those eyes made her skin crawl, and they caused a slight panic in her heart. She silently prayed that after the next few minutes, she would never see this man again in her life.

Desmond R. Devaney was the name his Alabama driver's license gave him. But if Meredith had to guess, she'd say that New England was more likely the area of the country where he'd come from.

The judge entered the courtroom. Meredith and her client stood, as did everyone else. After being seated, the county attorney rose and said, "Your Honor, due to new information that has just come to my attention, I am, in the interest of justice, moving the court to dismiss the state's case of aggravated assault against Mr. Desmond Devaney."

"Is that so?" the judge said as he leaned forward and peered menacingly at the prosecutor. "Twenty minutes ago you talked like you were ready to set the matter for trial. What sort of new information are you basing your motion on?"

"Ms. Marchant, counsel for the defendant, just revealed to me that she has located several witnesses who are prepared to testify that the defendant was at a social gathering in Roosevelt at the time the assault occurred in Duchesne."

"I see," the judge said. His stern gaze turned on Meredith. "How many witnesses?" he asked.

"Six, Your Honor," she said as she rose to her feet.

The judge continued to stare at her for several seconds as if that figure were suspect, then looked in the direction of the prosecutor. "Your motion is granted; the charges are dismissed, and we are adjourned," he said with a shake of his head and rap of his gavel.

There was a groan from behind her, and Meredith turned in her seat. Luke Osborne and the new detective, Enos Fauler, were shaking their heads in dismay. Her client rose to his feet and pushed his chair back. Two men on the second row of seats were looking right at him as he turned toward them. One, a good-looking fellow of maybe twenty-one or twenty-two, grinned at him and gave a thumbs-up. The second, older, sober, and with a surly face, simply nodded. Then they both left the courtroom. Meredith's client turned to her and said, "Maybe those two detectives learned a lesson today," before quickly moving away.

Meredith gathered up her papers and then followed him into the lobby. She spotted the rich, auburn hair of her young daughter and smiled in her direction. Deedee's face was flushed and her hair wind-blown. *She must have ridden her bike up here from town,* Meredith thought to herself. She froze as her client approached Deedee and she heard him say, "Hey, babe, you're very pretty. Need a lift to town?"

Meredith stepped forward quickly and shouted as she neared them, "Get away from her, Desmond!"

He turned around, apparently surprised at her protest, but didn't say a word until she walked up and put a protective arm around Deedee. His attempt at an innocent smile was marred by the slight leer, and he said, "Just being friendly to the girl, Counselor. Know her, do you?"

"She's my daughter," Meredith fumed, "and she doesn't need a ride with you."

Desmond's face grew dark, and he turned to Deedee. "Would you like a lift?" he asked again defiantly.

Meredith was suddenly so angry that she clenched her fists, ready to claw his eyes out if he so much as touched Deedee. Then a tall presence appeared beside her, and Enos Fauler said, "Why don't you just leave, mister? Is this any way to thank the lady who just saved your guilty hide?"

Desmond bristled and looked up at the tall detective. "It won't be any too soon. Not exactly my kind of town." He moved toward the door, but as he pushed it open, he made one last parting shot, looking straight at Meredith's thirteen-year-old daughter. "I'll see you again, beautiful."

For a big man, Enos Fauler moved awfully fast. He had to, or Meredith Marchant would have lit into her former client. Enos deftly stepped in front of her, effectively blocking the way as Desmond smugly left the courthouse.

Everyone in the lobby had been watching the tense drama unfold, and Meredith was suddenly embarrassed. "Thanks," she said to Detective Fauler, whose gaze suddenly dropped to the floor.

"He's not a nice man," the detective said without looking up.

Deedee moved to her mother and clutched her arm. Her eyes were wide. "Who was that horrible man?" she asked with a trembling voice.

Meredith tried to appear calm. "No one you ever want to know. He was a client of mine."

"He scares me," Deedee said.

"He scares me too, sweetheart," Meredith replied even as she was trying to stop her shaking hands.

"I don't dare ride my bike home now," the girl added.

At that moment, Detective Luke Osborne arrived. "Enos and I will see that your bike gets back to your house. You go on home with your mother."

"Thanks, Luke," Meredith said, then added, "I've defended some creepy people over the past few years, but that guy takes the cake."

"You got him off," Luke reminded her with a lopsided grin.

"Well, I did have six signed affidavits from people who are willing to testify that he was in Roosevelt the night your victim got himself beaten up. And you've got to admit that your victim is not exactly a nice guy himself."

Luke nodded in agreement, then turned to Deedee, who was still clinging to her mother. "He'll be out of town in no time. You don't need to worry about him. He knows that if he ever shows up here again, Detective Fauler and I will be on him like glue."

At the mention of the new detective's name, Meredith glanced at Detective Fauler. She met his eyes, and he immediately dropped his gaze. Luke smiled and said, "We'll be seeing you around. We'll get that bike back down to your place in a few minutes."

Just then the sheriff's secretary came in. "Luke," she said breathlessly, "a detective from Los Angeles says he sent you an e-mail you might want to look at. It's about the case you have today. He says it's very important."

Meredith felt a sinking in her stomach as Luke replied, "The case is over, but I'll come have a look anyway. Maybe you'd like to join us, Meredith."

As they walked the few yards to the sheriff's office, Luke couldn't help but notice the way Enos glanced at Meredith. *Maybe I ought to try to line those two up,* he thought. He also thought about Deedee, her young daughter. She was already as pretty as her mother, and even though she was only thirteen, she looked every bit of sixteen. *The boys will be after her long before her mother's ready for it,* he concluded.

Meredith interrupted his thoughts as they entered the lobby of the sheriff's office. "Did you notice those men who were seated two rows behind me in the courtroom, Luke?"

"I did notice, actually. The young one is Stuart something-or-other. I've never seen the older one before. Why?"

"Oh, nothing, I just wondered what they were doing in the courtroom."

"I wondered too," Luke said.

Deedee visited with the sheriff's secretary while Luke, Enos, and Meredith checked Luke's e-mail. None of them looked more distressed than Meredith over what they learned. The man who called himself Desmond R. Devaney looked suspiciously similar to a man the detective in Los Angeles knew as Jim White, a man suspected of international slave trading—women, mostly young prostitutes, who came up missing from time to time. Yet there was no way to know if they were actually the same person.

"Probably not," Luke said when he noticed the anguished look on Meredith's face.

"He saw Deedee," Meredith said softly. "He threatened her."

# CHAPTER 1

**Two years later**

"You don't even know Stu!" Deedee screamed in anger as she leaped to her feet from the sofa.

"I hardly know you anymore," her mother answered, willing herself to stay calm.

"It would be better for you if I hadn't ever been born."

"Maybe better for you too," Meredith said. "Don't think it's easy raising a teenager."

"Maybe I ought to just leave," Deedee shouted. "You don't want me here anyway."

"Sometimes you make me feel like that," her mother retorted. "Don't think my life wouldn't be more peaceful without you." She regretted those horrible words the second she'd spoken them. Deedee was her life, and she loved her more than anything in the world.

The fifteen-year-old glared at her mother for a moment, then her eyes filled with tears, and she spun away as she shouted, "I hate you!"

Meredith took a deep breath as the door to Deedee's bedroom slammed. She wiped at her eyes and slowly sank to the sofa, dropping her head into her hands. Deedee's stinging words cut deep.

Being a single parent was not an easy thing.

Being an only child wasn't easy for Deedee, who had also been rejected by a father she never got to know. Meredith's marriage had lasted just over a year. She'd married too young, hadn't really gotten to know her fiancé, and had seriously underestimated the strains of married life. He'd left her when Deedee was only a couple of months old. She hadn't seen him since, and the one who had paid the greatest price for his treachery was Deedee.

It was hard not to cry. Meredith loved Deedee, and she'd worked hard to provide for her, to raise her and give her the opportunities she deserved. But earning a good living meant many hours spent away from the girl, many hours that Meredith now realized should have been spent building more of a relationship, with the stability Deedee needed. Life had become a balancing act, one at which she thought she'd been doing quite well. She now admitted in her sorrow that it hadn't been quite so successful.

The years she'd spent getting through college and then law school had meant many days during which she'd interacted very little with her young daughter. But the time they did have together had always been special, and she'd always believed they'd been as close as a mother and daughter could be. Following admittance to the Utah Bar, money became less of a problem as Meredith established a successful law practice in rural northeastern Utah. But finding time to spend with Deedee became more of a problem as Meredith found herself working long, hard hours.

There had also been several men in her life, for Meredith was both attractive and fairly well off. However, she had resisted all serious advances, choosing to sacrifice romance during some of the best years of her life in deference to her daughter. While her decision may have broken some hearts along the way, the only heart she really cared about had been Deedee's.

Even though there was never enough time to do everything she would have liked to have done with or for her daughter, things seemed to be going fine. Then . . . well, Meredith was unsure just when the serious problems between her and Deedee began to develop. It was almost as if she woke up one day to discover a stranger in their house. And now, scarcely a day went by without a serious disagreement. Deedee was sluffing school occasionally, and she was balking at going to church, sometimes outrightly refusing to go. Something had to change, Meredith decided, and only she could bring about that change. She had to sacrifice whatever she must, for Deedee was her life.

Meredith stood, wiped her eyes as she entered her bedroom, and approached a mirror. She brushed her long red hair, applied some makeup to her cheeks, then brushed on a little eye shadow in an attempt to give life to her green eyes, eyes that usually were bright but were now dull with pain, worry, and regret. She hated what she'd just said to Deedee. She couldn't believe she'd done it, and she certainly hadn't meant it. She forced a smile onto her face and then looked herself over, resolving to mend things with Deedee, to treat her with more respect, more trust. And for some strange reason, she felt she had to look good for her.

Finally, feeling that she looked as cheerful and pretty as she was capable of at the moment, she turned away from the mirror and headed for Deedee's room. There would be no shouting, no recriminations, no anger. She'd offer a sincere apology and somehow demonstrate to Deedee that she loved her. She tapped softly on the door.

"Deedee, honey," she called softly.

She wasn't surprised when there was no answer. Deedee had recently perfected the art of administering the silent treatment. Meredith turned the knob and stepped into the room. "Deedee," she said as she looked around the room for her daughter, "I love you, sweetheart. I'm sorry for what I said. I didn't mean it. We need to talk. You talk, and I'll listen."

Meredith stopped. A cool breeze stirred the curtains of Deedee's open window. The closet door was also open. Dresser drawers were pulled out, their contents spilled carelessly about; clothes were strung across the floor and bed. A quick check in Deedee's bathroom revealed that her makeup kit and other essentials were gone. A hollow pit developed deep in Meredith's stomach as she looked in the large walk-in closet for Deedee's suitcase, also missing from its usual place.

Deedee had threatened to run away before, but she'd never seemed to mean it and had certainly never attempted it. Meredith approached the window as if in a trance and parted the curtains, peering into the deep blackness of the night. In despair she realized that she didn't have any idea where Deedee might go. She didn't know where to begin to search. But search she must.

And search she did after several intense and tearful minutes on her knees, pleading with her Father in Heaven for both forgiveness and help.

By morning Meredith realized that Deedee's anger and determination had run far deeper than she'd thought. None of the girl's friends had seen her or heard from her, and the sheriff concluded shortly after ten in the morning that Deedee must have caught a ride out of town. Meredith was enveloped with fear and pain that threatened to destroy her sanity.

Deedee, though only fifteen, looked three or four years older than that. At 5'5", she was still a couple of inches shorter than her mother, but she had inherited her good looks and attractive figure. Her auburn hair was long and thick, hanging halfway down her back. Her eyes, a dark brown like her father's, were expressive as well as pretty. Slim, willowy, even a little athletic, Deedee attracted boys much older than her.

It had been about one of those older men that they had argued. Meredith had reminded Deedee that dating before sixteen was simply out of the question—especially dating someone like Stu Chandler, a seemingly well-to-do twenty-four-year-old from the eastern end of the county. Meredith knew Stu had been giving Deedee some attention lately, and she had forbidden her daughter from seeing him again when Deedee mentioned that Stu had asked her out.

And now, looking back, Meredith couldn't even be sure if Deedee had been asking permission to date him or if she'd only wanted someone to talk to about the whole thing. Meredith had blown up so quickly that she hadn't even taken the time to learn what Deedee's response to Stu had been. Now, with her despair deepening, she suspected where Deedee had gone—toward the very man she had hoped to stop the girl from associating with, a man she feared might not be unlike Deedee's own unfaithful and unstable father.

# CHAPTER 2

Enos Fauler knew that staring at the door of his office wouldn't relieve him of the resentment at his new assignment. Because he was single, had very little social life, and had only been on the department for a little over two years, he seemed to always get the jobs others didn't want. In this case, it was an assignment that could possibly take him out of town for days. No one cared that he had dogs to be fed, horses to be taken care of, wheel lines to be moved, a garden to weed, and a dozen other chores that he attended to daily. It was not like he could pick up and leave to work on a case out of town any easier than any of the men who had families. In fact, it was probably harder for him, for he didn't have sons to do his chores and a wife to watch after the place. For him to leave took considerable arranging. And to think that he was going to be looking for the badly spoiled daughter of that lawyer, Meredith Marchant, a woman who was so attractive that he found it hard to even talk to her. It was almost more than he could bear.

A corner of his mind forced him to admit that he wouldn't mind finding Deedee for Meredith if it meant impressing her a little. But how could he just leave town for who knows how long and leave his farm unattended?

Enos pushed himself back from his desk and stood up. He stretched his long, lean, muscular frame and then reached for his sport coat, thinking mostly of Meredith Marchant. She'd never given him a second look, he was sure. He felt like she always looked down at him, even though she was only about 5'7", and he was four inches over six feet. It was foolish of him to even think about her the way he did. But he couldn't help it.

Her daughter had been gone for a week, and he knew he'd better get busy and see if he could find where she'd gone. Within a few minutes, Enos had discovered that Deedee's bank card had been used only once, and that was in Cedar City, where she'd withdrawn a thousand dollars from her account the very day she'd been reported missing!

What was Ms. Marchant thinking, letting a girl that young have access to that kind of money? Enos asked himself. But who was he to question what she did? After all, he'd never even been married, let alone tried to raise a child. It was probably very difficult for Meredith.

Enos knew that Stu Chandler was also gone, as was his car. Normally, Stu being out of the area would have meant nothing to anyone. He was viewed by officers all across the county as a lazy playboy. They all wondered where he got his money, but they'd never really tied him to any crimes. Yet the fact that he'd disappeared when he did—the same time Deedee Marchant vanished—was too much to be considered a mere coincidence. And now he, Detective Enos Fauler, was expected to find and bring the two of them back— Deedee Marchant to her harried mother and Stu Chandler to jail! He prayed that by some miracle he could pull it off.

* * *

"You assigned Enos Fauler?" Meredith asked the sheriff doubtfully. "Isn't he too shy for an assignment like this? When someone tries to speak to him, he just ducks his head and goes red. Maybe you should assign Luke Osborne."

Sheriff Robinson grinned. He liked Meredith, and he'd noticed several times the way Enos looked at her. He also knew that if it wasn't for the stress she was under, she'd probably never suggest that anyone else be assigned. "Meredith," he said as he wiped the grin from his face, "Enos is a little shy, but not like you think."

"I can hardly get him to look at me," she argued.

"Oh, he looks at you, Meredith, but maybe not when he's speaking to you. He's just fine around most people, women included," the sheriff said. "Around you he's shy."

Meredith blushed. She'd never realized it before, but the sheriff could be right. She had certainly noticed Enos. And she admitted to herself that if he'd ever had the courage to ask her out, she probably would have accepted. But this was not the time for those kind of thoughts. The question was whether Detective Fauler could find her daughter. She asked the sheriff just that.

"Yes, I believe he can, Meredith," the sheriff said with such conviction that it surprised her. "Enos is real smart, and he's persistent. I was lucky to get him away from Weber County. He was one of their top detectives. He worked every kind of case imaginable for them, including kidnapping and murder. They offered him a lot more money to stay there when I offered him a job. I could never have persuaded him to come if it hadn't been for the farm he found and bought out here. He was looking for a place in a rural area where he could have a few animals and a quiet life."

Meredith shook her long red hair and rubbed a hand over her tired eyes. She still wasn't totally convinced that Detective Fauler was the man for the job, despite his experience in a much larger department, but if the sheriff was that confident of him, she guessed she'd better make the best of it. Then an idea struck her.

"All right, I'll take your word on his ability, Sheriff. I just hope he'll talk to me because I plan to find someone to handle my cases for me if he has to leave the county, and it looks like he will. I'm going with him," she announced.

The sheriff rose to his feet. "Don't be silly, Meredith," he said. "You'd only make it harder for Enos. You'd make him very uncomfortable."

"Not as uncomfortable as I'd be sitting here worrying about Deedee while he's out following leads. I've made up my mind. I'm going if he does."

Sheriff Robinson walked around his desk. "Please, Meredith, don't make this more difficult than it already is. You know I can't send a civilian with an officer, especially a woman with a man."

Meredith forced a grin. "You're not sending me anywhere, Sheriff. I'd be doing it on my own. Anyway, we're both single, and if you're worried about us getting *romantically* involved, I doubt that very much."

"You're a civilian, and he's— " the sheriff tried again.

"Look, forget it. You're probably right," Meredith interrupted as her mind leaped ahead. "Send him, but I pray that he can find my little girl."

Tears moistened her eyes as she turned away, but resolve settled in her heart. She was going to look for her daughter herself. She'd follow Enos Fauler if he would let her, and she intended to use whatever powers she possessed to convince him to do so, no matter how uncomfortable it might make him.

\* \* \*

The unmarked patrol car idled in the street outside Stu Chandler's apartment in Roosevelt. Enos, after an hour of failed effort in finding someone to care for his animals, had been grateful to Luke Osborne. Luke had offered to take care of things free of charge for however long Enos was out of town. The two had been good friends since meeting three years earlier while working on a case that had roots in both Weber and Duchesne Counties. When they discovered their common interest in horses, Luke had invited Enos to his ranch for a few days, and Enos had made up his mind that he would one day find a place of his own where he could have a few horses and a few acres.

Then a detective position had come open in Duchesne at the same time the ideal little ranch was listed for sale. Luke had given Enos a call, and the rest was history. Enos had a left a relatively big and bustling department for a small one. And he'd never regretted it.

Enos turned off the ignition and approached the door to Stu's apartment. He didn't expect an answer to his knock, and there was none, but he had to begin somewhere. He turned his attention to the neighboring apartments. He found someone home at the apartment of the third door he knocked on. A young woman who was clearly both pregnant and suffering from a hangover leaned against the door frame. "Stu's gone," she said with a slur. "Ain't you heard? He run off with that lady lawyer's kid."

Enos thanked her and started to turn away. He jerked back when she added, "They cleaned out a bunch of his stuff before they left."

"Before they left?" Enos asked in surprise. He thought that Chandler had hurriedly left his apartment a week earlier and that he had left his belongings behind.

"Yeah, they woke me up when they come. They wasn't long. They just got a bunch more of his stuff and took off again."

"When?" Enos asked.

"Last night," the girl said as if Enos should have known. "They was arguing too. She said she wanted to go home, that she'd only meant to run away for a little while. He said a few more days wouldn't hurt her mom none, that they hadn't been gone all that long. She said she'd have been home days ago if it was up to her. He said that maybe her mom wouldn't be so stupid if the girl stayed away a little longer. She finally said okay, for just a few days."

"What else did you hear?" Enos asked.

"Nothing. I wasn't *trying* to listen. Ain't none of my business," she said with a shrug and shut the door with a bang.

Enos turned away, worried. Now he *knew* that Deedee was with Stu. And he feared that Stu was influencing her in a way that could cause her to do things she might not really want to do. If his neighbor was right, Stu was manipulating Deedee into staying with him. But Enos also wondered if Deedee might, by some miracle, have changed her mind after leaving Stu's apartment and persuaded him to take her home, as she seemed to want to get back to her mother. He hurried to his car and punched in the Marchants' number on his cell phone.

When Meredith answered, he fumbled for a moment for words, irritated that he had such a difficult time talking to her. It had always been this way when he tried to approach single women whom he was attracted to. It was especially difficult with women like Meredith, who were not only pretty but much more educated than himself. While he knew he was a very good detective, he still felt inferior to Meredith.

He forced the words out. "Good morning, Ms. Marchant. Have you seen Deedee this morning?" he asked, praying that she'd give a positive response but fearing that she would not.

"No," she said tentatively, a tone of hope in her voice. "Is she back in town?"

Disappointed, Enos wasn't sure what to say next. He had only called to make sure Deedee had indeed left again after returning to the area with Stu Chandler the night before. He hadn't meant to build up Meredith's hopes unnecessarily. As he searched for what to say next, he heard her sniffle and realized she was crying. He felt somewhat foolish. As much as he thought he might know about how she felt right now, he realized he couldn't possibly understand.

"I'm sorry, Ms. Marchant," he mumbled, then hesitated.

"So why are you calling?" she demanded. He could hear a touch of anger in her voice.

Enos was certain she was hurting and frightened, and it made his own heart ache. "I just left Stu Chandler's apartment building. He and Deedee were there for a little while last night during the night," he said.

He heard her gasp. "She came back?"

"It appears that way," he answered. "I'm just trying to find out if she might have returned home."

"She's not here," Meredith reminded him a little curtly. "Have you checked with her friends?"

"Not yet. I just wanted to be sure she wasn't there before I started looking again." He paused, wondering what to say next. Not that he needed to say anything. He'd found out what he called to know. Deedee was still missing. He was tempted to just hang up right then. Meredith was so hard for him to talk to. But Enos Fauler was not rude, and he definitely didn't want to risk making Meredith angry. Instead he said, "Thanks for your help, Ms. Marchant. I'll let you know as soon as I know more. I'm sorry if I startled you. I'll call when I find something else out."

Enos took a deep breath after telling Meredith good-bye and disconnecting. He had a job to do, and he'd better keep at it, he told himself. Deedee Marchant was in trouble. It might be of her own making, but she was just a kid and she needed help. Then he thought of one more question he should have asked Meredith, one that could be critical. He started to redial his phone, then decided against it.

His one last question would best be answered if he were to go to the Marchant home, in spite of how difficult that might be. So he headed back to Duchesne, using his cell phone to check with the list of Deedee's friends he'd been given.

* * *

Meredith dropped her head into her hands and sobbed. She was so frightened for Deedee, and she was ashamed that she'd been sharp with Detective Fauler. He was only trying to do what he'd been asked to do, she admitted reluctantly to herself. She resolved to be more patient with him, to try to be as helpful as possible. After all, if he had to leave town to search for her daughter, offending him or adding to his distress wouldn't make him want her around.

She absently ran a comb through her hair and wondered why, if Deedee had been in Roosevelt last night, she hadn't come home. She was startled when the doorbell rang. Surely Deedee was missing her by now, Meredith thought sadly as she turned toward the front door.

"I'm sorry to disturb you again," Detective Fauler said when she opened the door and stared at him in surprise.

She remembered her resolve and said, "I'm sorry if I was a bit sharp with you when you called. I'm just so worried about Deedee. Have you learned something else already? Is she with a friend?"

Enos shook his head, dragging his eyes up until they met hers. She forced herself to smile at him, and he turned just the slightest shade of pink. "None of them have seen her. But there's also something I forgot to ask you," he said.

As his eyes darted away, she admitted reluctantly that he was really quite an attractive man. But she quickly rid herself of that unbidden thought and said, "Please come in, Detective."

Enos stepped timidly across the threshold, brushing her blouse lightly as he passed her. She closed the door behind him, then turned and said, "Why don't you sit down." As he moved toward the sofa, she, to her absolute dismay and his discomfort, choked up and had to fight to keep from embarrassing herself with a flood of tears.

Enos spoke in his usual soft manner. "I'm sorry if I've upset you," he said after sitting down. "I'll do whatever I can to find your daughter. But I do need to know one other thing."

She nodded as she took control of her emotions. He paused, took a breath, forced himself to look Meredith Marchant in the eye, and then asked, "Is there any chance at all that she came here last night and got any more of her things?"

Meredith looked at him blankly for a moment, then said more sharply than she intended, "She hasn't been here. I told you that on the phone."

"Well," he began, anxious to get this over with and leave, "I know you didn't see her, but they were at Stu's during the night, and his clothes and some personal property were apparently taken. I'm glad she hasn't been here and taken anything else. It's a good sign that maybe she intends to come home soon. A neighbor who overheard them talking said that it sounded to her like Deedee wanted to come back but let Stu talk her out of it."

A sharp pain developed in the pit of Meredith's stomach, and she suddenly felt very weak. "Of course she wants to come back," she said, wringing her hands and fighting for control of her emotions. "She knows I love her. What did he say to make her decide not to come home?" she asked.

"The witness, a neighbor, wasn't really clear on what she heard, but Stu apparently argued that you'd want her back more if she was gone longer, and that you'd . . ." Enos paused. He didn't know how to say what he'd heard.

"Go ahead," Meredith insisted. "He said I'd what?"

Enos took a deep breath, then said, "He told her you'd treat her better."

"I guess he's right," she said forcefully, surprising Enos. "But then, I already know that I have to do that. I want to do that. I wish she were here so I could talk to her, to tell her how I feel."

"You're sure she didn't sneak in during the night and pick up any more of her things?" Enos asked.

"I don't think so, but let's make sure," Meredith mumbled as she rose shakily to her feet and motioned for him to follow. She led the way through the house to her daughter's room and gasped when she opened the door. She had spent over an hour straightening up Deedee's room a couple of days ago. She remembered shutting every drawer after picking up the things the girl had left behind. And now, again, a couple of drawers were hanging open.

Enos watched helplessly. He knew without Meredith saying anything that Deedee had indeed returned and that she had taken more of her belongings and left. But Meredith finally turned to him and said, "You were right. She's been here. She must have taken one of my suitcases and put more of her clothes in it."

"I'll send the APB nationwide," Enos said awkwardly as Meredith's voice broke. "And I'll get a warrant for Stu if the county attorney will give me an information document, charging Stu with kidnapping."

"And why wouldn't he?" she asked. Then she nodded her head sadly and answered her own question. "She went willingly. Kidnapping charges might not stick."

"Maybe, although we don't know for sure that he didn't force her at some point to leave the state with him," Enos said. "It appears that he might be using some psychological force against her. I hope to convince the prosecutor to sign an information document, and if he will, I'm sure I can get a judge to issue the warrant. Stu will get stopped somewhere," Enos said. "We'll get Deedee back, and we'll find a way to put Stu behind bars."

Meredith nodded, or at least it looked like a nod to Enos. He took that as agreement, mumbled an awkward good-bye, and turned to leave. But Meredith stopped him when she said, "Detective, I've never met Stu. I saw Deedee and a couple of her friends with him one day, but they were across the street and I didn't get a good look at him. From everything I've heard, he's not anyone a mother would want her daughter to be with. But no one can tell me anything really bad about him. What about you? Do you think he's dangerous?"

Enos turned back and forced his eyes to meet hers. "I don't know. I hope not. I'm told he is actually a local boy, born and raised in Roosevelt. He's been gone from the area a few times, sometimes for long periods, but he always returns. He doesn't hang out with the right crowd, but other than that, we really don't know much about him."

However, Enos also remembered something he thought Meredith must have forgotten, but he wasn't sure he wanted to worry her more by reminding her. It was probably not important, he tried to convince himself. She noticed his hesitation and asked, "You know something you're not telling me, don't you?"

"I really don't know anything more about him. Nobody seems to," he said evasively, dropping his eyes and turning partly away from her.

"Please, Detective, if you know something about him, please tell me," she urged. "I don't ever remember seeing him in court, and I'm there a lot, you know."

Yes, he knew. And she *had* seen Stu there at least once; she just didn't recall it. "I better get going," he said to her.

But Meredith was convinced that Enos knew more than he was saying. She pressed harder. "Have I seen him in court?" she asked. "Please, if I've forgotten something, help me remember. I handle so many cases that I can't even remember all my own clients, let alone others in court that I'm not dealing directly with. Please, Detective, I have to know all I can about the man my little girl is with."

Enos had a hard time looking her in the eye, but finally, knowing that she deserved the truth, he forced himself to face her again and look up. Then he said, "He wasn't your client. He wasn't even in trouble. He was just there once during one of your cases. You asked Luke if he knew who he was."

The memory suddenly came back to Meredith. She covered her mouth, tears filling her eyes. "Oh, Detective," she whispered, "he's the one Luke told me was called Stuart, isn't he? I never made the connection. He's the one who seemed to be a friend of that terrible man I helped beat the charges you and Luke had brought—the one who threatened Deedee."

Enos could only nod.

"He, I mean my client, was possibly involved in terrible crimes where young women were being kidnapped and sold into slave trade in third world countries," she said as she pulled out a chair and collapsed into it.

"We don't know that," Enos said, trying to reassure her.

"But he could have been," she said. "And Stu was his friend . . . Would Stu . . ." She couldn't complete her thought.

Enos backed toward the door. "That other man hasn't been around since then. Believe me, Luke and I have watched. I'm sure Stu doesn't have anything to do with him now. Probably barely knew him then," he said. "Like I just told you, Stu doesn't seem to hang around with the best people."

Meredith didn't answer. Her head was in her hands. Enos opened the door and quietly left her to grieve and worry alone.

* * *

With her legs curled up beneath her, Deedee stared out the window at the countryside as it flew by. Not a word had passed between her and Stu for over an hour. Her attraction to him and her fascination with him were gone. Oh, they'd had fun these past few days, but he was becoming possessive of her. She actually had to get angry with him to stop his unwanted advances. She knew exactly what he ultimately wanted, and it had alarmed her when he tried to book them both into the same motel room that first night, the one they spent in St. George before leaving the state and going on to Los Angeles. The thought that such a thing might be on his mind had made her angry, and she'd let him know she wasn't *that* kind of girl.

He hadn't tried it again, but he obviously wanted to. As angry as she'd been at her mother when she left, she wasn't ready to throw away *everything* she'd been taught. And she felt lucky that Stu hadn't pressed her about it since. But she was homesick now; she couldn't believe they'd been back in Duchesne and that she'd let Stu talk her into leaving again. She'd been ready to forgive her mother, and had hoped her mother would forgive her. But Stu had somehow convinced her that she needed to make her mother really worry if she wanted to have more freedom in her life when she returned. He'd told her that if she went back now, things would be better for a short time, but after that, her mother would treat her just as she had before.

He'd told Deedee that he'd been through the same thing with his parents. He also reminded her of what her mother had said—that she would probably be better off without her. While Deedee hadn't really believed that her mother had meant that, Stu was persuasive, partially convincing her that her mother was serious. Still, Deedee knew that her mother would be worried. Surely Stu wasn't completely right, she thought now. Things would probably be better if she went home. She missed her mother a great deal, and she had to admit that all the contention had not been only her mother's fault.

"What are you thinking about, Deedee?" Stu asked.

"Things," she said evasively as she rubbed away her tears.

"Like what?" he asked, his voice gentle. She looked away from the window, and he smiled at her. "You're getting prettier every day,

Deedee," he said in a husky voice that suddenly frightened her. Despite enjoying some of her time with Stu these past few days, Deedee was beginning to admit to herself that he not only wanted more from her than she was willing to give, but he was probably capable of simply taking it. That thought frightened her. She found that she missed the security of her mother's rules. After all, she told herself, she was only fifteen, even if people thought she looked a lot older than that. Turning back to the window, she again gazed morosely at the rolling scenery.

"Your thoughts?" Stu pressed. He sounded understanding, his voice gentle and sweet. Maybe he'd understand now, she thought hopefully.

Without looking at him, she said, "I think I better go back now, Stu. Mom's probably worried enough. I don't want to make her worry more."

Deedee was not prepared for the response she got from Stu. When she'd hinted before that she wanted to go home, he'd convinced her that a little more time would make her mother more understanding of her when she returned. That response was long gone.

"Go back!" he shouted furiously. "You don't really think that's possible, do you? Your mother is glad to be rid of you, Deedee. I'm sure she doesn't even want you back. And they'll charge me with kidnapping if I take you home! No, girl, we can't go back. Not now. Not ever. You made your decision—now you've got to live with it."

A chill rippled through her, and Deedee suddenly became very frightened. What had she done? "Kidnapping?" she asked, her voice quivering. "They can't do that to you, can they?"

"Yes, they can," he said angrily with a sideways glance at her. "They can and they will."

"But why? You didn't make me go with you," she said even as she realized that he had probably used every means of persuasion to keep her with him.

"It's the difference in our ages," he said. "Your mother could have me arrested. If I take you back, I'll go to prison. You don't want me to go to prison, do you, after helping you get away from a mother who really doesn't care about you anymore?"

"Of course not, Stu, but—"

"I'll take care of you, Deedee," he interrupted, his voice softer now. "I've got money, you know. We can travel and have a good time."

He reached across the car and touched her quivering shoulders as he drove. "I care about you," he said. She moved a little closer to him at his insistence, and he put his arm around her. She didn't want him to go to prison, but she also didn't want to be with him anymore. He was beginning to frighten her. His dark good looks and easy flow of money weren't everything. What should she do? Then she had a thought.

"They don't *know* I'm with you, do they?" she asked. "There's no way anyone knows where I've gone. And I promise, Stu, I won't tell anyone when I get back. Then they can't arrest you. I'll just catch a bus and tell them I've been riding buses for the past few days. They can't prove I wasn't."

Stu's fingers dug into her shoulder. "What about my nosy neighbor?" he asked. "You don't think she'll tell the cops she saw us together?"

Deedee gasped. They'd both thought the woman was peeking out of the window in the middle of the night as they carried things to his car. "Oh." She felt sick.

"Yeah, oh," Stu mocked. "You see, it's me and you now, baby. You can't ever go back unless you want me to go to jail."

Deedee said nothing more. She simply pulled her legs more tightly beneath her and turned her face to the window, blinking back the tears that were stinging her eyes. What had she gotten herself into? What could she ever do now?

# CHAPTER 3

So far, Enos hadn't had to leave the county or his farm in the course of the investigation. There was no place to go. Three more days had passed, and not a single serious lead had developed as to where Stu and Deedee had gone. He came into the office that morning to find Meredith waiting for him. She looked tired and worn, and it made him feel terrible. She didn't deserve to be so miserable. When she looked at him, he noticed that her eyes were red and puffy. They were always red these days, he thought sadly, and he wondered how much time she spent crying.

"What are you doing now to find my daughter?" she asked, her eyes blinking rapidly as if she were fighting back more tears. "Is there something I can do to help?"

Enos felt himself redden, and he looked awkwardly at his highly polished boots. He couldn't quite make out his reflection in them, but he knew that if he could, he wouldn't like what he saw. He couldn't help the shyness he always felt in her presence, but he was ashamed of it at times like this. He knew that he had to look her in the eye when he answered. He squared his shoulders, dragged his eyes from his boots, and looked in Meredith's general direction. "I'm doing everything I can think of," he answered.

"*Exactly* what are you doing?" she asked before he could elaborate. "And *exactly* how can I help?" She suddenly sounded very lawyerlike, and he felt intimidated in a different way.

Enos gritted his teeth and nodded in the direction of his little office. Without another word, he headed there himself and, upon entering the cramped confines, pointed to a chair. She sat. He sat, again failing to meet her steady but anguished gaze.

"I've had her picture distributed nationwide along with a picture of Stu and the license number and description of his car," he began. "And I've put a tracer on Deedee's credit card and her bank card as well as on three cards that I've located in Stu's name. Airports have been notified. The FBI has been notified, but they say that unless we have proof that Stu has left the state with her and that it was against her will, they won't get involved. Oh, and I've also talked to all of your daughter's friends again, as well as every acquaintance of Stu Chandler's I can locate. They all insist that he isn't with her, despite his neighbor's comments to me that indicate otherwise. And I have the warrant that I obtained listed on NCIC, the National Crime Index Computer. I honestly don't know what you can do to help."

Enos had just completed an amazingly long speech considering who he was talking to, but he wished he could tell her something more positive. He squirmed as a silence settled over the office. Finally he managed to force his eyes to meet hers, unable to help but notice what a bright green they were but how sad and worried she seemed. "Do you have any suggestions, Counselor?" he asked in a very formal tone. "I'm open to any idea that might get your daughter back to you."

Meredith could tell that he was sincere, and she was grateful for that, but she couldn't think of a single suggestion beyond what he'd already done. So she rose to her feet and said softly, "Thank you, Detective. Please keep me posted," and left his office. She hadn't meant to leave so quickly, but the last thing she wanted right now was for him to see her tears, and they were flowing freely by the time she turned up the hallway.

Enos rubbed his square jaw, feeling a sudden sadness come over him. He knew Meredith was suffering in ways he couldn't possibly understand. He honestly wished he knew what else to do. In the meantime, he could only wait for further developments.

* * *

Several states and hundreds of miles to the east, further developments were occurring. "Why do you need to buy another car?" Deedee asked. "What's wrong with this one? It's almost new, isn't it?"

"Nothing's wrong with this car," he told her sharply. "I just don't want to get stopped in it and have the license plate number come up hot."

"Hot?" Deedee asked. "What do you mean?"

"Your mom's friends at the sheriff's office might have put out one of those APB things on it," he told her. "You know, an all-points bulletin. The cops are probably looking for us all across the country. Your mom doesn't want you to come home, I'm sure, but she might want me put in jail and you in foster care."

"But Mom's a defense attorney," Deedee said with some confusion. "She defends the people the cops arrest. The cops aren't her friends—she works against them."

"Don't kid yourself, Deedee. All the lawyers and all the cops are in it together." He smiled smugly. "I ought to know."

Deedee suddenly remembered her mother telling her that Stu seemed like the kind who had probably been in trouble with the law sometime in his past. Even though she hadn't believed her mother then, she realized now she'd probably been right. Still, she didn't want to be responsible for him going to prison, and he'd convinced her that it would happen if she returned home.

Stu went on. "Anyway, as much as I hate to part with this car, we don't have much of a future if I don't. Come on, we're in this thing together. I'll let you help me pick one out. It'll be *our* car, Deedee."

Deedee didn't want to share a car with Stu, but she tried to cheer up as he began to walk across the used-car lot. An hour later, they were loading their belongings into an older brown Buick. As they pulled onto the interstate and headed east, she said, "This is an ugly car, Stu."

He just laughed. "That witless salesman, he thought he was really taking me," Stu bragged. "But I practically stole this car from him. He really wanted that one of mine."

"Yeah, I guess he would," Deedee said snidely.

Stu gave her a smug look. "You don't get it. I got one up on that salesman. Look at the fistful of cash I got. I made a really good deal."

Deedee wasn't convinced. "But this old thing's so ugly," she said. "And yours was nice—almost new."

He showed her the cash he'd stuffed in his pocket. "Count it," he offered.

She forced a smile and shook her head. "Okay," she said. "I guess you did get him." But she didn't really believe it, and she once again felt what was becoming a far too familiar and painful twist in her stomach and another twinge of homesickness when she thought about her mother and friends.

\* \* \*

Harvey, the car salesman, and his wife were neighbors to a police sergeant. As soon as the young couple finished loading all the stuff from one car to another and drove away from the car lot, he phoned his neighbor at the police department.

The neighbor, Sergeant Andrew Jones, ran a check on the license number of the car Harvey had just taken in trade. When he called Harvey back a few minutes later, he told him, "You should have been a cop, Harvey. You have an uncanny instinct."

"What's wrong with the car?" Harvey asked, anxious to confirm his suspicion about Stu Chandler.

"Did he have a girl with him?" Andrew asked. "She'd be very pretty, long auburn hair, looks about eighteen or twenty?"

"Yeah, he sure did. I assumed she was his wife, although she was very quiet, seemed sad or depressed or something. Maybe it was because they were giving up a good car for an old junker. They sure had a lot of personal belongings that had to be moved from one car to the other. What did they do?" Harvey pressed.

Andrew smiled to himself. He could picture the look of anticipation on his friend's face. "They're not married, Harve. Her name's Deedee Marchant, and you're right about her maturity. She's only fifteen."

"That makes sense," Harvey agreed. "She looks almost twenty, but she didn't act that age at all."

"And that's not everything," the sergeant continued. "She's a runaway. Police in Utah are looking for her."

"They must also want him for kidnapping, with her being a minor and all," Harvey said.

"Yep, there's a warrant on him. We need to find them again, the sooner the better."

"She didn't act like she wanted to get away from him," Harvey observed. "She just seemed quiet and withdrawn."

"The detective from Utah will be here as soon as he can get a flight. In the meantime, I'll need all the information you can give me—the temporary sticker number and so on. I promised Detective Fauler that I'd get a bulletin out on them right away. Fauler made it sound like it was almost a personal case to him too."

* * *

Detective Enos Fauler was anxious to get on a plane to Mississippi. Stu was there, and he had Deedee with him. He'd just received the confirming phone call. A flight awaited him in Salt Lake. But before he left town, he knew he was duty bound to call Meredith Marchant. This time, he was glad he had something to report. "Have you heard something about my daughter?" Meredith asked hopefully before he'd finished his first sentence.

"They're in Mississippi," he said. "I'm on my way there now, or will be shortly."

"Where in Mississippi?" she asked.

"Stu bought a car in Jackson just an hour ago," Enos said, and before Meredith could ask him anything else, he added, "I'll call you from there. I've got to run now."

"How do you know he bought a car there, and why would he do that?" she asked quickly. But then she realized why. "He was afraid his car would be spotted, run on NCIC, and he'd be arrested," she stated.

"That's got to be the reason," Enos agreed. "So I've got to hurry. I need to get on my way. I'll do all I can to find Deedee when I get there and bring her back. Oh, by the way, there is something I need to know. I should have asked you earlier. Does Deedee have a passport?"

Meredith felt a pain deep inside. She had taken Deedee to Europe two years ago. "Yes," she said. "Why would you need to know that?"

"Just covering all the bases," Enos said. "Do you know if she took it with her?"

Meredith allowed herself a sigh of relief. She'd placed their passports in a small, fireproof safe she kept in her closet after they'd returned from their trip. She couldn't imagine that Deedee would have thought to take hers when she ran away, but she said, "Just a minute. I'll check."

Enos glanced at his watch. He had plenty of time to catch the earliest flight he'd been able to arrange, but he was still anxious to get on his way. He waited impatiently, pacing nervously. Her minute was actually a couple, but when she came back to her phone, he could feel the relief in her voice. "It's still there," she said. "You weren't thinking he might leave the country with her, were you?" she asked.

"Just covering all the bases," Enos repeated. "Thanks for looking. I'm glad she didn't take it."

\* \* \*

At that moment, Stu was crossing yet another state boundary and taking Deedee into Alabama. Deedee was becoming increasingly depressed, and she was feeling very much her tender age. She'd again asked Stu to let her go home, promising to not say anything that would get him in trouble. She even offered to fly home if he'd just get her to an airport. But Stu was firm. He'd said there was no way she was leaving him now. He'd even told her that she could also be arrested and would probably end up in detention if she went home. He was persuasive, and Deedee believed him.

She looked over at Stu as regret welled up inside her. He wasn't what she'd thought he was. He wasn't as fun to be with now as he'd been those first few days. He didn't make her laugh anymore. What a fool she'd been. Now she was stuck with him. She looked away.

He'd told her that her mother probably didn't even want her now. She hadn't believed that at first, but now she wondered if it might actually be true. That thought shook her up. She admitted with regret that she hadn't been a very good daughter lately. Her mother probably thought she'd done things with Stu that were worse than what she'd ever do. There were things Stu wanted her to do that she didn't want to and would resist with every ounce of strength she had. That thought frightened her now. She knew how terrible it would be if he got his way with her.

If she could just talk to her mother, maybe she'd feel better. Or maybe she'd feel worse!

"Deedee."

She looked again at Stu, right into his eyes, and suddenly, she was very afraid of him. He had a look that made her tremble. She'd noticed it a few times before but had ignored it. Now she didn't, and the realization of what it meant made her gasp. He was on some kind of drugs.

She knew about drugs; everyone knew about drugs. She knew kids at school who were into drugs, but she'd never actually been directly exposed to any of them. She'd tried to make herself believe Stu would never do drugs, or drink . . . or rape.

She had no idea what kind of drugs he was using or even when he took them. She supposed it was in his motel room at night, and she wondered how much longer she could insist on a separate room.

"Aren't you talking to me, girl?" he asked angrily.

Deedee blinked and pulled her eyes away. "Yeah, I guess so," she said.

"Not mad, are you?" he asked.

"I really should let my mother know I'm okay," she responded sullenly. "Even if I can't go back, it would only be fair to let her know I'm not hurt or anything."

"Oh, sure, and who you're with and where we're at."

"I won't do that, Stu. I promise," she said. "Stu, I wasn't thinking. I was just mad at my mother. Running away was stupid," she admitted.

"And permanent," he reminded her in a menacing whisper before finally diverting his glazed daze to the road.

Chills snaked through her, and she began to sob.

"Deedee, quit it!" Stu suddenly screamed at her. "Just quit the bawling."

Deedee quit crying. She knew it was her fault she was here with him, and she also knew she'd have to make the best of it, but that didn't keep her heart from aching with sorrow and regret. Then she made a decision. She'd call her mother tonight from the motel like she should have done earlier. At least she could let her mother know she didn't hate her like she'd told her the last time she'd seen her.

Late that afternoon, they exited the freeway, and Deedee was surprised when Stu found a seedy-looking pawnshop. When she asked him what they were doing there, he said, "We have too much stuff in this car. We need to pawn a few things." Using a false name, Stu literally pawned everything he'd taken from his apartment in Roosevelt except for a large suitcase that was filled mostly with clothing. When they turned into the long-term parking area of the Atlanta International Airport late that afternoon, she felt panic clutch her chest.

"We're going to catch a plane," Stu told her smugly. "I'm not telling you where we're going just yet. It'll be a surprise, and I know you'll love it. You'll need both your ID and the birth certificate I had you bring along," he said.

Deedee felt like she might be very sick. Was Stu planning on leaving the country? He'd told her that a picture ID was necessary to get on the airlines, and he'd also had her take a copy of her birth certificate but had not explained what that was for. She didn't have her passport, and for that reason she hadn't worried about leaving the country. But why had he brought her to an international airport? Was there a way to leave the country without a passport? She didn't know, but maybe Stu did.

# CHAPTER 4

Enos had left his cell phone in the car as he packed a suitcase for the trip to Mississippi. After throwing his luggage into the backseat of his patrol car, he climbed in and started the engine just as the cell phone rang. He was surprised to hear Meredith's voice on the line and couldn't imagine what she wanted. He soon found out.

Meredith began. "Enos, I have what you'll probably think is a crazy idea. The sheriff thought so too, but I have a favor to ask. Have you left town yet?"

"No," Enos replied, tensing up. "I'm just leaving my house now."

"Good, then maybe I'm not too late."

"For what?" Enos asked cautiously.

"I'm going crazy here not knowing how Deedee is and worrying every minute about her. I'm useless at work, probably cheating my clients. But I need to be doing something," she said.

Enos knew she was leading up to something, and he had a feeling he might also know what it was.

"I'd like to go to Mississippi with you," she finally blurted out. Then, before he could think of a polite way to tell her that might not be such a good idea, she added, "I can be packed by the time you get to town. I've already arranged for a couple of the attorneys in Roosevelt to cover my cases while I'm gone. I did that yesterday, just on the outside chance that I would need to leave. One call will let them know that I'm leaving now. And I promise I won't interfere with your work. If I get in your way, just say so and I'll come back."

Enos was silent for a moment as he considered her request. Initially he thought that the most prudent thing would be to politely tell her he'd keep her informed, that it would be best if she stayed in Duchesne. But as he pictured her in his mind, he admitted to himself that her company might be nice. What could it hurt? He couldn't see how she would be a problem unless a situation developed where some kind of confrontation with Stu might occur. In that case, she would just have to stay behind. But Enos knew that a confrontation wasn't likely. In fact, he feared that by the time he got to Mississippi, Stu and Deedee might not be around.

Enos finally decided his response, hoping he wasn't getting himself and her into something they would later regret. "All right, Ms. Marchant," he agreed. "But you'll need to call the airport right away to see if there are any seats left on my flight." Then he gave her the flight number.

"Thank you, Detective. There are still seats," she said. "I've already called to see. I told them that I'd call back if I decided I needed a reservation. I'll call right now while I'm packing. I'll be ready when you get here."

True to her word, Meredith was halfway to his car with her suitcase before he was able to get up the sidewalk to help her. "Thanks," she said when he took the luggage from her hand.

He pulled into the street, wondering what he'd gotten himself into after they were seated in the car. She smiled at him, a pained but sincere expression, and he suddenly felt terribly awkward. Her smile did things to him that he hadn't experienced much in his life, and even though she tried to strike up a conversation with him, his tongue had suddenly become very thick, and he was afraid he'd sound like a fool if he talked.

While Enos drove, his eyes focused on the road every moment, Meredith wondered what she'd gotten herself into. She'd begun to feel more confident about him these past few days, but now she wondered if she had been wrong. Maybe she'd made a mistake by coming with him. If her presence made him uncomfortable, he might not be able to conduct an effective search for her daughter when they arrived in Mississippi. But she pushed her concern aside. She was glad she was going. She wanted to be there when Deedee was picked up, and if she had to endure an almost silent trip to make that possible, it would be worth it.

Thirty minutes later, the thickness in the detective's tongue had gone away, and he felt an obligation to speak. But it still wasn't easy. Enos had never been good at small talk. "We'll find her, Ms. Marchant," he said at last.

She looked up in surprise. He sounded so sincere that it actually gave her hope. Maybe it wouldn't be such a long and silent trip after all. "Thank you, Detective," she said. "We've just got to."

"She must be a good student," Enos said, feeling foolish in his awkward attempt to begin speaking.

"She is. She's a very intelligent girl. That's why I'm surprised she ran away like this. But it's also why I think she'll soon grow tired of Stu Chandler."

"Tell me a little more about Deedee," Enos suggested, unaware that he was providing the very opening that Meredith needed. While she talked about her daughter for the next half hour, Enos listened, and he actually glanced Meredith's way occasionally. There was little doubt in his mind of the love she had for her daughter, and he was surprised at the sacrifices she'd made in the girl's behalf. He was also convinced that, despite the recent rebellion, Deedee was a good girl, and someday she'd regret this whole incident.

By the time Enos and Meredith reached the Salt Lake International Airport, much of the awkwardness between them had dissolved. Enos was thinking that maybe this wouldn't be such a bad trip after all, that Meredith really was good company, and Meredith was thinking that Enos was a very decent and likable man.

They were both secretly disappointed when they found that they couldn't sit together on the plane, but neither said anything to the other. Enos was disappointed because he was honestly finding it quite pleasant to be in the company of a lovely and educated woman; Meredith was disappointed because she wanted to be able to speak to him some more, to get to know a little about him. Of course, she told herself, it wasn't for any reason other than she wanted to prevent awkwardness when the two of them found themselves in one another's presence on a purely professional basis in the future.

As the plane lifted into the sky, Enos found himself wanting to succeed in this assignment more than any other in his life. Meredith offered one silent prayer after another that somehow, when they got to Mississippi, the end of this terrible ordeal would come quickly and happily.

* * *

While waiting for their suitcases, Enos called the police department and asked if there were any further developments in the search for Deedee. The negative answer put a damper on both their spirits. They said little for the next few minutes, and after renting a car at the airport, they loaded their luggage, and Meredith asked what Enos was going to do now. "I think we'll go first to the car lot where Stu sold his car. Maybe there's something to be learned there."

Meredith couldn't imagine what they could possibly gain by going there, but she didn't have any better ideas, so she said, "Okay, let's do that."

After arriving at the car lot, it was only minutes before they were given access to the car Stu had traded in. It hadn't yet been cleaned for resale, and Enos began a thorough inspection of the interior.

Meredith had promised not to get in the way of Enos's work, but she couldn't imagine what good he was doing here, and her tension began to build. She was making a concerted effort not to criticize him, but as she stood watching him claw about in the front seat of the car, she just couldn't keep her mouth closed. "If you'd tell me what you're looking for, I could help," she offered.

Without looking up from where he was currently rummaging, Enos said, "I appreciate that, but I don't know what I'm looking for."

That was too much for Meredith's organized mind. She was used to planning her court cases very carefully and then sticking to her plan. Her confidence in him faltered, and she honestly wondered if he knew what he was doing. Finally she said, "Why don't we make some plans, Detective? I think we're wasting valuable time here."

"I have a plan," Enos mumbled, not wanting to offend Meredith but trying hard to concentrate on what he was doing. "I'm searching this car."

"But you don't know what you're searching for," she said as her frustration grew. "Every minute we spend here could be minutes my daughter is getting farther away."

Enos took a deep breath. Maybe this had been a mistake, letting her come with him. He wasn't sure just how to reassure her that what he was doing could actually be important while admitting to himself that he might very well find nothing that could shed any light on the case at all.

After a few moments, Meredith spoke again. "Please, if you'll let me know what I can do, I'll help."

Enos eased his way out of the car and slapped his hands against each other to get the dust off them. Then he looked at Meredith, who was becoming increasingly upset. "I need to search this car, Ms. Marchant. I don't know what I'm looking for specifically, but there may be something in here that could prove to be helpful."

"But how can I help you?" she insisted.

"I'm sorry, but this is something I need to do myself. Maybe you could call the sheriff and let him know we're here. Hopefully he won't be too upset with me for allowing you to come."

Meredith wasn't worried about that, but she needed something to do to keep her busy while Enos finished searching the car. "Okay, I'll do that." She pulled her cell phone from her purse, and as she punched in the number of the sheriff's office in Duchesne, she began to absently wander toward a long row of used cars. When the phone was answered, she learned that Sheriff Robinson was away on business. She then asked for Luke Osborne.

"Meredith, what can I do for you?" Luke said when he came on the line.

"Just get a message to the sheriff for me," she told him. "I'm in Mississippi, and—"

"What in the world are you doing down there?" he broke in.

"Deedee was seen down here," she responded. "I needed to get away, so I talked Detective Fauler into letting me come with him. He asked me to let the sheriff know we were here."

"And what's Enos up to at the moment?" he asked, marveling to himself that these two people had actually traveled all the way to Mississippi together.

"Stu traded his car in on another one. A salesman here was suspicious and called the local police. I was hoping they would have found them by the time we got here, but so far, no one's seen them.

Detective Fauler is searching Stu's old car right now, the one he left here when he got a different one, but I can't imagine what good that's going to do. It seems unlikely Stu would have been careless enough to leave something behind that would indicate his whereabouts. Frankly, I'm afraid Detective Fauler is wasting valuable time."

"Maybe, maybe not," Luke said cautiously.

"What do you think we should be doing?" she asked, and Luke could tell that Meredith didn't have a lot of confidence in Enos at this point.

He thought for a moment. He didn't want to undercut Enos by saying the wrong thing, but he finally took a chance and said, "I'd probably do just what Enos is doing and search the car."

Meredith was surprised. "What would you look for?" she asked.

"I don't know," he answered. "For whatever was there, I suppose. Police work's that way, you know. Not all of the answers have questions. They're just answers that are waiting to be found. Be patient, Meredith," Luke went on. "Enos is smart. Give him some space and let him just do what he feels needs to be done."

With her confidence in Enos restored, Meredith bid Luke good-bye and began strolling absently through the long lines of used cars. She scarcely looked at them, but she knew that she had to follow Luke's advice and give Enos some space.

And hope he found something useful.

"Can I give you a hand finding a car?" a voice behind her said.

Meredith turned. A man of about thirty was smiling at her. "Name's Harvey," he said. "Are you looking for something in particular?"

"Actually, I'm not looking for a car. I'm looking for my daughter," she said faintly.

"Oh," Harvey said, apparently taken aback. "I haven't seen any young women here today, at least not one who was alone. Is she looking for a car?" He smiled at her.

Meredith felt her emotions begin to surface, and she fought to control them. "I'm sorry if I seem confused. My daughter is missing, and the man she's with bought a car here. I'm with an officer who's searching that car right now. I'm just trying to stay out of his way while he works."

Harvey's smile had vanished as she spoke. "I'm the one who's sorry," he said. "I sold them the car. I wish—"

Meredith interrupted. "You saw my daughter? How was she? Was she hurt or anything? You can't imagine how worried I am."

"She seemed fine but rather sad, Ms., uh . . ."

"Marchant," Meredith said. "I'm Meredith Marchant. My daughter is Deedee."

"Yes, well, as I was saying, she seemed physically fine, but she didn't act like she was very happy. The fellow, Stu, he did most of the talking."

"He would," Meredith said bitterly. "Did either of them say anything that might have given you an idea where they were going?"

"Not really," he said. "I explained all this to my neighbor, Andy Jones. He's a police sergeant."

"Yes, I know about him," she said. "I was just hoping you might think of something, anything, that would give me some idea of what they were planning to do."

"Sorry, Ms. Marchant. I wish I could help more. I wish I'd called Andy before they ever left here. The guy just seemed too slick, too much like a crook. But I was—"

"I understand," Meredith broke in. "And I thank you for what you've done. Here, let me give you my card," she said, "in case you remember something you think might be helpful." She pulled out a business card and pointed to one of the numbers on it. "This is my cell number. Call it if something comes to mind."

Harvey took the card. "You're an attorney?" he asked.

"I am. You'll call me if you think of something, won't you?" she pressed.

"I sure will. I'm terribly sorry about this whole thing."

After Harvey had gone in search of a more promising customer, Meredith returned to where Enos was still occupied in his search of the car. He had the trunk open and was lifting the spare-tire cover as she stepped up. "Any luck?" she asked hopefully.

"Yeah, one thing," he said.

Meredith moved closer and peered past him as he worked. "What did you find?" she asked.

"I'll show you in a moment," he said as he began to lift the tire out. "What did Sheriff Robinson say?"

"He wasn't in. I talked to Detective Osborne for a minute, though. He said he'd let the sheriff know when he gets back."

"Thanks," Enos said. When he was finished, he brushed himself off and turned to her. "Well, I guess we're done here. Now I'll show you what I found." He pulled a small plastic evidence bag from his pocket and held it up. There was a tiny note that appeared to have been torn from a larger piece of paper. He held the bag so that she could read the note. On it was one word: *Rapper.* And there was a phone number.

"Looks like a nickname and a phone number," she observed.

"That's what I thought," he said with a smile that she found very welcome. "What we need to do now is find out where area code 242 is."

* * *

Stu kept Deedee back out of the way while he spoke to a ticket agent. Then he signaled her over and said, "She needs your student card. It will work for a picture ID. She also needs to look at your birth certificate."

Deedee felt a rush of panic as she reluctantly pulled out the card and birth certificate and handed them to the ticket agent. The lady looked closely at them, then wrote down some information and returned Deedee's documents to her. Deedee was again shuffled out of the way as Stu finished. He never let her see the tickets, and he managed to keep her from learning where they were going when he obtained boarding passes.

He checked their suitcases with the agent and then told her to follow him. "Our flight's not for a couple of hours or so," he told her. "We'll just have to wait."

After an hour, Deedee was getting so tense she thought she'd explode. If she only knew where they were going, she'd maybe feel a little better. Stu had purchased a magazine and was thumbing through it, but he suddenly handed it to her. "I need to run to the men's room," he said. "Stay right here."

Deedee watched him disappear into the crowd. She'd been eyeing a nearby bank of pay phones since they sat down, and she dug out some change from her purse and walked over to them, nervously glancing over her shoulder. She dialed her home, and her own recorded voice informed her that she'd reached the Marchant residence and that no one was available. She waited for the tone, then said, "Mom, I'm so sorry. I'm fine. I wish I could come home, but I can't now. I love you, Mom." Then she hung up.

She hesitated for moment before placing a second call to her mother's office. The secretary answered. Attempting to disguise her voice, Deedee asked for Ms. Marchant. "She's not in," the woman said. "She's out of town right now. May I ask who's calling and—"

Tears stung Deedee's eyes as she slammed the phone into the cradle. Devastated, she realized Stu was right. Her mother didn't care. She'd simply gone on vacation!

She jumped as she felt a hand on her elbow and heard Stu say, "Thinking about making a call?"

She turned to face him. "Yeah, I was, but I've changed my mind."

"I think you already did," he shot back.

"Okay, I tried," she admitted. "I just wanted to tell my mom that I was okay and to forget about me. But her secretary said she wasn't in, that she was *on vacation*."

"She really cares, doesn't she?" Stu mocked, and real tears flowed from Deedee's brown eyes. "Can you forget about her now?"

Deedee nodded sadly, her spirit crushed and her heart broken.

"Good. I'm glad I didn't tell you where we're going or you might have let it slip. You won't do that if I tell you now, will you?"

"No," she said, and she meant it.

Stu's anger had dissipated, and he pulled her away from the phones and shoved her gently in the direction of the ladies room. "Better go in there while you can," he said.

She had the feeling that Stu was going to keep a closer eye on her, but he didn't need to. Not now. There was no one to go home to anyway.

# CHAPTER 5

As her phone began to ring, Meredith pulled it from her purse, glanced at the number, and answered.

"Meredith," her secretary said, sounding excited and out of breath, "I was just ready to leave the office when the phone rang. I almost didn't answer it, but when I did, I couldn't believe my ears. I think it was from Deedee!"

"You think?" Meredith asked as she began to tremble. Enos was just pulling in to the parking lot of the police department. He glanced over at her as she listened.

"The caller didn't identify herself," the secretary explained. "The voice seemed a little low for Deedee, like she was intentionally trying to keep me from telling who it was. Before I realized it might be her, she asked if you were in, and I told her you were out of town."

"What did she say after that?" Meredith asked.

"Nothing. She just cut the connection. That's when I began to wonder if it was her. So that's why I'm calling now. I'm so sorry if I screwed up," she finished, sounding almost in tears.

"You did fine," Meredith assured her even as she wondered what kind of damage might have been done. "If she calls back, try to keep her on the line and get her talking if you can. Maybe you could even call the sheriff's office and have them set up a trace, just in case she does call back. Find out what she wants, where she's at, that sort of thing."

Enos looked over at her as she ended the call. "Did Deedee call home?"

"She might have called my office," Meredith answered.

"Good," he said as he searched for a parking spot. "And you did right, requesting she set up a trace. In fact, I'll call my office right now and get them working on it. Do you think she'll call back again?"

"Probably not," Meredith said sadly as she explained about her secretary telling Deedee she was out of town. "She's going to think I've abandoned her, and I'll probably never know why she called," she cried, leaning back in the seat and shutting her eyes while Enos made his call to his office in Duchesne. She tried to relax but couldn't. Her mind was swirling. Was Deedee in terrible trouble or some kind of danger? There had to have been a reason for her call. Meredith tried to offer a silent prayer. She needed help, and Deedee needed help.

Enos turned to Meredith after finishing his call. "I was just thinking that it might be a good idea to call your home phone," he suggested. "Maybe Deedee called there first. She might have left a message on your answering machine."

"I never thought of that," Meredith admitted, impressed that he *did* think of it. She dialed and then accessed her messages, listening impatiently to all of them but the last one. Then she hung up, sobbing quietly. Enos waited patiently, knowing that Meredith would talk when she was ready. It took a minute before she spoke to him. "You were right. Deedee called home. She left a short message."

"What did she say?" Enos prompted gently, but Meredith just shook her head and placed her face in her hands.

Enos turned to her. "Ms. Marchant—" he began.

"I'm Meredith," she cut in softly. "Please call me Meredith."

"Okay," he agreed, touched at her gesture. "Would you mind dialing your number again and accessing that message once more? I'd like to listen to it."

Meredith complied silently. When she was ready, she handed her cell phone to Enos. He listened as the girl's voice said, "Mom, I'm sorry. I'm fine. I wish I could come home, but I can't now. I love you, Mom"

He handed the phone back, and she silently put it in her purse. Enos opened his door, thinking about what he'd just heard. It worried him. Deedee wanted to come home, but for some reason she felt that she couldn't. Stu must be the reason, but what had he done or said to convince her that she couldn't return to her own mother? Anger slowly began to seethe within him as he considered how Stu might be taking advantage of an innocent girl.

As they walked toward the police department, Meredith spoke first, stopping before they reached the front door of the police station. She grabbed Enos by the arm and faced him. She had her emotions under control now, and only the red of her eyes gave away the fact that she'd been crying.

"Detective Fauler," she said. "What do you think about what my daughter said?"

"Enos is my name," he said, amazed that he'd found the courage to say it. She nodded in agreement, and he went on. "Stu has somehow exerted control over her, either physically or psychologically—perhaps both. And as long as he has that control, we'll only get her back by taking her from him."

Hearing Enos say what she'd been thinking was almost more than Meredith could bear. She loved Deedee more than life itself, and the thought that she might never return was overwhelming. What if Stu had taken her to that horrible man she'd once defended, the one suspected of selling young women in foreign countries? She steadied herself against the brick building, forcing herself to take deep breaths.

Enos involuntarily reached out and lightly touched her arm in an attempt to comfort her. His face began to burn, and he stiffened. Finally, he spoke. "We'll get her back, Meredith. The Lord will help us, I know He will." And he meant it with all his heart. Enos suddenly wanted more than anything to make this woman happy again. He was afraid of his intense feelings, so he simply tried not to think about them anymore. But he was determined to succeed at his assignment no matter where it led him or what it might involve.

Several people passed by them, and Meredith finally relaxed a little. She wiped her eyes with a tissue, then said, "I'm sorry, Enos. I just keep thinking of that horrible friend of Stu's, and I can hardly stand it."

"We can't worry about that. It's so unlikely, Meredith," he told her. Or was it? He'd never felt so strongly about solving a case, and he didn't want to overlook anything. He'd also never felt such a growing concern for someone else. He finally managed to stammer, "Let's go talk to the officers inside."

Meredith looked at him for a moment, reassured by his faith, drawing strength from him. She found that she was grateful to have someone so strong to lean on at such a difficult time. Over the years she had yearned for someone to support her, to give her encouragement and strength when she was faced with trials. It was easier when someone didn't have to face things alone, she now realized. She prayed that Enos would be there to help her until this nightmare was over. She needed him and felt a strange sort of peace wash over her at that thought.

\* \* \*

Deedee was so relieved she felt like bawling. She'd been sure they were going out of the country, but when he finally handed her a ticket, it had indicated Miami as the destination. Of course, she couldn't understand why they didn't just drive there like they'd been doing for so many days now or why he'd pawned his TV, his stereo, and the other things that they'd taken from his apartment.

She realized with dismay that once they got off the plane, they'd be without a car. He'd left the old Buick in Atlanta. She had no idea what he was planning to do or where he planned to go in Florida, but nothing about what Stu did made sense to her anymore.

Deedee got another worrisome surprise as soon as they'd gotten off their plane in Miami. Stu informed her that they were catching another flight in an hour, but again, he wouldn't tell her where they were going. "You'll know soon enough," he said. "And you'll be excited. You'll need you ID and birth certificate."

"Okay, but where's our luggage?" she asked as panic threatened to overcome her.

"It'll be on the plane we'll be getting on next," he informed her. They were approaching a bank of phones, and Stu veered toward them. "You sit down here and wait," he ordered. "I need to make a call." Trembling, her stomach rolling and her mind in a blur, Deedee sat down next to an elderly lady with perfectly manicured nails and snow-white hair. She had an ornately carved cane leaning against the seat beside her and was holding a large black purse on her lap. She smiled at Deedee, but Deedee found it impossible to smile back.

There was nothing in her life right now that gave her a reason to smile.

The elderly woman reached out and patted her hand. "Whatever it is, it can't be that bad," she said in a surprisingly soothing voice.

Deedee felt her eyes begin to fill with tears, and she looked away from the woman. She spotted Stu at the phones. He was rummaging through his pockets and looking very agitated. She wondered if he'd lost something. Finally he gave up, dropped a quarter in the slot, and began to dial.

"Are you with him?" the woman asked, nodding toward Stu.

Deedee glanced at her, rubbed her eyes to clear them, and said, "Yes."

"Handsome young man," she remarked.

Deedee nodded.

"Sometimes it helps to talk about things with someone who's a good listener," the woman said. "Did you two have a fight?"

Deedee didn't want to say anything, but the lady was so nice. Finally, she spoke. "I think he's taking me someplace I don't want to go."

"Is he your husband?" the woman asked.

"No."

"Your boyfriend?"

"No," Deedee said, unable to keep the bitterness from her voice.

"He must be your brother then," the woman said gently.

Deedee shook her head.

"Then you don't have to go anyplace with him," the woman told her.

"But I don't have anyone else," Deedee said, surprised she was talking like this to a complete stranger. She glanced at Stu, who was now talking animatedly on the phone, his free hand gesturing wildly. She looked back at the woman at her side. "I ran away with him," she revealed.

The elderly lady looked shocked. "But you said he's not your boyfriend. Do you even like him?"

"No," Deedee said.

"Then you don't have to go anywhere with him—not tonight, not anytime."

"You don't understand." Deedee's voice took on a tone of desperation. "My mother doesn't want me anymore, and I don't have anyone else in my life."

The woman looked at her, scrutinizing her for a moment. "How old are you?" she asked.

"Fifteen," Deedee admitted, casting a glance in the directions of the phones again. "Oh no, here he comes," she said. "I can't be seen talking to you." She turned away from the woman.

Stu stopped in front of her, and she started to get up, but he stopped her. "Stay put, Deedee. I just need some change for the phone. Do you have some in your purse? I need a bunch of quarters."

Deedee opened her purse, finding only five quarters. "I need more than that," Stu grumbled as he took them.

"Maybe I can help," the elderly lady said as she opened her huge purse and pulled out a smaller one, popping it open. She soon handed Stu a dozen more quarters. He took them wordlessly and headed back to the phones.

"You didn't have to do that," Deedee said.

"We aren't through getting acquainted," the woman responded with a bright smile, her blue eyes flashing with delight. "I just bought us some time."

"Thanks," Deedee said.

"So your name is Deedee?" her new friend asked. "What a cute name for a truly beautiful young lady. What's your last name?"

"Marchant."

"Deedee Marchant. Very nice. There's a ring to it. It's a modern name. I have an old name," the woman said, frowning. "I'm Victoria Deveaux."

"That's not an old name. I know a girl named Victoria," Deedee said.

The charming smile returned. "But it's a name that's been around for centuries. Deedee is a modern name, and an unusual one. In fact, you're the very first person I've ever known by that name. And I'm pleased to get to know you. Where are you from?"

"Utah," Deedee said without thinking.

"Oh, what a lovely state that is," Victoria said. "Are you from Salt Lake City? I've been there, you know. I love Temple Square."

"I'm from Duchesne," Deedee said.

"Oh, that sounds like a French name. Like my last name. Duchesne," Victoria said, glancing, as Deedee did, toward Stu. He was still busy on the phone. "Surely you have someone in Duchesne," she added.

"Just my mother, and she doesn't want me around anymore. That's why I'm still with Stu. He's all I have."

"Is your mother a Mormon?" Victoria asked.

"Yes, but . . ." Deedee began.

The old lady put a finger to her lips. "I know several Mormons. They are good people. Why don't we call her? I'd be glad to talk to her, tell her that you want to go home to her. You would like to go home, wouldn't you?"

"Yes, but she doesn't want me," Deedee's voice quivered. "She's on vacation somewhere. I don't even know how to get ahold of her."

"How do you know she's on vacation?"

"I talked to her secretary. She told me."

"What does you mother do?" Victoria asked.

"She's a lawyer."

Victoria shook her head. "I can't imagine that your mother doesn't want you to come home. You're such a beautiful young woman. I'll bet your mother is absolutely worried sick over you being gone."

Just then, Stu headed back toward them. Deedee's stomach began to roll. "Come on, I gotta find some more change," he said angrily. He was clearly upset about something

Deedee began to get up, but Victoria put her hand out. "Let her stay with me," she said to Stu in a disarmingly sweet voice. "She was just telling me how good you are to her and what a fun trip the two of you are having. I'll keep her company while you find some change."

Stu flashed a look that Deedee knew was a warning, then looked at the elderly woman. "I'll be right back. Don't go anywhere," Stu said and strode quickly up the concourse.

"Why did you tell him that?" Deedee asked. "I'm not having any fun at all. In fact, I'm afraid he's about to take me out of the country."

"Do you think that he'd have left you here with me if I'd told him that you didn't want to be with him anymore? Here, let's call your mother."

"But you gave Stu your change," Deedee said.

"I don't need change. I've got a cellular phone," Victoria told her as she reached for her purse.

"We need to hurry. He'll be back here soon."

It took a moment for the call to go through to Meredith's office, but when it did, her secretary answered on the first ring. Victoria told her who she was and then said, "I have a young woman sitting beside me here who says her mother doesn't want her anymore and—"

Meredith's secretary interrupted. "Deedee is with you?"

"Yes, and as I was saying—" Victoria began again.

But the secretary was suddenly desperate and again interrupted. "Her mother *does* want her! She's sick with worry. How did she get away from Stu?"

"He's not far away, so we have to hurry. How can this young lady get back to her mother?" Victoria glanced at Deedee and smiled, attempting to reassure the young lady.

Deedee smiled back and then gasped. She was almost certain she'd seen Stu coming down the concourse. She grabbed the woman's arm. "Please help me!" she cried. "He's coming!"

Victoria also saw Stu, and her conversation became rushed and panicked. "I need to put my phone away. Stu's coming, and I need my hands free for my purse and my cane. We're in the airport in Miami," she finished desperately as she dropped the phone into her purse, grabbed her cane, and hurried with Deedee into the concourse. The two mixed with the crowds of people and raced away from Stu, the old woman's cane tapping the floor with a quick staccato beat.

# CHAPTER 6

At the airport in Jacksonville, Enos and Meredith were trying to arrange flights and not having much luck. They'd received a fax from Luke, a copy of Enos's birth certificate, which it turned out he now needed. But it was getting late, and both Enos and Meredith were worried and on edge.

With the help of Sergeant Jones and some of his colleagues, Enos had learned that the phone number he'd found in Stu's car was from the Bahamas, specifically an area called Abaco. He'd never heard of it, but Sergeant Jones told him it was a lightly populated island surrounded by a whole host of small islands that were collectively known by that name. These tiny surrounding islands were each referred to as a cay, pronounced *key*, Enos was informed.

There had been considerable discussion among the officers about the possibility that Stu intended to take Deedee to Abaco. Meredith, who was part of the discussion, was convinced of this and worried out loud what his purpose might be. She was prepared to fly to Abaco as soon as possible, and Enos had to admit that there was the distinct possibility that they might be going there. But he didn't rule out anything. "What if he realizes he's lost the slip of paper with the phone number on it?" Enos had asked. "Isn't it possible that he might suspect we could come up with it, and couldn't that cause him to become nervous and go somewhere else?"

"That is a possibility," Sargeant Jones had agreed, "but on the other hand, he might not have any idea where he lost it. If that's the case, it's likely he wouldn't give any thought to us having found the number."

Meredith turned to Enos, making him blush lightly, much to his embarrassment. "It's the best lead we have, Enos," she'd pleaded. "Please, let's make arrangements to go there now." But then she'd realized that it wasn't easy leaving the states. They would both need a photo ID and a birth certificate. She had her passport with her. She'd impulsively stuck it in her purse when she'd checked for Deedee's that morning, but Enos only had ID.

"I can call Luke, tell him where I keep one at the house, and have him fax it to us," Enos had said.

But even now that they had the birth certificate in hand, arranging for flights that would take them to Abaco was proving to be very difficult due to the lateness of the hour. And Enos could feel Deedee slipping away from them again. They might not even be going to the right place, but he didn't honestly know what else to do.

* * *

Mrs. Deveaux's heart was pounding painfully in her chest. She didn't have the strength to keep up their pace. She stopped and turned with Deedee as Stu shouted from right behind them, "Hey, old lady, where are you taking my wife?"

"Your wife?" Victoria said sternly. "She's not your wife!"

"That's a lie!" Stu shouted as he grabbed Deedee's hand.

There was a sudden sharp pain in Victoria's chest. She caught Deedee's eye and tried to speak, but the pain was dragging her down, gagging her. Deedee interpreted the look on the woman's face as one of doubt, and she immediately felt betrayed and hopeless again.

Stu was pulling her away, and Victoria made one last effort to stop him. Unable to, she felt her feet collapsing beneath her.

"Come on, Deedee. We don't have much time," Stu insisted as the distance began to grow between them and the lady. Deedee caught Victoria's eye one last time, but the woman seemed to have forgotten her already. Victoria's gaze fell away.

Deedee followed Stu, who was almost dragging her along. She looked back once more, but a throng of people stood where Victoria had been only moments before. Deedee gave up all resistance and followed Stu to another bank of phones. "I don't know what you and that old woman were doing, but I'd guess you were trying to call your mother. She doesn't want you. You better get used to the idea and not try something stupid like that again."

Deedee nodded numbly. And Stu dropped a quarter in the slot.

\* \* \*

Enos and Meredith were growing increasingly frustrated. It appeared that it would be the next day before they could go to Abaco, and they had to fly to either Miami or West Palm Beach first. Enos was talking to a ticket agent, his patience growing very short when Meredith's cell phone rang. When she picked up, she heard her secretary talking so fast that Meredith had to calm her down to understand her.

"Slow down," Meredith said impatiently. "What's happened?"

"I stayed late at the office like you asked, and I just got a call from an elderly lady. She said Deedee was with her and that Stu was coming and that they were in the airport in Miami. Then she must have dropped the phone, so I called the airport there. They said they'd see what they could find out, but that's a big airport—"

"Are you sure she had Deedee with her?" Meredith cut in, trying to remain calm herself.

"I think so. She said that Deedee said you didn't want her anymore, and I told her that you did. That was all we got to say before she got frightened and said Stu was coming," the secretary explained.

Meredith made a quick decision. "Call Sheriff Robinson. Have him call Miami. Enos and I will fly there as soon as we can."

"It's going to take some time to get to Abaco," Enos said in frustration a moment later. "Nobody seems to care about our problem. Who were you just talking to?"

"Forget about Abaco," Meredith said, her eyes shining. "That was my secretary, and Deedee is in the airport at Miami. We need to catch a flight there right now."

Not waiting for an explanation, Enos turned quickly back to the ticket agent.

# CHAPTER 7

Several uniformed officers surrounded the boarding gate of the flight Stu had booked to Marsh Harbor, the very last flight of the night. It seemed impossible that anyone could have figured out where he was headed. Then he thought about the call the old lady had made, and he knew that the cops might know he was here in the airport in Miami. But that still didn't explain why the cops were right there waiting at his flight. He wasn't about to risk finding out. Fighting back the urge to panic and run, he simply steered Deedee back up the concourse. He hadn't told her exactly where they were going, only that it was to an exotic and beautiful island in the Caribbean. He'd felt compelled to tell her that when they went through customs because she'd begun to press him about their destination. When he'd told her they were going to a place everyone wished they could visit, she actually cheered up a little.

He still wasn't ready to give her an explanation about how he knew Rapper, the man whose phone number he seemed to have lost. Nor did he want her to know what he and Rapper were planning to do. Stu had received a letter from Rapper that was postmarked New York. The letter had been delivered to his apartment in Roosevelt sometime after he and Deedee had left Utah the first time. It had been waiting for him when he came home to pack more stuff for what he knew could be a permanent departure from his home state.

He thought about the letter as he rushed Deedee up the long concourse. It was a semicoded invitation to meet Rapper in Abaco at the end of the month. There was work to be done, the letter had indicated, and it would pay well. Stu had planned to go, and though he hadn't mentioned it to Deedee, that was why he'd headed east when they left Duchesne that last night. Rapper wanted him in Abaco by the end of June, which didn't leave a lot of time. Stu figured that with Deedee accompanying him, the sooner they could both get out of the states, the better it would be.

Rapper was not the man's real name, and Stu didn't even know what the real one was. Rapper changed names frequently, but Stu could care less about what his name was as long as Rapper called him often to work. The last time he'd assisted the man, he'd been paid well. It didn't matter to him that other people's lives were destroyed when Rapper was doing a job. All that mattered was that Stu made a lot of money.

The letter had informed Stu that Toby Liner, the middle-aged man from Los Angeles who had helped them in their last job, was also coming to Abaco. The three had been in Duchesne for a short time together, but after Rapper had gotten in trouble and almost lost his freedom, they'd gone their separate ways. Stu thought it was funny that it was Deedee's mother who had helped Rapper get out of trouble, along with some shady friends of Stu's who were willing to lie for Rapper. And it hadn't really cost them that much, he remembered. Meredith had only been required to convince the prosecutor that the witnesses were for real. She'd done her job, and Rapper had left.

Before he left, though, he'd promised Toby and Stu that he'd contact them when he needed them again. This was the first time Stu had heard from him since. However, Stu had stayed in touch with Toby, and after receiving the latest invitation from Rapper, he'd called Toby late one night from a motel where he and Deedee were staying.

Toby had already made contact with Rapper, and he gave Stu Rapper's phone number, which Stu had promptly lost. He'd tried unsuccessfully to reach Toby and get the number so he could let Rapper know that he was on his way to Abaco. He'd finally decided to simply fly to Marsh Harbor and contact Rapper once he was there.

"Where are we going?" Deedee demanded as they left the airport. "I thought you said we were catching a plane tonight."

"I changed my mind," Stu said sharply. "Don't worry; we'll get where we're going."

"But most of our luggage is on the plane. You told me that yourself," she complained.

Stu hadn't thought about that, but Deedee was right. Their luggage was going to Marsh Harbor on the flight he'd booked—whether they did or not. "Don't worry about it. We'll pick it up later when we get to where we're going," Stu said. "We'll get along without it for a day or two."

"Why don't we just get on the plane like you'd planned?" she asked. Not that she was anxious to leave the states with Stu Chandler, but after failing in her attempt to contact her mother and possibly get away from Stu earlier that day, she'd resigned herself to spending more time with him. And if they were going to simply hang out, the Caribbean seemed like a reasonable place to do it.

They were out of the airport now, and Stu couldn't see any cops. He stopped, faced Deedee, and said, "The cops were waiting for us back there when we turned around. We couldn't just let them grab us. We'd both end up in jail if that happened."

Deedee shivered at the thought of being thrown into a jail cell. She didn't recall seeing any officers, but then she hadn't been paying a lot of attention. "Why would they—" she began.

"Your mother wants you locked up," Stu lied coldly. "And she must have connections. I'm telling you—they were there, whether you saw them or not. And they were looking for the two of us."

Deedee finally admitted to herself that if Stu said the cops in the airport were after the two of them, he was probably right. She certainly didn't want to go to jail, but what would they do now?

She asked Stu that very question, and he said, "We'll find another way to get where we're going. You just leave it to me."

Thirty minutes later, a taxi dropped them off at a motel in the southern part of Miami. "We'll stay here for a day or two, then we'll go on," Stu told her, knowing that he couldn't stay there too long or he'd miss the job with Rapper—and with the money Rapper paid, he didn't want that to happen. With a girl as beautiful as Deedee to support, Stu knew he could use the money. He was convinced that money and the things it would buy were the way to a girl's heart, and he intended to keep this girl.

"I'll book a room while you stay back here out of the way," Stu told Deedee. "I don't want the people here to know we're together."

"But we need two rooms," she insisted.

"One will have to do this time," he said firmly. "I need to keep an eye on you after what you tried to pull with that old woman."

Deedee felt a rush of emotion, and tears welled up in her eyes. "I won't try to call home again or to run away," she promised. "I can't."

"You won't," Stu said with a voice that was more than a little intimidating.

\* \* \*

Early the next morning, Stu made a series of phone calls and located Toby at last. He quickly explained his problem to his older and more experienced partner. "I don't dare fly there now," he admitted. "The cops might be watching all the airports. Any idea what I can do? My girlfriend and I need to get out of the country right away."

"You didn't mention a girl before," Toby chuckled. "Is she good-looking?"

"A knockout," Stu bragged. "You won't believe her when you see her. But we've got to get to the Bahamas as soon as we can."

Toby didn't bother to ask why. Instead he said, "I'm flying out there today. I know some fishermen in Miami. Maybe we can get a ride on a boat."

Stu told Toby where to meet him, smiling and gloating as he hung up. They'd get to Abaco, and they wouldn't have to go through customs again to do so.

\* \* \*

After being forced to spend the night in the airport in Jacksonville, Enos and Meredith finally arrived in Miami and made reservations for a flight to Abaco in the early afternoon. In the break they had before their flight, they made a trip to a nearby hospital to speak with Victoria Deveaux, but she was very ill and they were not able to learn any more from her.

They made the short flight to Abaco, secured a rental car, and found rooms in a small hotel in Marsh Harbor. They were both very tired but only stopped long enough to freshen up a little before making a visit to the local station of the Royal Bahamas Police Force.

The man who seemed to be in charge that day introduced himself as Inspector Samas. He was a stocky, middle-aged man who was quick to let them know that this island had a very low crime rate and that he didn't want any unnecessary trouble stirred up. "We keep a very low profile," he explained in his Bahamian dialect. "We have only a small force here, and the people see very little of us. We'd like to keep it that way."

Enos glanced at Meredith, wondering if she was having as much difficulty telling what the officer was saying as he did. "We only want to find Ms. Marchant's daughter and take her home," Enos said. "We know that once she knows we're looking for her, she'll cooperate fully."

"Are there warrants for this Stu fellow?" Inspector Samas asked.

"Yes, several misdemeanors and one for kidnapping, a felony," Enos explained. "The girl may have left willingly, but we believe she is no longer with him willingly. We want him arrested and sent back to Utah."

"We'll help you find the girl," the inspector promised. "And we'll arrest her friend if we find him."

"Thank you," Enos said. "Now, about my pistol. What will it take for me to be allowed to pick it up from customs and to carry it on my person while I'm here?"

It took a lot, but before the day was over, Enos was finally armed. He was admonished to keep his pistol out of sight at all times unless it was absolutely necessary. Enos promised to abide by that condition. He was just glad to have it, for experience had taught him that crooks, no matter what the local laws dictated, always found a way to arm themselves. He didn't want to be at a disadvantage, or allow Deedee and Meredith to be at one, should a dangerous situation arise.

While working on getting his pistol, both Enos and Meredith had asked a lot of questions around the airport. One of the customs officers recognized the names of Deedee and Stu and told them that unclaimed baggage was being held for both of them. "They never arrived on the plane," he said. "They never picked up their luggage."

That piece of information shocked both of them. "Then where could they be?" Meredith had asked.

"Maybe they decided to fly over later," they were told.

Meredith looked at Enos with dismay. "They aren't here," she said. "Now what do we do?"

"Their luggage is here. My bet is that they're still coming. The best thing we can do is wait and see." He turned to the customs agent. "Would you spread the word for the people here at the airport to be watching every flight for them? When they come, arrest the fellow on this warrant." He handed the customs officer a copy of the warrant that had been issued for Stu on the charge of kidnapping. "And will you make sure that the girl is detained here?" Enos asked. He'd given the officer a photograph of both Stu and Deedee. "The girl is only fifteen even though she looks a lot older than that. Hold her and we'll come right away and meet her. The police know where to find us. And they will hold Stu until we can arrange to have him extradited back to the states."

The young officer had seemed quite impressed that he was asked to assist in such an important case. There were seldom serious problems at this little airport, and he acted like he might welcome something a little more exciting than the normal, everyday tedium of his job. He assured Enos and Meredith that if Deedee and Stu arrived by plane, they wouldn't get past customs.

After Meredith produced a copy of Deedee's birth certificate, she attempted to persuade the officers that she was the mother of the girl the luggage belonged to. Meredith described some of the clothing they would find in the suitcases, Deedee's makeup kit, and several other items she knew Deedee had taken. Finally convinced that the luggage did in fact belong to her daughter, the customs officials allowed Meredith to take Deedee's luggage, which consisted of two large suitcases.

After leaving Meredith to go through Deedee's things at the motel, Enos again went to the police station. He showed the police officers the phone number he'd found in Stu's car and was told the easiest way to find out whose number it was would be to dial it and ask. He already knew that but didn't think that doing so would be such a good idea. The last thing he wanted was to tip anyone off that the authorities knew about the number and the fact that Stu and Deedee had planned to come to Abaco.

When Enos returned to the motel, it was starting to get dark. He tapped on Meredith's door and found her very withdrawn, even sullen, when she let him in. He could see that she'd been crying. He really didn't have any idea what he should say or do in this situation, and he felt the urge to simply put his arms around her and comfort her. But the thought of doing that was terribly frightening.

Enos finally did the only thing he could make himself do. "I'm going to go eat. Would you like to come?" he asked.

Meredith had moved from the door after letting Enos in and was now standing in front of one of her daughter's suitcases. It was open, and several of Deedee's belongings were carefully stacked beside it. She'd been meticulously going through everything. At Enos's invitation to accompany him to dinner, she looked up at him. "I don't think I can eat, Enos. You go ahead if you're up to it," she said sadly.

Feeling defeated and surprisingly lonely, Enos turned toward the door, opened it, and was about to leave when Meredith said, "Look at this, Enos. She brought her scriptures." There was a sudden lightness to her voice, and Enos stopped and looked back. Meredith was kneeling beside the big suitcase, holding her daughter's scriptures. They were in a pink-and-blue-flowered cloth case. Deedee's name was embroidered in white on the front. "I can't believe she took them with her. Now that I think of it, I didn't see them in her room, but the way she's been acting lately, it never occurred to me that she might take them with her."

Enos nodded an acknowledgment. Once more he fumbled for words, not wanting to appear rude by saying nothing. He finally spoke. "That's good. She was probably reading them."

Meredith's face brightened, and she looked up at him. "You think so?" she asked as if he could truly shed authoritative light on the matter.

"Why else would she take them with her?" he asked, honestly having no idea if she'd been reading them. In fact, it occurred to him that it was highly unlikely she'd actually been using them.

Meredith rose to her feet, holding the sacred volumes tightly. "That makes me feel better," she said. "Can you give me a minute, Enos? Maybe I will go with you."

"Sure," he mumbled, confused by her rapid mood swings. He stepped back into the room and closed the door as she disappeared into the bathroom.

"I'll be just a minute," she shouted from beyond the door she'd just closed.

The minute was closer to ten, and Enos spent five of them wandering restlessly around the little room. Then he stopped and picked up the scriptures from the table where Meredith had laid them minutes before. He knew he was snooping, but he was suddenly compelled to open them. He unzipped the case to find inside a single volume with a blue cover, the same kind he owned.

He thumbed through Deedee's volume and was surprised to find that she had marked a lot of verses. She even had notations in the margins on a few pages that he turned to. He read what she'd written and was quite impressed. Despite the problems of late, he could tell Meredith had done a good job of instilling something within Deedee that had caused her to spend some serious time studying the scriptures. He felt it was a positive sign.

As Meredith opened the door and reentered the room, the scriptures in Enos's hands fell open to the sixth chapter of Ephesians in the New Testament. Deedee had underlined the first three verses of that chapter, and in the margin she'd written, *I'm sorry, Mom. I'm so very sorry.*

Enos felt like a kid with his hand in the cookie jar when Meredith walked over to him and said, "She really did read them faithfully at one time. Our bishop always encourages her to read them every day, and for a long time she did."

"Look at this," he said, handing the book to her. "It fell open to this page as I was thumbing through just now."

She took the scriptures from him without another word, choking back a sob as she turned the book sideways and read the notation in the margin. In a voice cracking with emotion, she said, "This is a note to me. You were right, Enos. She's been reading them."

Meredith swept a long lock of fiery red hair away from her eyes and read once more. Finally, she shut the scriptures, rubbing her eyes and sniffling softly. "Thank you," she said as she put the scriptures back in the case. "I don't think I'd have had the courage to open them. This gives me so much hope."

Meredith was standing close to Enos as she laid the book back on the table. She turned toward him, her eyes still glistening. "We've got to find her," she said in a pleading tone.

"We will," he responded, praying fervently that his promise would not become a lie.

"She'll be okay when we get her back," she added hopefully.

"Of course she will," he said.

"But they aren't on this island. What can we do now?" she implored.

"Like I told you earlier, we can wait," he said, "and we can pray. The Lord will help us," he said. "And He will help your daughter."

"You have such strength," Meredith suddenly said. She touched his arm in a grateful gesture. Her eyes filled with tears, and she said as she quickly drew her hand back, "Let's go find something to eat."

Thirty minutes later, they were waiting for some outrageously expensive food while enjoying the fresh smell of the sea and the sound of waves licking at the nearby harbor. Some of the ships and boats moored there were lit by cabin and deck lighting. Soft music played in the background. The lighting in the restaurant was dim, and as Enos gazed shyly at Meredith's face across the table from him, he wondered if this was the closest he'd ever get to having a romantic dinner in his life. It was certainly beyond anything he'd experienced previously.

He felt like he was under some kind of spell, a magic spell cast by the beauty of his companion and the serenity of their surroundings. But when she spoke a minute later, the spell was shattered. Cold reality returned. "Maybe we shouldn't wait here in Marsh Harbor longer than tomorrow sometime. Maybe we should catch a plane back to Miami," Meredith suggested. "If they didn't dare fly here like they'd planned, then maybe they'll go someplace else instead."

Enos almost closed his eyes in the hope of bringing back the spell, but he didn't. Instead he said to Meredith what he'd told her twice before. "We better wait. Their luggage is here in Abaco. They'll follow it."

"There's nothing she can't replace with enough money," Meredith said. "And Stu must have money. So does Deedee, for that matter."

Enos slowly shook his head, and his eyes met Meredith's across the table. "She can't replace those scriptures," he said. "They're personal to her."

"That's true," Meredith admitted. "But they aren't to Stu. And he's controlling her right now. Anyway, how could they get here? Surely they don't dare fly. I just can't believe Stu would be reckless enough to try that."

"I suppose they could come by boat," Enos suggested.

Meredith's face lit up. "Yes, of course," she said with hope once again surfacing. "There must be ferries or something—" she began.

"No," Enos said thoughtfully. "They'd probably come illegally. And at night. First thing in the morning, let's start checking the ports. They may come tonight."

"Okay," Meredith agreed. "Could they already be here, I wonder?"

"I doubt it, and they haven't gone after their luggage," Enos reasoned.

"I wish we could start looking tonight, just in case, but I'm too tired. My brain is about to shut down," Meredith told him.

Enos sighed inwardly with relief. He was beginning to think this woman didn't require much sleep. He'd feared that she'd insist that they begin tonight when he mentioned the possibility of their arrival by boat. He was careful not to let his relief show, for he didn't want to offend her. He was finding that he enjoyed her company, but he needed rest if he was to work effectively.

Meredith watched Enos and wondered what he was thinking. She'd found a new respect for him. He was really very good at his job, she admitted, and she needed to help him stay focused on the task he had to do. She wondered if her emotions were distracting to him, and she resolved to work harder at keeping them under control. Finally, she also allowed herself to think about how much she liked being with him.

They finished their meal with very little further conversation. A cool breeze gradually turned into a stiff wind. When they left the restaurant, both worried about the storm that was blowing in, but neither commented on it to the other. They didn't want to even think of the possibility that Deedee might get on a boat and head out to sea in bad weather. And both hoped that it was just a little storm, an isolated one, that would blow over soon.

# CHAPTER 8

Choppy seas caused the fishing boat to rock continuously. The captain sat at the controls on the bridge several feet above the cabin, working to keep the boat moving steadily in the rough water. Stu was up there with him, as he had been for most of the journey. The captain had even let him take the wheel for a little while when Stu had told him he'd operated a boat similar to this one. "You do okay," the captain had said after Stu had been at the wheel for a half hour or so. "Ever consider doing this for a living?"

"No, I just like to boat for fun," Stu said. "I have easier ways of making money."

"Like what?" the captain had asked.

"Oh, just things," Stu had responded. "You wouldn't be interested."

He'd said it in such a way that the captain didn't pursue the topic. When the sea had begun to get rough, Stu had turned the wheel back over to the captain.

Deedee sat in one of the fishing chairs that faced the foaming, churning sea. To both her right and her left were large fishing poles, each with a line trailing into the choppy water behind the boat. The captain, who was the only other person aboard besides Deedee, Stu, and a man Stu had introduced as Toby, had insisted that they fish for a while before they made the illegal run for Abaco. That wouldn't occur until after darkness had set, which wasn't far off now, making it less likely that they would be spotted by the Coast Guard.

Deedee had watched as the men stood on a smelly dock and negotiated a price for the trip. While the agreed-upon sum had seemed awfully high to her, they'd willingly forked over the money in hundred-dollar bills. Early in the evening, they'd set a course to the east. The wind had come up very suddenly about an hour later and had been gradually increasing in velocity ever since. Dark clouds had also gathered overhead. The captain had already assured them that it was early in the year for hurricanes but that a storm warning had been issued. He'd told them it couldn't be anything too serious and didn't seem to be concerned. Deedee, however, was feeling increasingly ill. The constant motion was more than she could take.

Stu came down from the bridge and occupied the seat next to her. Both he and the man Stu had introduced as Toby Liner, to whom Deedee had taken an instant dislike, appeared unfazed by the rough seas. Deedee felt Toby's eyes on her back from where he sat in the shelter of the bridge. She loathed the way Toby leered at her. How Toby and Stu knew each other was a mystery, but she was smart enough to realize it couldn't be a good thing. Stu refused to explain Toby's identity to her, but the man looked like a thug. He was not a pleasant person to be around.

Deedee's worries of Toby were soon forgotten as she found herself kneeling at the side of the boat, vomiting violently. She only felt marginally better when she'd finished, and she returned on unsteady legs to the chair and sat with her head in her hands, trying not to look at the churning water of the boat's wake.

Toby laughed at her, then turned to Stu and said, "You better go take care of the babe, Stu, before I take over for you."

Stu had already started back toward the empty chair beside Deedee, but he swung around and stalked toward Toby as the boat pitched and swayed. "You stay away from her," he warned darkly, poking the older man in the chest with his finger as the two stood swaying toe to toe.

"I think she likes me," Toby said with a grin as he pushed Stu's hand aside roughly. "And don't go poking no fingers at me."

"The girl's mine," Stu retorted possessively. "I risked a lot bringing her here, and no one's going to take her from me. You touch her, and so help me I'll—"

Before Stu had spelled out his threat and further escalated the disagreement, the captain shouted down from his perch above them where he was fighting to control the vessel. "You two shut up and sit down! I don't need no distractions here. This is getting worse by the second, and if you got any brains you'll get some life jackets on."

Toby and Stu looked up at him. "Thought you said there wasn't no hurricane," Toby shouted.

"This is not a hurricane, but it's a lot worse storm than predicted. Now get them life jackets on. And don't forget one for the girl."

Toby and Stu glared at each other for another moment before they turned away wordlessly. The distressed look on Captain Earnestine's face and the tightness of his voice had alarmed them both. He was clearly worried about his boat's safety, which frightened the two men. Stu retrieved life jackets for Deedee and himself. "Better get one," he said as he passed Toby.

"Ain't that bad yet," Toby growled. "I don't plan on leaving this boat till we reach shore anyway."

Deedee was aware that Stu took his chair beside her a moment later. She didn't look toward him as she said in a broken voice, "We aren't going to make it, are we?"

"Of course we are," Stu said, although he'd begun to entertain similar bleak thoughts himself. "This ain't nothing for the captain. He's out in this kind of weather all the time. If it was a hurricane, we'd have waited for a day or two. They see those things coming days in advance, you know. This is just a normal old storm at sea. Won't last long. Nothing to worry about. Here, put this on."

If it was nothing to worry about, why the life jacket? Deedee wondered, but she was too sick to ask Stu that question. She knew in her heart that the storm was something to worry about, and she worried a lot.

It took several minutes, but Stu and Deedee eventually had their life jackets secured. The next few hours dragged by interminably. They were making very poor time, and Deedee felt continually worse. She didn't ever remember being so sick or so cold or so frightened in her entire life. She tried to pray from time to time, but her heart wasn't in it. Fear of death pressed down on her weak, chilled, and shaking body. She wept bitterly for herself and for her mother, and she regretted more than ever the foolishness that had led her into this wild and deadly ocean voyage.

The darkness of the storm seemed to add to the darkness of the night as the captain coaxed his boat toward the Bahamas. Electric lamps lit the interior of the boat and the raging sea ahead of them, but the constant spray of ocean water and the rain that was beginning to fall made it difficult to see. Toby continued to prowl about the boat, still seemingly unaffected by the turbulence. As the rain began to fall more steadily, Stu helped Deedee into the limited shelter beneath the bridge, where they sat together, holding one another while hanging on to a steel pole that rose from the floor between them. Toby eventually sat down beside them, uncomfortably close to Deedee. Leaning around her, Stu said to Toby, "Can he dock this thing in the storm?"

"Got to," Toby replied. "He can't run around out here forever. He'll run out of fuel if he tries that."

"Go up and ask him when we'll get there," Stu suggested.

Deedee thought Toby was going to refuse, but after a sharp look at Stu, he did as Stu asked, climbing the ladder as the boat swayed wildly. When he returned a few minutes later, he reported, "Captain says we'll make land by the middle of the night if the storm doesn't get any worse. Says he knows a place where it'll be sheltered from the worst of the wind. He called it the leeward side of the island—that means the sheltered side, for you dummies. He'll take us to shore there. He says not to worry."

Stu glared at Toby. "I knew that. I've probably been at sea a lot more than you have," he growled.

An hour later, the storm seemed to let up a little, and for a couple of hours, the boat surged steadily forward. Captain Earnestine set and locked the controls and came below with the others. He reeled in the fishing lines and stored the poles. "Ain't nobody else crazy enough to stay out in this," he said. "We can quit pretending to fish."

"Is the storm about over?" Stu asked.

"I suspect it is," he said.

But he was wrong. The winds picked up again and were soon stronger than ever. At times, the little fishing vessel seemed lost in the mountainous waves. Water surged over the sides of the boat when it was near the bottom of a trough, then drained back out as it was lifted high on some monstrous wave. Then once again, water poured in as it slipped into another trough. The crests seemed increasingly higher and the troughs ever deeper.

Even Toby lost his optimism after a while. "Captain can't possibly know where he's going," he said glumly. "We could be clear past the Bahamas and halfway to Europe before this thing lets up."

Deedee was almost beyond caring. She didn't expect any of them to get out of this trip alive. They should never have come. She should never have run away from her mother. She would die now for what she'd done, and as sick as she was, fear of death receded a little. She actually thought of it as a welcome release from the torture she was suffering.

Still another hour dragged by, but it made no difference to Deedee. She just wanted this nightmare trip to end. She clung tightly to her pole and sat, her head down, her stomach churning. Suddenly the captain, dressed in his yellow rubber clothes, appeared at the top of the ladder. He hurried down and joined them. "Hey, you, get back up there," Toby ordered in anger. "This thing can't drive itself in this kind of weather!"

"For a minute it can," the seaman said. "We'll be getting to Abaco soon, but before I let you off, I need more money."

"More money!" Toby roared. "We paid you too much already."

"You paid me *fair weather* money," the captain said. "This ain't *fair weather*. I need another thousand now. Then we'll get you to land."

"We had a deal," Toby said darkly.

"Deal's changed," the captain said. "Hand over the thousand now. And don't try telling me you ain't got it. I know you do 'cause I saw it."

"And if we don't give it to you?" Stu asked from where he remained seated beside Deedee.

Captain Earnestine threw a dangerous look his way. "Then we'll all go back to Miami together."

Toby spun around and faced the captain. "We had a deal," he shouted darkly. "Now go steer this thing or whatever it is you do up there."

The captain held out his hand. Toby stood resolutely. The boat dipped dangerously forward, then rose and tipped to the side. Toby and the captain slid into one another, and for a moment they grappled angrily, each trying to overpower the other. Deedee gripped the steel pole beside her, her hands locked on it. Stu also continued to hang on tightly.

The boat righted itself, and Toby shoved himself free of the captain. Both of them were beyond the shelter of the cabin. A colossal wave rose above them, and they both looked up, their mouths open, eyes staring in mortal fear. Then, with a loud clap and fierce roar, the water descended, the boat tipping again until it was nearly on its side.

Deedee shut her eyes, her head spinning. Water flowed above her ankles as the boat again righted itself. She didn't open her eyes until she heard Stu shouting. "Toby, get back here!"

She stared toward the back of the boat and saw—nothing! The captain and Toby had disappeared. Stu swore. Deedee screamed. The boat tipped the other way. She continued to stare, her eyes stinging, but all she could see was water, mist, and occasionally a glimpse of the empty fishing chairs at the back of the boat. It took a minute for the gravity of the situation to sink in. Then it hit her. Toby and Captain Earnestine had been washed overboard! She and Stu were alone on the boat.

The boat continued to fight its lonely way eastward through the rough seas. Stu and Deedee were stunned. "Should we look for them?" Deedee asked, her voice choking with sobs she couldn't control.

"Where would we look?" Stu asked. "They clearly aren't on the boat anymore. And that water . . . well, you can see for yourself. There's nothing we can do. Neither one had a life jacket on. They're gone." With that, Stu struggled to his feet.

"Where are you going?" Deedee protested. "You just said you can't search for them. And you can't leave me here alone."

"I'm going up there," he shouted, pointing toward the bridge where the boat continued without anyone at the wheel. "I'm not ready to die! And that's exactly what will happen unless somebody takes over the controls. I have had some experience, you know. I'm our only chance to make it to land alive."

Before she could protest further, Stu swung onto the ladder and disappeared above. He might have operated a boat similar to this, but Deedee was sure he'd never done it in a storm like this one. Hope had surged inside her momentarily when the captain had insisted on more money, indicating he'd clearly expected to make it safely to land. But now, with Stu at the wheel, she was almost certain of death. Terrified, she continued to hang on to the pole, closing her eyes and again trying to pray. She found that she agreed with Stu on one point. She wasn't ready to die either.

Several minutes passed. The boat, though continuously dipping and tipping dangerously, also continued to press steadily forward. Suddenly, the wind abated and a calmness seemed to settle in. The boat slowed down, and though it continued to rock, it was no longer the wild and dangerous ride it had been the past few hours. Deedee had no idea what Stu was doing up above, but she guessed he actually did know enough about operating the boat to get them safely to shore.

Deedee began to relax and actually let go of the pole, her lifeline, and wiped at her stinging eyes. She shivered from the chill. It occurred to her that she was cold and weak, but she was no longer as sick to her stomach as she had been.

The lights seemed brighter now without the heavy rain and mist blowing past, and Deedee made her way to the steel ladder. She called up, "Stu, what happened?"

"I think we just drove into the shelter of the island or something. The leeward side is calmer in a storm." He was silent for a moment, and she thought about climbing the ladder. Before she'd made up her mind, he shouted again, "I can see land in the lights. I'll steer for it."

"Go slow," Deedee warned.

The wind was still strong, but nothing like it had been out on the open sea. Deedee decided to join Stu on the bridge. Despite the weakness and cold, she successfully negotiated the ladder, then peered through the windshield in front of them. She was now able to see what Stu had been watching. There were definitely trees ahead, but that was all she could see. They were blowing back and forth in the wind, and the boat was approaching them very rapidly.

The boat's speed decreased a little more as Stu eased back on the throttle. "There's got to be sand before we reach the trees. We'll just let the boat push up on it, and then we'll make our way through the trees. I'm sure there'll be a road close, and we can catch a ride to the nearest town and get warm and dry soon."

"Stu, I can't see anything but the trees," Deedee said a moment later.

"There's got to be sand," Stu insisted. "Brace yourself. When we run up on it, the boat will stop pretty quickly."

But there was no sand, and the next thing Deedee knew, the boat was plunging into a dense thicket of branches. The boat slowed so suddenly that she flew forward, hitting her head on the glass. Then she was thrown back and fell in a heap dangerously close to the ladder and the long drop to the deck below. She scrambled frantically until she was able to grasp the metal railing that circled the bridge.

Stu was also thrown from his seat and landed near Deedee. His head struck the floor just a fraction of a second before the windshield shattered. They could hear branches breaking all about them. The boat's engine continued to run, and the boat forged a little farther ahead before it suddenly shuddered, the engine died, and the boat began to settle into the water.

Deedee didn't realize it at the moment, but it was not land they had encountered but a large grove of mangrove trees that grew from the shallow ocean floor, their branches intertwining above the water. The boat had broken its way several yards into the thick conglomeration of branches before it had finally been forced to a stop.

Stu moaned and struggled to sit up. The boat continued to settle down through the thick branches. As Deedee helped Stu, she kept thinking that the boat would hit the ground at any moment. But when it didn't, she began to panic. Stu, groggy for only a moment, soon snapped out of it and said, "Are we sinking, Deedee?"

"I think so," she said in alarm.

"Hang on to something," Stu ordered.

Deedee had already grasped the metal railing. "I am," she shouted.

"No, I mean we've got to grab a branch of one of the trees. I don't think there's anything beneath us but water. And there must be a hole in the boat, so it's probably filling with water."

The boat was clearly sinking. Loud pops and bangs continued as branches broke beneath its weight. Then the back end of the craft began to sink faster than the front, and Stu shouted, "We've got to get out of here."

At that moment, the lights flickered and went out, throwing them into thick blackness. They began to slide across the deck and were soon clinging to the rail that was now above them. "We've got to swim," Stu ordered.

Deedee didn't want to let go, but the sheer weight of her body dragging down as the boat settled forced her to do so. She slid into the water, mildly surprised that it wasn't nearly as cold as she'd imagined it would be. Stu called to her from only a few feet away, and she began to struggle to reach him. Branches scratched her face, and the water, though not rough like it had been in the open sea, still lifted her weakened body up and down. The life jacket she wore kept her from sinking, and she was grateful to have it. She pushed small branches aside and used bigger ones to help her work her way toward Stu.

She finally reached him and was actually relieved when he took hold of her hand. Together they found a large limb and steadied themselves against it. They didn't see the boat when it finally sank beneath the surface, but they did notice when the branches quit breaking and eerie silence took over.

"It's gone," Stu said.

"What do we do now?" Deedee asked through chattering teeth. "We can't stay here."

Stu moaned. "My head hurts."

"I hurt all over," Deedee countered. "But what are we going to do?"

"Wait until we can see," Stu said. "Then we'll make our way to land. It can't be far. These trees are growing in the water, so it can't be very deep here. We'll have to wait for daylight though. Then we'll go to the shore. It couldn't be more than a few feet from here—a hundred yards or so at the most."

He sounded confident, and Deedee took comfort in that. She despised him, but right now she was awfully glad that he was with her, that she wasn't alone. She tried not to think about Toby and the captain or what would have happened if Stu had been washed out to sea with them. The thought of being alone was too horrible to contemplate.

# CHAPTER 9

Enos had not slept well during the night. Instead of blowing over, the storm grew in intensity. Fierce wind and pelting rain had kept him from sleeping deeply. When he had tapped on Meredith's door at dawn, she answered almost instantly, and from the dark rings around her eyes, he knew that she had suffered similarly. But he was pleased to see in her hands a copy of the Book of Mormon and was impressed that she'd been reading the scriptures so early in the morning despite the distractions of the night. He, too, enjoyed the comfort they offered, and he seldom missed a morning without spending a few minutes reading them. Somehow, there was solace to be gained from them, encouragement, faith, and guidance. He and Meredith certainly needed those things now.

Meredith closed the Book of Mormon and said, "I was reading about the sons of Helaman just now. They had such great faith and courage."

"Which they obtained at their mothers' knees," Enos reminded her.

"Yes," she agreed. "I might not be the best mother in the world, Enos, but I really have tried to teach Deedee the gospel."

"And she'll remember those things you taught her," Enos said, "even as the stripling warriors did."

"I hope you're right," Meredith said as she moved with him toward the door. Enos turned as if to step out, but Meredith stopped him. "Would you shut the door for just a minute?" she asked almost timidly.

Surprised, he did as she had requested, wondering what she was thinking. Then she said, "We can only do so much, you and I. Deedee's fate really is in the hands of the Lord. Would you pray with me?"

Enos was both surprised and honored. Prayer was such a sacred thing, something he'd always felt was deeply personal. He'd already been on his knees that morning—he always began his day that way even before he read from the scriptures. He suspected that Meredith had already prayed as well, but she wanted to pray with him! She wanted their combined faith to reach heavenward. He was deeply touched by the gesture and listened in a sort of awe as she offered a fervent prayer to her Heavenly Father, first thanking Him for her life, for her daughter, and for Enos's help. Then she went on by asking that He watch over Deedee that day. She prayed that wherever she was, she had not been lost to the terrible storm. She also asked that she and Enos would be blessed with wisdom, that they would receive divine guidance in their search for her daughter. After she'd finished and as they rose from their knees, Enos felt a closeness to Meredith that had not been there before. She smiled at him, touched him lightly, and said, "Thank you. We can go now."

When they left the motel, a warm breeze carried salty air from the sea, and they both breathed it deeply, hoping that their search would end this day. The sky was clear now, the storm had passed. They were joined by several police officers who seemed less than enthusiastic to check the harbors, explaining that there were actually hundreds of places a savvy person could dock a boat on Abaco and the surrounding cays. But as disheartening as that sounded, they stressed to the worried mother that Deedee and Stu would surface soon if they had managed to sneak in on a boat during the storm and come to shore somewhere.

"However," one of the officers said, "I'd be surprised if anybody got to the island by boat last night or even attempted it. That was a fierce storm. Nobody who knows the power of the sea would try such a thing." He went on to explain that even though it was a far cry from a hurricane, it was a strong storm, and no sea captain in his right mind would try a crossing from Florida on a night like that.

Enos and Meredith looked at one another with concern. Enos could see that Meredith was close to tears, but she composed herself and said, "Would you mind helping us check the main harbors, just in case?"

They agreed, but just a few minutes later, the same officer again approached Meredith and Enos. His face was grim, and Meredith felt her heart sink. "What is it, officer?" she asked, her voice trembling. She leaned against Enos for support, and he found his arm encircling her shoulders.

"This may be nothing," the handsome young officer said, "but we received a report that a fishing boat from Miami set out to sea before the storm last evening and hasn't returned."

Enos gripped Meredith a little tighter as he felt her body tremble. He asked, "Has it some significance as far as our missing girl is concerned?"

The officer explained that there was no way of knowing at this point but that a witness claimed to have seen the boat departing its port the previous evening. He told them that the authorities in Miami believed that the captain of the missing boat usually took out small groups of people by himself to a full day of deep sea fishing. However, that particular captain was one who seldom stayed on the ocean overnight, and then only in good weather. But in this case, it appeared that the boat had not returned, and the U.S. Coast Guard was concerned that it might have capsized and sunk during the storm.

"Is he someone who might try to smuggle people from the U.S. illegally?" Enos asked

The officer didn't have an opinion on that, but he gave Enos the name of an officer in Miami who might be able to at least hazard a guess. He offered to call him.

"Thanks, we might take you up on that. But in the meantime, did they give you any idea who might have been on the boat?" Enos pressed.

"There were two men, one woman, and the boat's captain, according to the report we got."

"A woman?" Meredith asked tentatively, and again Enos's arm held her firmly.

"A young woman," the somber officer answered. He went on to explain that she was older than Meredith's daughter, more likely in her late teens or early twenties, according to the report from Miami. But when the officer described her as having long auburn hair, Meredith's hand went to her mouth.

\* \* \*

By the time daylight had arrived, there was little sign that there had been a storm during the night. The ocean was still, the salty air fresh, the sky blue, but Stu and Deedee were anything but fresh. Cramped, cold, and hungry, they had eventually managed to climb from the water and into the tangled branches of the mangrove trees, where they had spent the balance of the fateful night.

With the sun shining brightly, they were shocked to see that there was no land anywhere near the trees. They appeared to be growing from the bottom of the ocean, which didn't seem to be very deep at that point, for they could see the fishing boat where it rested not many feet below the surface. There were more small groves of trees nearby that appeared to also be growing from the ocean floor. Each little group of mangrove trees appeared, from their vantage point, to be a small island, but were, in fact, nothing but more groves similar to what they were perched in. Farther away, however, was a long, unbroken line of trees that they decided had to be the island. After some debate, Deedee finally agreed that their only chance for survival was to drop back into the water and swim for that distant shore.

"At least we have these life jackets, so we can rest as often as we need to," Stu told Deedee.

"What about sharks?" she asked.

"This close to land?" Stu asked, as if that meant anything. But it calmed Deedee's fears a little, and she agreed to swim for shore.

After offering a short and desperate prayer in her mind, Deedee entered the water. She followed Stu from the thicket of branches, and then they both began to swim eastward. Deedee was already weak, and she knew that it would take a long time to get there. But she had survived the storm, the boat crash, and the night in the branches, and she was not about to give up now. As long as sharks were not a danger—and Stu seemed confident that they weren't—she could make it to the island. So with all the energy she could muster, she swam, matching Stu almost stroke for stroke.

\* \* \*

After giving considerable thought to the officer's offer to call his colleague in Miami, Enos realized that he wasn't content to let a Miami cop do the legwork for him and maybe miss an important clue. But when he announced to Meredith that he was going to fly back to Miami, she insisted on accompanying him. "No, why don't you stay here," he suggested, "just in case Deedee happens to show up. I'll find out all I can there, then return. I should be back by morning at the latest."

"You don't honestly believe they'll turn up here," Meredith said sadly. "And neither do I. I'm coming with you, Enos. And I think we should take our bags. We might not need to come back here at all."

Enos was worried at how despondent Meredith had become, how convinced she was that Deedee had been lost at sea. He knew that was a distinct possibility, but he wasn't ready to give up, not by a long shot. He'd been assigned by his boss to find Deedee Marchant, and as long as there was any chance at all, he intended to do just that.

It never occurred to him that he might be trying to impress Meredith. He'd never consciously tried to impress a woman in his life, but had he taken the time to think about it, he would have had to admit to himself that he wanted desperately to make her happy, and finding her daughter was a definite way of accomplishing that. But even more, he found that Deedee's life had become very important to him. He barely knew her, but he couldn't bear to think that she might never be reunited with her mother.

Enos continued to argue that Meredith should wait in Marsh Harbor, and she continued to insist that they should pack up and leave. A compromise was reached; all but one overnight bag each of their luggage was left behind in the motel. They both caught the first available flight back to Miami, and upon arrival there, they took a taxi to the small harbor that the missing fishing boat had sailed from the day before.

Meredith followed Enos around, trying not to interfere as he questioned everyone he could find that might know anything about the missing boat or its captain. She also tried to be positive about Deedee, wanting with all her heart to believe that her daughter was alive and well but finding it hard to assume. That was especially true after Enos learned that the captain was an excellent sailor but also a bit of a rogue. Many of his competitors believed he'd do about anything for anyone if the price was right.

The worst bit of news, the most crippling to Meredith's faint hopes, was received from the man who'd watched the three people climb aboard with the missing captain. He instantly identified Deedee from a photo Enos showed him, and then he nodded and said, "That's the younger of the two men," when shown a photo of Stu. He described the other man the best he could, and neither Enos nor Meredith had any idea who he might have been.

Once they were positive that Deedee had in fact sailed on the small fishing vessel, Enos contacted the Coast Guard. He was told that when an unexpected storm like the one from the previous evening struck the area, fishing boats routinely headed for the nearest safe harbor. After the weather settled down, they returned to their own port. The missing captain had not done so, and his wife was the person who had sounded the alarm that he was missing at sea.

Enos decided to talk to the woman himself. They found her, distraught and crying, with a drink of whiskey in her hand beside the pool in her flowering backyard. Enos approached her sympathetically and learned that her name was Sandi Earnestine. A pretty woman of about thirty-five, she was deeply tanned and seemed quiet by nature. "I'm sorry about your husband," he said after introducing himself and Meredith.

"He's not coming home," Sandi said as tears began to flow, and she took a big swallow of the drink in her hand. "He'd be here if he could." She looked up at Enos, who was standing awkwardly in front of her. "He sometimes fishes at night, but never in a storm."

That surprised Enos. From the conversations with the men at the harbor, he'd learned that most fishing boat captains took clients deep sea fishing in the day. It suddenly became clear to Enos what was going on in this case, and it was also clear that it wasn't the first time the man had smuggled people to or from the coast of Florida. But his wife might not know that, Enos realized.

"I'm sorry," he said to her again. Then he pulled up a chair for Meredith and then one for himself. After they were both seated, he said, "We believe one of the people on the boat with your husband was Ms. Marchant's daughter."

The lady's face became even sadder. "Oh, no," she said.

Meredith could hardly stand it. She didn't need this woman's doubts thrust in her face. They only served to frighten her worse. Yet the situation caused Enos to suddenly become more assertive, which surprised Meredith.

"Mrs. Earnestine," he began, "Deedee Marchant, Ms. Marchant's daughter, was not going fishing."

"But you said—"

"I said she was on the boat. The man she was with, one of two men who also went with your husband, was illegally taking her to the Bahamas. They had planned to fly, and their luggage arrived in Abaco. But for some reason they never got on their flight. We have cause to believe that they decided to go by boat instead."

Sandi Earnestine looked genuinely puzzled. "Then why would they get on a fishing boat?" she asked.

"That's what we'd like to know," Enos said. "Apparently your husband is involved in more than just fishing."

Sandi's face darkened. "My husband would never sneak people out of the country illegally."

"Do you ever go with him when he takes clients fishing?" Enos asked.

"No, I don't like the smell of his boat," Sandi answered. "Anyway, I get seasick too easily."

"Do you ever see the fish he's caught when he returns?" Enos pressed.

"No, I don't like the smell," she insisted. "He never brings any of them home."

"But sometimes he's gone all night?" Enos asked.

"Not very often, but when he is, it's because he's fishing."

"Do you know that for a fact, or is that what he told you?"

Sandi suddenly seemed to be not so sure of herself. She looked down at the drink in her hand, then took another large swallow, coughed, then said, shaking her head slowly, "He told me. And I believed him."

Enos said nothing more right then, wanting to give the woman time to think. Suddenly her face brightened, and she looked back at Enos. "Maybe that's why he's missing. Maybe he's still alive." Her dull eyes began to shine with a glimmer of hope, but it didn't last. "He'll be in trouble now, won't he?" she asked.

Enos nodded. "But when he comes back, if he'll tell us where he took Deedee and the man she's with, Ms. Marchant and I will do all we can to help him, won't we, Meredith?" He looked sternly at Meredith, who nodded her reluctant assent.

"Ms. Marchant is a criminal defense lawyer," Enos added impulsively. "And she's a very good one. She would know how to help your husband." He didn't mention that she wasn't licensed to practice anywhere but the state of Utah.

"Oh, will you do that for us?" Sandi implored, her reddened eyes on Meredith's face. "I'll make him tell me where he took your daughter if you'll promise to help him get out of trouble."

"I'll do what I can. You have my word," Meredith said, biting her tongue to keep from adding, "if he comes back." She was becoming increasingly convinced that Sandi had seen the last of her husband and that she had seen the last of Deedee.

After leaving Sandi's home, Enos again checked with the Coast Guard. There was nothing new on the fate of the missing fishing boat, and a call to the police in Marsh Harbor revealed nothing new from there either, so the two weary travelers found a hotel for the night.

* * *

Two even more weary travelers were also trying to find shelter once they reached the shore. After the harrowing trip and many hours in the water, Stu's wallet and his substantial supply of money was gone, as was Deedee's purse. They had nothing with which to pay for a motel room, but Stu was a great talker, and he eventually prevailed upon the motel attendant that his friend, a resident of the island, would pay the next morning.

Their clothes were dirty and torn, but after they walked through the dense and rugged forest to a two-lane highway, both Deedee's and Stu's clothes were dry.

A friendly islander had given them a ride into Marsh Harbor in his badly rusted, older-model Chevrolet pickup. From a phone booth in town, Stu had tried to call Rapper, but even after several attempts, there was no answer. Finally they gave up and went to the motel. Deedee was starved, but since they had no money for food, Stu assured her that his friend would feed them in the morning.

Deedee entered room number 244, right next to the one where Stu was to spend the night. She showered and then put on her badly soiled clothes, wishing she had her suitcase so she could dress in fresh ones. Little did she know that the very suitcase she longed for was sitting on the bed in a room a few doors down and the scriptures she was missing terribly were lying open on the nightstand in that same room.

It was nearly noon the next day before Stu finally managed to make contact with Rapper. "We're at the motel, and we're—"

Rapper cut him off sharply. "Just be watching for me. I'm in a silver Mercedes," he said. "I'll be there in ten or fifteen minutes."

Deedee, who had never been so hungry in her life, watched from her window while Stu met Rapper in front of the motel. She couldn't see the fellow Stu called Rapper very well, but she could tell that he was clearly angry. The two seemed to be arguing. After a minute or two, Stu and Rapper finally started toward the motel office. They weren't gone long, and when they came back, Stu hurried up the stairs, knocked on Deedee's door, and said, "Come on, Deedee. We're all set."

Stu opened the door to the Mercedes, and Deedee climbed in ahead of him. Rapper looked over at her, his face angry. "Who's the chick?" he demanded. "And where's Toby? You told me he was still in the room."

"It's a long story," Stu said.

"Start telling it," Rapper demanded. "Toby was a valuable man. I trust he'll be along soon."

As he spoke, Rapper was eyeing Deedee. She'd never seen eyes so cold in her life . . . or had she? There was something sickening familiar about this man. And yet there was no way she could have ever seen him before, she reasoned, trying to calm her sudden intense fear.

"This is Deedee," Stu said desperately. "She's with me. We're going to get married."

"Oh, really?" Rapper said. "Maybe I have other ideas, Stu. Maybe you *are* actually helping out here."

The way he said this sent chills over Deedee. Even worse was the reaction of Stu. "No, you can't do that, Rapper. She's my girl." Stu's voice was unnaturally high, and for some reason, Deedee had the feeling that Stu was afraid of this man, this man he'd told Deedee was a friend.

Rapper kept looking at Deedee, and a feeling of uneasiness snaked over her. She reached over Stu and said, "I think I'll get out, Stu. I don't mean to be a bother to Rapper." She knew her voice was giving away her intense fear of this man, but she couldn't help it.

Rapper stepped on the gas, and the car shot into the street. "We gotta get moving. She can come to the house. We'll decide what to do about her after you tell me where Toby is," he snapped sharply. "And you better have a good explanation for things, Stu." His tone was menacing, and Stu squirmed uncomfortably. "Like where's your luggage? Don't you have some somewhere?"

Deedee dropped her head into her hands and rubbed her eyes as Stu fumbled with his answer, which was a clumsy mixture of truth and fiction.

\* \* \*

Enos and Meredith didn't know which way to turn next. Finally they'd decided that they could once again check the ports throughout Abaco to see if Captain Earnestine had docked anywhere. He hadn't appeared in Miami yet, as they both had feared would be the case. And as of just a few minutes before their flight left Miami, Sandi had not heard from her husband, and she was becoming increasingly distraught.

As they pulled into the motel parking area a couple of hours later, a silver Mercedes sped away. Meredith caught just a short glimpse of a flash of long auburn hair as someone in the center of the car leaned forward. She caught her breath. "What is it?" Enos asked as he parked in front of the motel.

"Probably nothing," she said. "But did you see that silver Mercedes that pulled out as we drove up?"

"Sure did. Guy needs a ticket. And it seems like a fancy car compared to most of what we've seen around here. Why?"

"It's probably nothing," she said with a quiver in her voice.

Enos was instantly alert. His experience had taught him that it was often the things that didn't seem important that proved to break the case. "What did you see?" he asked sharply.

"Well, like I said, it's probably nothing—but there was someone in the backseat with hair about the color of Deedee's."

Enos had the car in reverse and was backing from the parking space before Meredith had finished her last sentence. He sped into the street and followed in the direction the Mercedes had gone. Just ahead was an intersection, and as he slid to a stop, Enos looked sharply in three directions for the Mercedes. "There it is!" Meredith shouted, pointing to the right. Enos waited for the intersection to clear, and the Mercedes rounded a curve and disappeared in that brief span of time. Enos gunned the rental car and headed down the street, but they were unable to find the car even after searching for over an hour.

Disappointed, they headed back to their motel. Meredith went straight to her room, but Enos paused, then turned away from his door and headed for the manager's office. "Did someone check out a little over an hour ago?" he asked when he arrived.

"Yes," he was told.

"Was this the man?" he said, producing his picture of Stu.

"Uh, it could be. I'm not sure though. All you white guys looks the same," the fellow said, grinning slightly.

"There was a girl with him," Enos said, not interested in humor at the moment. "Deep reddish-brown hair—auburn, I guess you could say. This would be her." He showed the picture of Deedee to the young man at the desk.

The man studied the picture for a while. "I'm not sure it's her. I didn't see her close. I know she was very dirty, maybe a little sick. Her hair was sure a mess." The man concluded that the girl he'd seen was probably not the same girl as the one in the photograph.

"Was there another man with them?" Enos asked, disappointed that he hadn't received a positive identification.

The manager explained there were only two of them when they'd checked into the motel the previous evening, but a third man actually paid for their rooms when they checked out. "The girl, she didn't ever come in here. Just the two men."

"But only one man and one woman stayed overnight?" Enos pressed.

"Yes. The other man, he came here just a minute or two before they checked out. He was driving a silver Mercedes," the fellow added, "a real nice car."

"What names did they give you?" Enos asked. "Stu Chandler and Deedee Marchant are their names."

"Nope, not them," the manager said. He then showed Enos the motel register, pointing out the names Sonny Thompson and Janie Bills.

Enos knew it was likely they were using false names now that they were where they didn't need picture ID to travel. It could still be Stu and Deedee, he thought. "Thanks," Enos said to the manager as he turned and slowly climbed the stairs to Meredith's room, wondering if he had enough information to bother her with right now. He decided he would tell her what he knew. He knocked softly on her door and waited.

It took Meredith a moment to answer, and when she did, Enos said, "I think it could have been Stu and Deedee." He still held the photos in his hand. "If it was them, then they spent the night here under assumed names. The guy in the Mercedes paid their bill."

Meredith stood for a moment, then slowly backed into the room until she came to a chair. She moaned softly as she seated herself and dropped her face into her hands. Enos, who'd followed her in, could tell that she was crying softly. He stepped beside her and put a callused hand on her shoulder. "Hey, the manager couldn't tell me for sure, but there is at least a chance it was them. If so, this is good news," he said. "It means they might be right here on this island. And best of all, it means Deedee's alive."

Meredith's body trembled beneath his touch, but she didn't look up or speak. "I'll go now," he said after a long pause. "I'll notify the police, let them know it might be them. Maybe someone else has seen them. And maybe it's time to call that number I found in Stu's car. If it was them, then Deedee can't be far away now."

His last sentence evoked a response from Meredith. She looked up, wiped her eyes with the back of her hand, then said, "Enos, I've been such a fool."

He was slightly taken aback. "You've been great," he said with more feeling than he'd intended to show. There was just something about this woman that was causing a stirring deep inside him that was unfamiliar, frightening, and yet very pleasant.

Meredith rose to her feet and faced Enos. "No, I have not been great, Enos. I prayed for wisdom yesterday morning, but then when you suggested a wise course of action, I wouldn't agree to it. I've blown it terribly by not following your advice and waiting here while you went to Miami. You didn't need me there, and if it was Deedee who stayed here last night, I would have known her even if she had tried to change her appearance. If I would have listened to you, I would most likely have had her back by now. The Lord might have tried to answer my prayer, but I wouldn't listen."

Enos was quick to reply in her defense. "We still don't know if it was her, Meredith. And don't go blaming yourself. I could have insisted that you stay," he said, looking deep into her beautiful eyes. As he spoke, he was thinking how much easier it was for him to work when she was there. He'd been secretly glad that she'd insisted on going to Miami with him. "But I didn't," he finished, "and so I share the blame."

This brought a quick smile to Meredith's face. "Oh, Enos, you know better than that. I'm way too stubborn. I admit it. But I'll try to do better after this. I just pray that I haven't blown my only chance of getting Deedee back."

"I'm sure *we* haven't," Enos said firmly. "And together, I'm sure we'll still find her." There was a lot more he wanted to say to her now that he seemed to be developing some courage. He wanted to tell Meredith that her very presence was becoming more of a help to him than she could ever imagine, that she inspired him, that she motivated him. He wanted to tell her that she was fast becoming an important part of his life and that her missing daughter was important to him in a very personal way. He considered giving it a try, but at that thought, the words that had begun to form began to twist inside his brain and become all garbled. He had to look away from her, afraid that if he attempted to say something to let her know that he was beginning to have feelings for her, he'd mess it all up. Anyway, there was no way that a beautiful and intelligent woman like Meredith would ever have feelings for him.

Instead he said, "You need rest, Meredith. I'll keep at it for a while. I'll show the pictures of Stu and Deedee around town. Maybe someone will be able to positively identify them."

But Meredith wasn't about to let him go without her. And even though she knew it was something that would shock everyone who knew her, most of all Enos himself, she was beginning to have feelings for the man, tender feelings. She wanted to be with him every minute that she could. Even in the midst of the pain and turmoil, she was beginning to actually enjoy his company. And he was someone she could lean on in this time of such terrible stress. In fact, he was much of what was keeping her going now. She wanted to tell him that, but concluded it wasn't the time or the place. She wiped her eyes again and spoke only a few thoughts. "Enos, I know I'm being stubborn again, but I'd like to come with you. I can't get my daughter back without you, and I don't want to be alone right now."

Then her thoughts returned to Deedee and how close they might have been to getting her back. Her wanting to be with Enos, to not be alone, might have allowed Deedee to slip from their grasp. As those thoughts came, she couldn't stop the tears, and she turned away, wiping her eyes and shaking with sobs. Enos stood helplessly for a moment, then stepped toward her, put a hand on her shoulder, and said, "Of course you can come. We're in this together, Meredith."

Meredith turned slowly toward him. When her eyes met his, he didn't duck his head. For a moment they looked silently at each other, and in that moment there was an unbidden transfer of feelings from each to the other. Meredith found new strength. Enos found renewed determination. She smiled at him. He reached out and took her hand, holding it silently. Then the moment passed and Meredith said, "I want Deedee back, and with God's help and yours, that just might be possible. If she is on this island, then you and I together can find her."

"Of course it's possible," he said. "Let's go see what we can learn."

As they left the motel room, each was thinking of Deedee and how close they might have come to getting her back. Each was also thinking how much the other was beginning to mean, wondering how to keep from blowing the beginning of something neither of them had expected—but both of them secretly wanted.

# CHAPTER 10

Rapper took Deedee and Stu to a very large and luxurious house on a hillside overlooking the sea and the small, distant island of Hope Town that lay across the broad channel. He pulled the silver Mercedes into a large, three-car garage and closed the door behind them. With a curt nod of the head, he led them into the house. It was clean, neat, and filled with things a man obsessed with power and risk might collect.

Deedee concluded from a comment by Rapper that he had a maid who cleaned and cared for his home. Acting as the perfect host, Rapper offered them drinks. Stu took a beer, and Deedee a Sprite. She was starving, but her hunger seemed unimportant now as they sat in comfortable black leather furniture and sipped their drinks in awkward silence for several minutes. Deedee noticed that Rapper, though he always had a glass in his hand, was drinking very little while encouraging Stu to tank up. Stu was finished with his beer and was on his third glass of some kind of hard liquor before Rapper offered Deedee some of that same liquor. She firmly declined. The uncomfortable atmosphere suddenly intensified.

Rapper's face grew dark, and his evil eyes flashed. "When I offer liquor, my guests drink," he said in a low, threatening voice. Deedee shivered with fright. This man with his shaved head and short beard looked unfamiliar, but she couldn't shake the feeling that she'd seen him somewhere before.

Stu attempted to come to her defense by saying, "She's only fifteen, Rapper. She's way too young to drink."

"Fifteen!" Rapper thundered as he turned on Stu in a fury. "Don't you think I have eyes, man? Don't lie to me. If she's fifteen, I'm twenty."

"No, I'm serious, Rapper. She's fifteen. She just looks older. Believe me, I wouldn't kid about that. She's too young to drink."

Rapper's face grew darker yet, and his eyes smoldered. He looked like the most dangerous man Deedee had ever seen. She looked anxiously about, wishing she could run. Then Rapper began to smile. "If you're not lying, my friend, then maybe you've done us both a favor," he said as he again looked Deedee over as if she were nothing but an animal at a livestock auction.

"No, Rapper, you can't do that. She's my friend," Stu said, but Deedee could tell he was afraid of Rapper too.

"This is my house," Rapper said, the awful smile slowly fading, but his eyes still watching Deedee closely. Rapper appeared thoughtful for a moment. Then his demeanor seemed to change. "She needs food and something to wear," he said. "And I suppose you're both probably starved."

"Yeah, we haven't had anything to eat for a while. Maybe she and I could borrow some money, walk to town, and find some food," Stu suggested.

It dawned on Deedee that Stu wanted out of this house as much as she did. She hoped he could be as persuasive with Rapper as he so often was with others. She didn't like Stu, but right now he was certainly the lesser of two evils.

"Oh no, I'll see that you get something real soon," Rapper said. "But before I do, tell me where Toby's at. That's one question you've avoided answering."

Stu looked at Deedee, but she was so terrified that she was clearly of no help. So he faced Rapper and said truthfully, "He got washed off the boat on our way over from Miami."

There was a tense silence for a moment while Rapper digested this information. Then he said in a low voice, "So he's dead?"

"I think so. He and the captain were fighting, and they both got washed overboard. Neither one of them had a life jacket on. I can't imagine how they could have survived."

Rapper shook his head for a moment, then asked doubtfully, "So you two brought the boat to the island by yourselves?"

"I've done some boating," Stu said. "It was the only choice I had."

"Congratulations," Rapper said snidely. "Where's the boat now?"

Stu told him where it had sunk, and Rapper shot back, "And you claim to have had experience." Then he added as if to himself, "So there's a boat and its captain missing from Miami. There's a female juvenile in my home who's a runaway. My surviving partner, who was supposed to meet me here so he could help me do a little job, is now wanted in the states for who knows what, probably kidnapping and a lot more. Most likely there are cops swarming this very island looking for him and the girl as we speak. This is a fine spot to be in."

He was talking so calmly now that Stu relaxed a little. He even found the courage to say, "I came to help you. And I plan to do that, Rapper. I just need a place where Deedee and I can stay."

Rapper nodded his head. "Of course you do, Stu. Of course you do. We'll make this situation tolerable, won't we? What are a few little snags after what we've been through together? We're partners, right?"

"Right," Stu said, breaking into a foolish grin.

Deedee could see that Stu was feeling better about things, but she was not. She was feeling very ill, terrified almost out of her mind.

"Okay, so we can stay here tonight and you'll help us find a place of our own tomorrow, right?" Stu asked.

Rapper nodded thoughtfully, then said, "Not a problem. I have a place in mind for you . . ." He drifted off. He looked at Deedee for a moment. "The girl needs something to wear."

"Yeah, she will," Stu said. "I'll need something too."

"Sure you will," Rapper said. "We wouldn't want people seeing you around the island looking like that."

Deedee could tell that Stu didn't grasp the gravity of their situation, that Rapper was toying with him for some reason.

When Rapper spoke again, he sounded reasonable even to her. "Let's get something right now for both of you. Stu, you come with me. You'll just need to kind of keep your head down while we're out and about. Deedee can stay here."

Deedee's heart suddenly leaped with joy. If they left her here alone in this room, she'd get away from both of them—she had to! Surely someone would help her when she got out of this house. Maybe she could go back to the motel and—

Her thoughts halted and her hopes plummeted as she heard Rapper say, "Deedee, I'll show you to a room you can stay in while you're my guest. It has a shower, so you can clean up. I'll find you something to wear until I get back with something more suitable for a woman so very beautiful. And I'll give you something to eat. Come with me."

The way he referred to her beauty gave Deedee the chills, but she rose from the couch and followed him. Stu smiled at her as she left the room. "We'll find you something pretty," he promised. "And we won't be too long."

Deedee didn't even acknowledge Stu, intending to be free of both him and Rapper in the next little while. Without a word, she followed Rapper up a long, winding stairway. At the top was a hallway. Rapper opened a door at the very end of it, went in, and she followed. It was a fully furnished bedroom. "You'll like it in here," he said. "There's a shower in that bathroom." He pointed to a closed door to her right. "Make yourself at home. I'll see what I can find for you to wear, and I'll rustle up a meal for you. Why don't you go ahead and get in the shower."

She entered the bathroom and locked the door behind her, glad to be alone. For a moment she stood there trembling, thinking about how badly Rapper frightened her. She had to get away, and it had to be soon. Finally, she stripped off her clothes and climbed into the shower, spending fifteen minutes there. When she was finished, she wrapped a towel around herself and reentered the bedroom. True to his word, Rapper had left her some clothes and a plate that contained a hot TV dinner. She dressed quickly, embarrassed at how silly she looked in Rapper's pants and shirt but feeling clean and refreshed despite the ill fit.

She rolled up the pant legs, tightened a belt around her waist to keep the pants up, and shrugged on the large T-shirt over her head. Then she attacked the food, literally shoving it down. She had no time to waste. When she'd finished, she walked barefoot to the window and looked out, hoping she might be able to escape through it. What she saw instead almost caused her to sink to the floor in despair. The house was built on a hill, and the room she was in was probably three stories from the ground. She took a deep breath. If she couldn't go out the window, she'd just have to try to get to an outside door to make her escape. She slipped her shoes on without socks and headed resolutely to the door she'd first entered the room through. She grabbed the knob and attempted to give it a twist.

The blood froze in her veins.

The door was locked from the outside! She was a prisoner. Slowly, she sank to the richly carpeted floor and sobbed as her hopes of getting away were dashed and the reality of her situation sank in. From somewhere far away in the house, she could hear the faint ringing of a telephone. Sobbing quietly, she curled up on the plush carpet.

\* \* \*

"There's no answer at this number," the police superintendent said. "And there's no answering machine."

Meredith groaned. Enos watched the superintendent thoughtfully for a moment. Sam Brown was a short, stocky black man of middle age with closely cropped graying hair and intelligent eyes. He was very businesslike and did seem genuinely concerned about Meredith and her missing daughter, although he was not convinced the girl was on the island and had stated as much. He seemed to Enos like a man who could be trusted, and he was grateful for that.

"Let's ask around town about the silver Mercedes. I remember seeing it myself a few times. I've never met the man who drives it, but he is bald and has a short beard. Someone will know him, I'm sure."

"Thank you," Enos said. "We appreciate all the help you can give us."

"That's why we're here," Superintendent Brown said. "We don't get much crime on this island, and that's good. I don't think she's here, but if I'm wrong, we'll find this little girl of yours, Ms. Marchant. People here look out for each other. Now if you folks will give me a few minutes, I'll send some officers out right now. I'll be back shortly."

Meredith and Enos were sitting across from one another at a small table. "He seems very efficient," Meredith said.

"Yes, and very nice."

"You know, I can't help but wonder if they have any nonnative officers on the department. I haven't seen any if they do."

Enos smiled at her. It was becoming easier to do that. "Neither have I. In fact, they don't seem to have many officers at all. From what I understand, the people are generally friendly and quite religious given the laid-back way of life. I'm surprised how few of Stu's kind there are," he said.

"That's comforting. Even though Stu is not a decent person, I'm glad that his kind aren't common here."

Enos agreed aloud, but inwardly he was wondering what kind of person or persons had attracted Stu here. He clearly had at least one friend or associate, and Enos couldn't help but think that whoever he was, it was almost certain that he was not a good man.

When the superintendent came back in, he was excited. "You folks may be right. We think we know where the missing boat from Miami is," he said. He told them that some young people were boating on the leeward side of the island, and as they passed one of the many groves of mangrove trees growing up from the shallow ocean bottom, they spotted a sunken vessel. "It's not far beneath the surface of the water. I'm going out there to have a look. Would you two like to come with me? There's nothing else you can do until we learn something more about the man with the Mercedes."

Meredith looked at Enos, who nodded. She felt renewed hope surge in her heart. Maybe Deedee and Stu really had made it safely to the island.

\* \* \*

Though only eighteen, Hank Prentice was much sought after for handyman services in both Marsh Harbor and Hope Town. He pedaled around Marsh Harbor on his bike to do whatever odd jobs people hired him to do. When he needed quicker transportation, he borrowed his elderly mother's old Chevrolet sedan. He also kept a small boat docked a short way from the house where he still lived with his mother, using it to go to Hope Town two or three times a week. Only in bad weather did he ride the public ferry.

Hank was pleasant to be around and worked hard. He didn't make much, but he didn't require much either. About 5'8" and stocky, Hank was both physically strong and very smart. His pleasant personality made him a favorite of the older people in the area. Soft-spoken and gentle, Hank also liked people, and he believed in treating others the way he wanted to be treated.

Hank had been pedaling up the street in one of the more wealthy parts of Marsh Harbor when Rapper pulled his Mercedes into his driveway. Hank had never seen the man with him before or the girl with the reddish-brown hair who sat between them. He didn't get a good look at the girl before the car pulled out of sight into the garage, but from what he did see, Hank had wondered if something was wrong. She'd looked right at him as the car passed by him, and for just the briefest moment, he'd caught her eye. Maybe, he thought now, he was just imagining it, but she'd seemed so sad at the time—as well as afraid.

That was silly, he told himself as he worked on the hinge to a shutter. But then again, he'd actually done a small job for Rapper once, and he promised himself he'd never do so again. The man frightened him, and he wasn't even sure why. Maybe it was his eyes, he had concluded, for the man had an evil stare unlike anyone Hank had ever met.

He remembered the first time he'd ever seen Rapper. It had been four or five years ago, and Rapper had come into the grocery store where Hank was working for tips carrying groceries to the tourists' cars. He'd taken Rapper's bags out for him, and after putting them in the man's car, he'd waited politely for a tip. But Rapper had ignored him and driven off. Hank hadn't thought too much about it at the time, for strangers who weren't accustomed to the way things were done in Abaco often failed to tip.

At that time, Rapper had a full head of dark hair and no beard. Now he wore a short, neatly trimmed beard and shaved his head. But one thing hadn't changed, and that was the sinister look in his eyes.

As Hank worked and thought about Rapper and his guests, he heard the garage door open. Rapper and the stranger emerged in Rapper's open-topped red Jeep, then pulled into the street and passed by Hank. They were arguing, and for just a few moments their voices carried to Hank's ears. He wondered if he'd misheard what Rapper had just said to the man he called Stu. If he hadn't, what Rapper had in mind was horrible. Apparently Stu thought so too, for Rapper said very clearly, "You want to die, Stu, just buck me on this. You brought her here. Now I do with her what I want. This is business."

Hank's imagination ran wild for the next few minutes. He could picture the girl tied to a chair with a gag in her mouth somewhere deep inside Rapper's huge house. He was certain, as he thought about the short conversation he'd overheard, that Rapper had mentioned taking the girl to a yacht, but not for a lovely cruise around the Caribbean. No, Hank knew that yacht wasn't for lovely rides.

Hank shivered as he thought about what he might have heard, and he began to wonder if there was some way to get her out of the house. If he tried to go inside, Rapper might return and catch him there. Anyway, he couldn't really be sure the girl was in any kind of trouble. Yet no matter how he tried, he couldn't get the girl off his mind.

He finished the shutter before Rapper had returned, and he asked the woman of the house if there was anything else she'd like to have done before he left. She thought about it for a moment, then she said he might check the flower beds for weeds and pull them. He told her he'd do that and charge her only half his normal hourly rate. What he really wanted was an excuse to stay near Rapper's house to see if Rapper did come back alone. Then Hank wanted to watch the house and see if Rapper brought the girl out. If he did, he wanted to follow him, although that would be very difficult on his bike. Of course, if he took her to his yacht, he knew exactly where that was, and he knew a shortcut by bike to get there.

Hank continued working along the edge of the property, watching the front of Rapper's house, waiting for Rapper's return.

\* \* \*

A diver accompanied Enos, Meredith, and the superintendent on the ride to the sunken fishing boat. After arriving at the spot where the boat could be seen not far below the surface of the water, the diver went down. He resurfaced after a few minutes, and when he was back in the boat, the superintendent asked him what he'd found.

"Not much," he reported. "It's the missing boat, but there aren't any bodies down there." He then described to them how it must have run right into the trees, punctured a hole low down, and sank fairly quickly.

After a short discussion, he and the superintendent concluded that the captain was not on the boat when it ran into the trees. There was some speculation as to the missing man's fate, but unless Deedee and Stu were found, both what happened to Captain Earnestine and the fate of the mystery passenger would remain unknown, as would the fate of Stu and Deedee, unless they could find more proof that they'd been on the island.

"We'll have the boat salvaged in the morning," Superintendent Brown said. Then he promised that they'd try to find out if Deedee and Stu had been able to swim to shore, and if so, where they had actually left the water.

As they rode toward the shore, Meredith sat very quietly beside Enos, drawing both strength and faith from him. Only once did she break the silence, and that was to say, "I can't believe Deedee was able to swim to shore. She's not that good a swimmer."

"I'm convinced that she did it, though," Enos said.

The issue was resolved a short while later when a pair of abandoned life jackets were found near the edge of the water. The police superintendent conceded that Deedee and Stu must have made it to shore at that spot.

Meredith's eyes filled, but she kept a brave face. "I hope it was them," she muttered.

"They must have walked to the highway from here," the superintendent observed.

To Enos, the facts were simple. They'd found one more piece of evidence that Deedee really was the girl who'd been at the motel, that she really had made it to Abaco.

\* \* \*

Deedee awoke, cramped and sore, after falling asleep on the floor. She hadn't intended to go to sleep, but her body was exhausted, as was her mind, and it had just happened. There was no way to know how long she'd been there on the floor. Her watch had stopped after the many hours in the salty water of the sea, and there were no clocks in the room. She shuffled over to the window and peered out. She looked for the sun through the tall trees outside her window, but the branches were too dense to the west, and she couldn't see it. She figured it was sometime in the afternoon because they had arrived at Rapper's house around noon, according to a clock in the room with the black leather furniture. She must have slept for two or three hours, at least, she guessed. But Rapper had promised that he and Stu wouldn't be long. She shivered. Time was wasting, and she desperately needed to get out of this house. There was a catch on the window, which she opened, and she pushed the window up easily and admitted refreshing air into the room. It only took her a moment to remove the screen, and then she leaned out. It was a long way to the ground, but she suddenly had an idea. It was dangerous, she knew, but she was desperate.

There were sheets and blankets on the bed. She could tie them together and lower herself down—provided that they reached far enough to allow her to get away. She hurriedly tied them, but when she was done, the makeshift rope reached less than halfway to the ground. Terribly disappointed, she pulled her makeshift rope back up and untied the knots she'd made. She even remade the bed so Rapper wouldn't guess what she'd been up to. Then she wondered if she ripped the sheets and blankets in two if she could make a rope long enough to do the job.

Wishing she'd thought of that before, Deedee turned back to the bed and grabbed the top blanket. There was a noise at the door, and in one swift movement, she leaped onto the bed and slid beneath the covers, pulling them to her chin. The door opened, and Rapper walked in. He had some clothing in his hand. "Put these on and get ready to leave," he said.

"Where are we—" she began.

Rapper cut her off. "Put these on. I'll be back for you in five minutes or less." He threw a bright pink blouse and pair of blue pants, some socks and underclothes, and a pair of shoes on the bed at her feet and stalked out. The foul mood he was in struck new terror in Deedee's heart. And where, she wondered, was Stu?

Rapper had no more than shut the door before Deedee sprang from the bed, grabbed the clothes, and hurried into the bathroom. She didn't want Rapper walking in on her while she was changing. She hurried and was surprised to find that the clothes fit well. She ran her fingers through her hair, checked her face in the mirror, and left the bathroom.

Rapper was waiting at the door. "Let's get moving," he said.

"Where's Stu?" she asked.

"He's in a bungalow over in Hope Town," he said. "That's where you two will be staying for a while."

Deedee nodded. As much as she'd come to distrust and even detest Stu, she'd rather be alone with him somewhere else than with Rapper anywhere. But she still intended to get away. She was convinced that Stu had no real influence with Rapper, and Rapper was a very bad person. She followed him reluctantly to the garage. A red Jeep and a large white utility van were parked beside the Mercedes. Rapper directed her to the van, which had windows only in the front seat and at the rear doors. He made her sit on a seat halfway to the back of the vehicle.

"We can't have anyone spotting you," he said. "We won't be long. My boat isn't far away. We have to use it to get to Hope Town, of course, as it is a separate island."

Deedee had figured that much out, but the thought of getting back on a boat after the nightmare she'd gone through didn't give her much comfort.

# CHAPTER 11

Hank was feeling desperate as he pedaled furiously toward the harbor where Rapper kept his yacht. He still couldn't believe what he had seen a few minutes earlier. He'd just happened to glance up at the high front window of Rapper's house when the rich, reddish hair of the girl caught his attention as she leaned out and looked down. He'd stopped what he was doing and crouched in the bushes, where he could watch that window and still see the street.

After a moment, she'd left the window. Two or three minutes passed, and then the girl had reappeared. To Hank's absolute amazement, she'd dropped a makeshift rope made of sheets and blankets from the window. It wasn't long enough to reach the ground, but it was very clear to Hank that the girl was desperate to make an escape. Despite the distance between them, he could see the disappointment she felt when she pulled the blanket and sheets back up and stepped away from the window.

About that time, the red Jeep had returned with only Rapper inside. The girl never came to the window again, and a few minutes later, Rapper left the house again, but this time he was in his white van.

* * *

The boat was unlike any boat Deedee had ever seen. It was a yacht, something from TV and the movies. Rapper led her below the main deck, and they entered a room that was richly furnished and very ornate. It appeared to be a living room of some kind. Round windows overlooked the water, and her feet sunk in the plush carpet.

From there he led her into a dining room, and then into a bedroom. She figured this was where he was going to leave her, but she was wrong. Rapper pushed a button concealed within a cupboard, and the bed moved several feet to the left. He leaned down, pulled a piece of carpet aside, and there, in the floor, was a trapdoor.

Deedee's blood ran cold as Rapper opened the door and said, "In there, Deedee."

She shook her head, and Rapper calmly pulled out a pistol. He pointed it at her and said, "Get moving."

She went, almost in a trance. It was dark down there, the ceiling so low she couldn't stand up straight, and there was a mustiness that stung her throat and burned her lungs. Before Rapper slammed the door shut and locked her into the darkness, she got one terrifying glimpse of what could only be described as a floating dungeon—iron rings in the wall with chains hanging from them spaced every foot or so apart. At the end of each chain was a handcuff!

Then the door slammed down, nearly striking her head, and she was alone in deep darkness. Deedee figured her life was over. Was what she'd done to her mother so terrible that she deserved this? Oh how she regretted her rebellion. She felt the urge to pray, knowing that only God could get her out of the fix she was now in. She dropped to her knees and bowed her head. "Please, Heavenly Father," she begged, "help me. I'm so sorry, so very sorry." She couldn't get more words out as violent sobs racked her body. Several minutes passed, and she remained kneeling below the trapdoor.

Finally, she crawled near the wall. She felt about her and touched one of the chains. There was nothing supernatural about it, yet it seemed to represent some terribly evil thing that happened from time to time in this place. She tried not to think what that terrible thing might be.

* * *

Hank had arrived at the harbor just in time to see the girl start down the stairs to the lower deck of the yacht. He trembled, almost feeling as though he were being forced into that place, not knowing what horrors awaited her below.

He hid himself and watched the yacht, expecting the engine to fire up and the vessel to move from the harbor into the open sea. But within just a few minutes, Rapper came back onto the deck alone, looked about, then jumped to the dock and hurried back to his van.

Hank's insides were churning. He knew he had to do something. The girl was in serious trouble, and he felt compelled to help her if he could. He thought about going to the police, but that might take too long. They might get back here to find the yacht gone. The sun was sinking in the west, and he knew his mother would be expecting him home for dinner soon. But he couldn't worry about that. This girl, whoever she was, needed his help.

Fear ran through Hank's body, and he hesitated momentarily before realizing there was no one else around to help her—he was the only one. So he summoned courage he didn't know he had and stole silently onto the yacht, slipping down the stairs to the lower deck and looking around. The lights were off, but there was enough light from fading twilight for him to see his way around. He hurriedly searched, expecting to find a locked door somewhere with the girl behind it. But as he went from room to room, he found nothing.

Hank rubbed his eyes in frustration. This was just too much. He'd seen Rapper bring the girl aboard and leave without her, so she had to be here somewhere. Then his imagination kicked into gear, and he began to envision secret chambers. He hurriedly searched the entire area again, tapping on cupboard doors, searching the pantry, sticking his head in every closet. He even looked beneath the bed. Nothing.

Every few minutes, Hank would slip back up the steps and peek outside, knowing he couldn't be much longer. Finally, frustrated, he left the yacht and returned to his bicycle. He felt like a complete failure. He looked back at the yacht. Surely she was in there. He stared at it for a long time, and then it hit him. There had to be space beneath the second deck, and there had to be a secret passageway that led into that space. The girl must be in there, afraid and in total darkness.

Though it would be dark in a little while, Hank felt compelled to once again go on board and search, this time for a way through the floor. But he had to have a flashlight, he decided. Without one, he wouldn't be able to see regular features, let alone secret passages, and turning on lights would be too suspicious.

He hated to leave for fear the yacht would be gone when he returned, but he had no choice. He jumped on his bike.

* * *

"Superintendent, we know who the Mercedes belongs to," a young officer said excitedly when the superintendent returned to the station.

"And do you know where the owner's at right now?" Enos asked quickly.

The officer shook his head. "We don't."

"Get a surveillance set up at his residence," Superintendent Brown ordered.

"We've already done that," the officer reported.

"Good. As soon as he comes out or shows up to go in, we'll pick him up." Superintendent Brown smiled at Meredith. "We just may get your little girl." Then he turned to his officer again. "Who is this man, the owner of the Mercedes?"

"It seems that his name is Darnel Sloan, but apparently he also goes by Rapper. He's from the states, but nobody knows what he does. He's got plenty of money, and he's here on the island most of the time. Would you like to see where he lives?"

"Yes," Meredith answered before the superintendent could do so. She not only wanted to see where he lived, but she also wanted to rush in and grab her daughter from him, but she knew that was something they couldn't do without just cause. However, there was nothing to stop her from sitting outside that house until Deedee came out. And then she'd do whatever she had to do to get the girl to come back to her.

* * *

Meredith and Enos looked at one another in amazement when they saw Rapper's house. It was large and modern, and unlike many of the homes they'd seen, it was not a pastel color, but white with dark blue trim. "Not the kind of place I'd expect any friend of Stu Chandler's to live. This guy, whoever he is, can't possibly be anyone in Stu's league," Meredith observed.

"Maybe a partner in crime," Enos suggested.

The way he said it made Meredith's stomach churn.

Enos said, "I understand that we can't enter without permission, but can't we knock and ask if Deedee and Stu are with him? Maybe he'd force Stu to give her up if he thought it might get him in trouble if they kept her. I mean, he might not even know that she's with Stu illegally."

The superintendent thought for a moment, then said, "I suppose that's okay, if you want to tip your hand."

"I just want Deedee back," Meredith said.

"Then let's give it a try," Superintendent Brown agreed. "Why don't you go, Enos. The rest of us will wait out of sight, and we'll have the house watched from the back side while you're up there just in case someone tries to slip out."

A bald man with a small, neat beard who appeared to be in his midthirties answered the door after Enos had pressed the button for the third time. "What do you want?" he asked.

Enos took a moment to size him up. His narrow eyes were almost as dark as his black beard, and his shaved head was tanned a very dark brown. He was a little shy of six feet in height, but his slender frame was knotted with muscles. Enos guessed there was a well-equipped weight room in this large house.

"I'd like to speak to the young girl you have here, Deedee Marchant," Enos said.

The man didn't even bat an eye. He simply said, "You've got the wrong house. Ain't no girl living here." With that he stepped back as if to shut the door, but Enos was too quick for him and had already slipped into the doorway.

"You brought her here from the motel," Enos said, "in your Mercedes."

"I don't know what you're talking about. Now if you'd kindly move, I'd like to close my door." The man talked rapidly and smoothly. His voice was rather high and had a nasal quality to it. He didn't look or sound like a nice man. And his eyes . . . well, Enos felt like he was staring at the devil himself when he looked into his dark eyes.

"Listen, Mr. Darnel Sloan, or Rapper as you're better known, I know who you are," Enos said.

"It's not hard to learn someone's name," Rapper shot back, appearing surprised when Enos called him by name. "This is not exactly a metropolis here."

Enos ignored his comment and said, "We don't take kindly to having young girls hauled off from their homes in Utah and taken out of the country." As he said that, he produced his badge. "We want to talk to Stu Chandler. We know he and the girl came with you to this house earlier today."

"Don't know any Stu," Rapper said, "but just to show you what a good guy I am, I'll let you have a look inside of my home, although we both know I don't have to do that."

Enos's heart sank. The man was too willing. Now he knew that they weren't going to find Deedee in this house, that she'd already been taken somewhere else. A search might be a total waste of time, but he wasn't about to turn down the invitation. So he shouted to the waiting car, "Superintendent Brown, Rapper has invited us to have a look inside his home."

When Meredith heard Enos shout, she also knew that Deedee must have been moved already or been taken someplace else from the start. And hope fled as she followed the superintendent around the corner of the house and joined Enos as he followed Rapper inside. Then Enos stopped and said, "Oh, Rapper, you might like to meet Deedee's mother."

Rapper turned just a little too quickly. "This is Meredith Marchant," Enos said. "You'll note the strong resemblance to her daughter."

Meredith was stunned. She knew this man—she was absolutely certain of it. She just couldn't remember when or where she had met him. There was definitely something familiar about the bearded face, and the eyes . . . well, they weren't the kind someone forgot.

Rapper smiled from his nose down as he said, "I'm sorry, I don't know your daughter, but she must be lovely like her mother."

Enos could have kicked the man in the shins. His arrogance was almost more than he could take. Meredith stared at Rapper, fighting the impulse to do something worse than kick him while she tried to place where she'd met him. But she kept her composure and nodded a terse greeting.

It took several minutes to tour the large house, and both the superintendent and Enos were watchful as they followed Rapper from room to room. There was absolutely nothing that would indicate that Deedee or Stu had ever been in the house. All the beds were made up neatly in each room, and there were no dirty linens or used towels in the laundry room that might indicate guests had been present. Every bathroom—and they'd seen three of them so far—were so clean they sparkled.

On the top floor, Enos entered the final room at the front of the house, following Rapper, who stopped just inside and waved his hand, inviting a quick inspection. "As you can see, I live alone. A maid cleans for me once a week. I like things orderly," he said. "I do entertain guests occasionally, and this is the room they all like the best."

"Yes, I can imagine," Enos said as he stepped past Rapper and walked to the window. He leaned forward and looked out. A magnificent view lay before him. The sun was just setting to the west, and it created a golden glow across the sea. He felt Meredith's presence as she stepped up behind him, the fragrance of her perfume pleasantly enveloping him. However, he didn't turn to face her, for his attention had been drawn to the windowsill. The maid Rapper had mentioned might be efficient, but she had missed a very small piece of fabric that clung to the wood.

"Okay, you folks can go now," Rapper said. "I've been more than generous, and there is no one here, as you can see."

"Yes, you've been very generous," Superintendent Brown agreed. "And we appreciate it a great deal. We're sorry to have bothered you."

Enos ignored them as he continued to study the tiny piece of fabric. Then he turned to the bed and knew what he'd found. The fabric, nothing more than a few threads really, appeared to be the color of the blanket on the bed.

Without a word, Enos opened the window and leaned out, gazing down thoughtfully. It was a long drop, and he considered again the trace of fabric. Finally, he shut the window and turned. There was another door to his right, a bathroom, perhaps. He stepped over, glancing at Rapper as he did so, expecting a protest. "Nobody's in there," Rapper said, "but you may look in if you'd like."

Enos took the opportunity and looked closely. Rapper and Superintendent Brown were out of sight when he entered the bathroom, and Meredith still stood near the window, gazing absently across the bay at the distant lighthouse in Hope Town. No one saw Enos lean down and pick up a single strand of long hair that lay—almost invisible— beside the toilet. He looked at it closely as his heart began to pump a little faster. In the less-than-perfect light in the bathroom, it was hard to be sure of the color, but Enos was quite certain it had a reddish tint to it. He carefully put it in his shirt pocket, figuring there would be no value in confronting Rapper with it at this point. He'd only come up with a logical explanation anyway, for he'd already told them that his guests preferred this room. But the strand of hair was enough to convince Enos that Deedee Marchant had indeed been there.

He scanned the room carefully once more, then turned and joined the others in the large bedroom. He still wasn't through and didn't fail to notice the look of impatience that crossed the face of Rapper as he opened the closet door across the room from the bathroom. But he found nothing of interest there and finally said, "We appreciate your help. This is sure a nice home you have here."

Meredith couldn't take her eyes off Enos as he spoke to Rapper and then as he moved into the hallway. She had to admit that she had no idea what he'd seen in this room that was different from any of the others, but she was almost certain that he'd found something. She had the good sense not to ask what it might be while they were still in the presence of Rapper.

At the front door, Rapper said to Superintendent Brown, "I would appreciate it now if you would see to it that these people don't bother me anymore. I'm a law-abiding citizen, and I bought this home on your beautiful island so I would have a place to get away from time to time. I think I should have the right to enjoy my solitude without such rude interruptions."

"You are certainly right," the superintendent acknowledged. "Thank you again for your time."

Back in the car, the superintendent said, "I think we've made a mistake. There must be another Mercedes on the island."

"We didn't make a mistake," Enos said, and the calculated tone of his voice made the superintendent look sharply at him.

Meredith leaned forward in the backseat and said, "You saw something significant in that last room, didn't you?"

Enos nodded. "Deedee *has* been in that room," he said, and the confidence in his voice was unmistakable.

"Then why didn't you say so while we were still there?" Superintendent Brown demanded. "We certainly looked the fools, you know."

"Better that Rapper think us fools than that he knows we know she was there," Enos said. "He undoubtedly knows where she is, but if he thinks we realize that, he'll be extra cautious and never lead us to her. But as it is, there's a good chance he'll slip up. It's absolutely essential that we keep watching him."

"What was it that you saw in there?" Meredith insisted.

"Three things," Enos answered, twisting in his seat so he could meet her eye. "On the windowsill there was a very small bit of fabric, and it was the color of the blanket that was on the bed. My guess is that someone hung that blanket out the window."

"That makes no sense," the superintendent said, appearing to be a little impatient.

Enos watched Meredith's face for another moment before he turned back to the superintendent. "It would make sense if you happened to notice that the doorknob on that room locked from the outside instead of the inside," he said solemnly.

Again the superintendent looked sharply at Enos. "Are you sure?" he asked. "I didn't notice that."

"Neither did I until we were leaving, and then I was looking for it. You see, I think Deedee was planning to use the blanket and sheets to try to let herself down to the ground outside that window. And considering the distance of that drop, she wasn't likely to try that if she could walk out of the room. She didn't make it down, though, either because she got caught trying or because she couldn't reach the ground with the sheets and blanket. It's a very long drop. Again, it didn't make sense to me that she'd try something so desperate unless she was a prisoner in that room. And if it locks from the outside, that room, as high as it is, becomes a fairly effective prison cell."

The superintendent was impressed. Meredith was shocked. "That's two things, Enos," she pressed. "What else did you see?"

Enos reached into his pocket and carefully extracted the single, long strand of hair he'd found in the bathroom. "This," he said as he again turned back to face her. "And unless I'm mistaken, I'd say it's about the color of Deedee's hair. When we get back to the police station, maybe we could have a closer look."

"That rat," Superintendent Brown said, more to himself than his guests.

Enos glanced at him in surprise, somewhat satisfied to hear him refer to Rapper in that fashion. Enos believed he'd regained the support of the superintendent, and that was important.

The superintendent grimaced. "We're not used to having his kind on this island. We do better when they're not here."

# CHAPTER 12

Deedee listened for what seemed like an eternity to someone move around on the deck above her. She couldn't imagine what Rapper was doing. She kept expecting the boat to move out, but all she could feel was the gentle rocking motions as it stayed tied to the dock.

She wasn't sure if it was Rapper up there, but she couldn't imagine who else it could be. When he began to tap something, then move something, then tap some more, she had really wondered what was going on. But she didn't dare do anything but sit there, her back against the wall, wondering what fate had in store.

Deedee kept picturing Rapper's face. She felt like she'd met him before. But was that possible? It certainly seemed unlikely. She thought hard and long about the face, trying to picture it clean shaven. She tried to picture Rapper with a full head of hair. She considered his black eyes. For a moment, she thought she almost had it, but she couldn't quite pull the fragments of memory together.

After a while she was again aware of someone coming aboard, but whoever it was didn't come down to the lower deck. Then to her absolute dismay, she heard the engine start up, and the boat went into motion. At that exact moment, she realized that she knew who Rapper was, knew where she'd seen him. Deedee passed out.

\* \* \*

Hank groaned in dismay as he slid his bike to a stop and dropped it in the dirt. The yacht was already pulling out of the harbor. But he hesitated only for a moment before picking up his bike again and heading toward his house, dropping it near the dock behind his neighborhood. He untied his boat, jumped aboard, started the engine, and made the fastest exit he'd ever attempted from the harbor.

Hank was grateful for the partial moon that lit the surface of the sea. He didn't want to run any lights this night. His boat was relatively small but the engine was large, and Hank could get a lot of speed from it when he wanted. Tonight, he wanted all the speed he could get. He kept as close to the shore as he dared while rounding the point. He didn't want to cover any more distance than he absolutely had to. Finally, he could see the distant lights of Hope Town, and he set a course in that direction.

Rapper was probably running without lights, like he was, Hank guessed. It was risky heading straight across the channel, but it was worth it. Rapper might not have been heading to Hope Town, but he could well be intending to sail east, and to do that, he had to pass close to Hope Town.

Hank had his boat running full throttle, and it was literally skimming across the waves. Ahead of him he spotted a light. As he drew closer, tension built within him, and he knew it could be Rapper's yacht. He finally cut back his speed as he continued to gain on the other vessel. Rapper had his lights on, and he wasn't going very fast, but it was his yacht, of that Hank was certain now. He slowed down and held back, content now to simply see where Rapper might be headed. He hoped it wasn't out to the open sea—he could never follow him there. He would run out of fuel long before the yacht did.

To Hank's relief, Rapper sailed the yacht right into the bay that ran up the center of Hope Town. Hank pulled his boat close to the shore and watched the lights of Rapper's yacht as it pulled up and docked. Hank did the same and then ran along one of the narrow streets until he'd come close to where Rapper was tying up his boat.

Then he blended into the shrubbery and watched.

\* \* \*

In her semiconsciousness, Deedee could tell that the yacht was moving quite quickly. But it wasn't long before it slowed to a crawl, and then a few minutes later she felt it bump against something and then begin to rock lazily in the water. She wanted out of this place she was in. She had already thrown up from the seasickness, and she was dizzy and weak, yearning for some fresh air. Yet the last thing she wanted was to see Rapper's face.

A couple of minutes passed, then she heard the bed above the trapdoor being moved aside. She could hear Rapper as he pulled the carpet back, and then light flooded in as he lifted the door. She squinted at the sudden brightness, and her stomach turned as she heard Rapper's voice.

"Get up here, girl," he ordered. "This is where you get off."

Without a word, Deedee obeyed. She climbed the short ladder and was soon in the luxurious bedroom. She could see the pistol tucked in Rapper's belt, but after all she'd been through the past few hours, she was mostly numb now and very weak. She knew she couldn't have gotten away from Rapper if she'd tried.

He closed the trapdoor, slid the carpet back into place, moved the bed to its proper spot, and then shooed her into the dining room. To her surprise, he had food on the table there. He ordered her to eat, but the seasickness prevented her from tasting more than a few small bites. "I'm sick," she said when he glared at her. "I have a problem with motion sickness," she added by way of explanation.

Rapper seemed to accept that, but he did say, "You better get used to the motion, girl, because you'll be riding on this boat for a long ways in a few days."

Her stomach turned again, nearly bringing what little food she'd managed to swallow to the surface. Rapper offered her a Sprite. "This will settle your stomach," he growled.

She took it and began to sip, and it did make her feel better. She'd managed to drink about half the can when Rapper began to gather up her meal. He put it in a bag, handed it to her, and said, "Take this with you. You might feel a little more like eating later."

Rapper then told her not to make any kind of scene when they left the yacht. He touched the butt of his pistol, and she got the message. He then ordered her to go to the upper deck. When she stepped into the clear, cool night, she breathed deeply. The air was so good she felt like she couldn't get enough of it. "We'll leave the boat now," Rapper said. "Step onto the dock right there."

She did as she was told, then he led her to what looked like a golf cart. He told her to get in, and he sat beside her and turned it on. After a short ride along a narrow street lined with brightly lit houses, he parked the cart and directed her to a small, bright pink house that he called a bungalow. She expected to see Stu inside and was mildly surprised when she saw he wasn't there.

She asked Rapper where he was. "He's gone," he said sharply. "You won't be seeing him anymore. Count yourself lucky that I didn't send you with him."

Deedee didn't say anything else, and she wondered and worried about what had happened to Stu. Yet she was smart enough to know that it was all out of her hands, so she quietly entered the room Rapper told her she would be staying in for a while. He flipped a light on, then turned and shut the door as he left. Deedee could hear it lock and Rapper's footsteps fade away through the house. The room she was in was ground level . . . and windowless! Not only could she not get out, she couldn't even see out. Other than a higher ceiling, fresher air, and a single light above her, this room was as solid a prison as the dungeon in the yacht had been.

* * *

Hank Prentice watched the bungalow that Rapper had taken the pretty girl into. He knew that he was dealing with a situation way over his head, but he had to find a way to save that girl. It was just something he had to do. He could never respect himself if he didn't.

Several minutes passed, and then Rapper came out. He walked quickly to the golf cart and rode it back toward where the yacht was moored. Hank followed in the shadows, wanting to be absolutely sure that Rapper was gone before he attempted to get the girl out of the bungalow. Rapper went directly to the yacht, started the engine, and pulled back into the bay. Within minutes he had sailed out of sight in the direction of Marsh Harbor.

Hank walked quickly back to his own boat, grabbed a handful of small tools, shoved them into his pockets, and then proceeded toward the pink bungalow. He could hear people laughing and talking in neighboring houses, but only a few ventured into the night, and none of them seemed to pay any attention to Hank. Once he was again near the place where Rapper had left the girl, Hank slid into the bushes and thought about what he should do next. He was reasonably confident that if he could get into the bungalow, he could get the girl out, whisk her to his boat, and then sail away with her from Hope Town before anyone knew what had happened.

Finally, he gathered up the courage to do what he'd convinced himself he had to and slipped quietly from his hiding spot. It only took him a minute to get through the front door of the bungalow. It was not a large place, and it didn't take him long to find the one interior door that was locked securely with a dead bolt. It caught Hank a little by surprise. Why would such a simple home need such a heavy door and lock, and inside at that?

He studied the door for a moment, then nodded in grim satisfaction. He pulled a screwdriver from one pocket and began to remove the heavy hinges. The screws were big, tight, and set deep, but in the end they were no match for Hank's skills.

\* \* \*

Deedee ate the rest of the sandwich Rapper had given her, and she'd finished the Sprite as well. She was feeling a little better when she heard someone scraping at the far side of her door. She was tempted to call out but didn't dare. More than likely it was Rapper, although she couldn't imagine what he was doing.

She shut the light off and hid in the far end of the tiny room, near the bathroom door. When the heavy door finally swung open, and light rushed in, she let out a little whimper. She hadn't meant to, but she couldn't help it.

When the figure in the doorway spoke, her fears slowly faded. "Hey, I've come to get you out of here. Don't scream," he said. "I want to help you get away from Rapper. He is a very bad man."

His voice was young and kind. He sounded like a good person. Deedee instantly made the decision to trust him, at least for now, figuring that no one could be worse than the man who'd locked her in here. "You promise you won't hurt me?" she asked.

"I promise. I came to help you. Come on now, we better get away from here as fast as we can," Hank said.

Deedee rose to her feet and padded softly across the hardwood floor. Hank reached out, and she took his hand. "Follow me," he said. "I'll get you away from here."

A few minutes later, the water lapped softly against the side of the little boat as it slipped from its small hidden dock and moved into the open channel that separated the main part of Hope Town from the towering red and white lighthouse on the far ridge. The lighthouse was lit with flood lights, and the surrounding foliage, usually deep green in the daylight, was dark and shadowy now. Hank kept the motor idling slowly both to keep the speed down and to keep from attracting undue attention to himself. The girl was lying on the bottom of the boat to conceal herself, only speaking a few words to thank him for helping her.

Hank slowly moved the throttle forward, picking up a little speed as he approached the sea. It was a beautiful night, not too cool, and with only a slight breeze blowing. He perspired heavily, but it was as much from worry and tension as from the humidity. He'd never done anything like he was doing now, and he was very nervous.

\* \* \*

As night closed on the small island, peering eyes traced Hank and Deedee's path.

# CHAPTER 13

Rapper didn't like complications. He'd made good money over the years, usually because he'd always planned well, made sure of the loyalty of his accomplices, and left a clean trail behind him. He'd planned an upcoming job that required the help of two other men, Toby and Stu. Toby had been a faithful accomplice for several years, and while Stu was a relative newcomer, he and Toby had worked so well together in Los Angeles two years ago that he'd chosen them to assist him again.

Then Stu had stupidly shown up in Abaco with a young girl, had lost Toby while crossing the ocean from Miami, and worst of all, had brought the cops to his house. Rapper had made sure Stu wouldn't do anything moronic like that again, although the girl he brought was not such a bad asset after all. Rapper had plans for her, but her mother was a problem, as was the nosy cop from Utah. Rapper couldn't help but think that Ms. Marchant had remembered him despite his change of appearance. He was almost certain her daughter had remembered him, although it had taken her a while. And he feared that if the lawyer had recognized him, the detective would also know him.

Rapper's Hope Town friend would not be back for a few weeks, so using his bungalow presented no problems. Even though the place really belonged to Rapper, it was listed in one of his many aliases, and it was actually helpful to have someone else appear to be the owner and live there for much of the year. Rapper's buddy didn't object. He knew that Rapper used the place for some kind of illegal business when he was away, but Rapper paid him well to live there and keep his mouth shut.

But Rapper wasn't sure how long it would be before he could take Deedee away. He needed more girls to make the trip pay, he needed time, and he needed help. That would mean a flight to the states to round up a couple of other former employees, as well as a quick foray through the late-night streets of New York.

Rapper wasn't particularly worried about the local police. They didn't deal with much heavy crime and seemed to like to keep a low profile. But that detective from Utah was another matter. Rapper couldn't imagine what the man had seen in the room Deedee had been in, but he knew he'd seen something that made him suspicious. Rapper was convinced that he had to do something soon or the cop would cause real problems for him. He and the woman were already a thorn in his side, and they may have just made it impossible for him to use Abaco as a base of operations in the future. Then he made a decision. He knew what he had to do, and he knew it couldn't wait.

Rapper began to carefully plan his moves. He would use only one accomplice, a man who now lived on the island and whose most valuable skill was with explosives. He knew that the man would take the money he was offered, do what needed to be done, say what needed to be said, and then keep his mouth shut long enough for Rapper to disappear from Abaco and begin a new life somewhere else. He didn't want anyone else besides that one man involved though—he had to accomplish what he planned to do and make a clean getaway with the girl in tow. He couldn't afford to make any mistakes. His future prosperity dangled precariously in the balance. Since there were cops watching his house who might follow him if he went out, Rapper picked up the phone and made a single call. When he laid the phone back down, he smiled. *That will do for now,* he thought to himself. Sometimes he had to make hard decisions that might actually cost him money in the short run but make it possible to make more in the future. That was the case now. He had also thought of a way to get some extra money from the woman who had been his attorney before he made his getaway with her daughter, before he made her pay with her life for interfering with his. And the Utah cop, he thought proudly, would suffer in a most unique way for what he was doing. He certainly wouldn't enjoy his fate, Rapper promised himself smugly.

He smiled as he thought about what he was going to make happen in the next few hours. Besides money, there was another element in Rapper's motivation. He liked to see people suffer, and other people were about to get hurt.

\* \* \*

Deedee lay in the bottom of the little boat and prayed that the sea would stay calm. She was already getting queasy, and it wouldn't take much to make her ill. The young black man spoke to her. "What's your name?"

"Deedee," she said.

"That's a very nice name," he said. "I'm Hank."

Hank had been very quiet as he guided his boat through the moonlit night. He'd scarcely said ten sentences since he'd led her from the pink bungalow. And at first she'd had a hard time understanding him, but soon she was used to his accent and had asked where he was taking her. His reply had been short. "Someplace where you will be safe from Rapper."

"How much farther is it?" she asked now as her stomach rolled uncomfortably and another wave of dizziness washed over her.

"You ask too many questions," Hank said with a chuckle.

Deedee tucked her head back in the crook of her arm and closed her eyes. How she longed for her mother and her friends and the solid, safe environment of home.

\* \* \*

Enos had a very difficult time sleeping that night. In fact, he simply couldn't do so. They'd come so close to finding Deedee, but now he began to wonder if they were too late to save her. Rapper was an evil man, a very depraved man. Enos was convinced that he'd do anything to further his own interests, which was too bad for anyone who got in his way.

His troubled thoughts turned to the woman next door. Enos no longer thought of Meredith Marchant as *the defense attorney.* No, when he thought of her, he saw her as a very special woman. He was approaching the point where he wondered if life would seem awfully bleak without her around. In a very real way, her sorrow had become his sorrow, her fear his fear. His heart ached for Deedee and for Meredith.

Enos paced the small confines of the motel room then stopped as he thought he heard the soft closing of a door. He strained to hear and was certain there were footsteps outside. He glanced at the clock beside the bed. It was two o'clock in the morning. He began to pace again. Then he heard a vehicle start up, and he moved to his window and parted the curtain. A red Jeep was pulling into the street. For a moment Enos stared at it. There were two heads in view, but he couldn't make out more detail than that. Then he remembered the garage at Rapper's place. Beside the silver Mercedes there had been a white van and a . . . red Jeep!

Clad in pajamas, fear nearly cutting off his breath, Enos rushed from his room and pounded on Meredith's door. There was no answer. "Meredith, are you in there?" he shouted. Still there was no response.

Enos ran down the stairs to the office and rang the bell until a sleepy attendant finally entered, grumbling about being awakened at such an hour. "I need a key to the room next to mine," he demanded. "Quickly."

"I can't let you—" the fellow began.

"You better come right now. Something's wrong over there. Grab the key and come."

The urgency in his voice spurred the attendant to action. He did as he was told, and the two of them ran up to Meredith's room. Enos broke into a cold sweat as the light was flipped on and the bleak emptiness of the room was revealed.

Enos felt like the life had been sucked out of him. In that instant, he was shocked by the realization of two significant and frightening facts. Meredith had been taken away from here by Rapper! And he cared about what happened to her in a way he'd never cared about anyone before.

He flexed his hands violently, almost as though they were around Rapper's neck. Anger and panic flooded through him. He stood for a moment, composing himself. Then he realized that the motel attendant was speaking to him.

"Sir, the lady, she's gone out. We can't stand in her room like this," he said urgently.

"The lady is my friend," Enos said fiercely. "And she was *taken* out of here."

"I don't understand," the attendant said, puzzled.

"She's been abducted, kidnapped! Give me that key and you can go," Enos shouted.

"But I can't—" the fellow tried again.

"Now," Enos demanded, his hand held out expectantly. "Then call the police. Quickly. I want Superintendent Brown here personally."

The attendant looked for one more moment at Enos's determined face and dropped the key silently into the outstretched hand. Then he ran out of the room, presumably to call for help.

Enos hurried back to his own room, dressed in record time, and then returned to Meredith's room, where he began to quickly assess the situation. Her suitcase lay open on the floor beside her bed, but everything appeared to be neatly in place. Hesitantly, he bent down to go through it when a knock came on the door. Thinking the police had arrived, he hurried over and opened it.

The attendant was standing there. "Well, say something," Enos barked. "When will the police be here?"

"Well, ah, sir, they're all busy now," he stammered.

"Busy?" Enos asked in astonishment. Then he felt some relief wash over him. They must have seen Rapper take Meredith.

The attendant's next words sent his spirits plummeting. "Yes, sir. There's a fire at one of the harbors. There's been an explosion on a boat. Even the superintendent is there."

Enos groaned. This quiet little island was suddenly not so quiet, and he was afraid he knew why. Rapper was likely behind the trouble at the harbor. He knew he was being watched by the police and must have planned a way to distract them. It had certainly worked. They'd left Rapper to do whatever he pleased.

As a result, Meredith, along with her daughter, were in his hands.

Enos felt like screaming. Instead he ushered the motel attendant out of Meredith's room and finished his examination of her suitcase. Everything was in order, and he put it all back exactly as it had been, embarrassed that he'd even looked through her things and not sure now why he had. The pants and blouse she'd worn that day were not in the suitcase, nor were they anywhere else in the room, but he found her nightgown hanging neatly in the bathroom. Enos considered the implications of what he'd observed. Meredith must have been desperately afraid if she'd dressed without raising a loud protest, and Enos knew she hadn't, for he would have heard her. He certainly hadn't been asleep. She had clearly gone without a struggle, so Rapper must have been armed and had most likely convinced her he'd harm her if she resisted in any way.

Enos was filled with dreadful urgency as he thought of what must have happened. Meredith would be defenseless against a dangerous man such as Rapper. Enos stood looking for a moment at the street, closing his eyes tightly and trying to picture the red Jeep as it drove away. He seemed to remember it turning left, which meant it was headed south, away from Rapper's home, away from Marsh Harbor.

But he couldn't be sure. He headed for his rental car with determination, then drew up short. There was a note stuck beneath a windshield wiper. Hands trembling, he opened it, angled it toward the nearest streetlight, and instantly recognized Meredith's neat handwriting. He opened his car door and slipped inside, where the lighting was better. He began to read, his empty fist clenched, the one holding the letter trembling ever so slightly.

*Dear Detective Enas P. Faulerr,* she'd written. He stopped and looked at those words again. Meredith was a very bright woman, and yet she'd misspelled both his first and last names and added an initial that didn't belong there. Shaking his head, he read on. *I know how to get Dedee back.* This was too much. She'd now misspelled her own daughter's name. Was she trying to tell him something? *I'm with a young fellow from the island who knows where she and Stu are hiding. He called me here in my room shortly after we got back tonight. He suggested that we needed to go in the middle of the night. He has other friends who will help us if Stu tries to cause any trouble when they awaken him. And my new friend says that Rapper hasn't had anything to do with my daughter or Stu. He's going to take me to them tonight. He doesn't trust cops, so he wouldn't let me bring you with us. Don't be angry. Please wait and I'll be back soon with my little girl. Don't worry, and please, please don't interfere. I know what I'm doing.*

*Merredith P. Marchant*

She'd even misspelled her own name and added the same initial she'd added to his name. There had to be a reason for the names written the way they were. But what could she possibly be trying to tell him?

Ignoring the problem with the names for the moment, Enos considered the note. If taken exactly as written, it meant that Meredith wanted him to believe she'd gone off with a perfect stranger whom she'd actually believed would help her. The note also gave an explanation about why she'd gone willingly with the man, offering no resistance. Did she want so desperately for Deedee to be okay and for her to come home that she believed this man, whoever he was? That just didn't sound like the Meredith he'd come to know so well. Something wasn't right, something that had to do with the red Jeep that just happened to be pulling out about the time Meredith was leaving.

Then it struck him. Meredith must have been trying to tell him something with the misspelled names. He looked at the note again and spread it out on his steering wheel.

He carefully examined the names as she'd written them, looking for a message of some kind. He pulled a pen from his pocket, and in the margin of her note, he jotted down the letters that were wrong. First he wrote an *a*, then he jotted down the *p* that didn't belong. Next he noted the extra *r* in his last name. There was an *e* missing from Deedee's name, as well as an extra *r* in Meredith and the *p* that she'd given herself for an initial.

He now had the following letters in the margin: *a, p, r, e, r, p*. He sounded it out, deciding it was definitely not a word, and if it was to was mean anything, he needed to rearrange the letters. It took him only a moment for the letters to fall into place in his head. *Rapper* was what she'd wanted him to see. Rapper had taken her, just like he'd first feared. He angrily shoved the note and pen in his pocket and started the engine.

* * *

Deedee could scarcely tolerate the smell, but she forced herself to ignore it the best she could. She'd promised the young man named Hank that she would wait here for his return. Even if she hadn't promised, the sounds of the night coming from the nearby jungle threw fear into her innocent heart.

Deedee had no way of knowing for sure what kind of creatures stalked the night in that dense, dark foliage surrounding her. She now hunkered down inside a gigantic tank, her knees pulled up beneath her quivering chin. However, having stepped in something that smelled a great deal like pig manure, she suspected that there were dangerous wild boars and probably poisonous snakes and other deadly creatures as well.

Hank had helped her climb through a jagged hole into the tank, where he'd told her she'd be safe if she stayed put until he got back. There was a partial moon when they'd tied up to the rusty harbor of what Hank told her used to be the shipping point for molasses that had been produced on the island many, many years ago. She could believe that by simply looking at the deteriorated state of the tanks and pipes as Hank shined his bright flashlight around in an attempt to reassure her that no one would find her here. She could see that the jungle had literally grown up and around everything. He'd only wanted to show her that this was a desolate place, a place where no one would likely come snooping around, but she'd seen it as a spooky place.

She'd begged Hank to take her someplace else, but he assured her that for now, this was the safest place he could think of. Rapper would not find her here, he'd promised. He'd also promised to hurry back with food and water as soon as possible. Then he'd hoisted himself through the opening and left. That had been hours ago, and after all she'd been through the past few days, she was more numb than anything. She was also afraid of being alone. Hank wasn't the company she'd have ever imagined herself choosing, but she looked forward now to his return.

Deedee was as tired as she'd ever been in her life, but she dared not sleep. She was sure there were snakes in the cavernous reaches of this horrible tank, and she tried to rouse herself from the numbness and listen for them. Even though Hank had assured her that she was safe in here, she didn't feel like she was really safe anywhere. She'd found a stick near the opening Hank had climbed through only moments after his departure, and she now held it with one hand and peered over her knees into the inky blackness in front of her.

Deedee prayed. It was a desperate prayer but one of the most sincere she'd ever offered. She thanked God that Hank had helped her get away from Rapper, and she also prayed for protection from any other unknown dangers in this place. She sought forgiveness for the terrible things she'd done to hurt her mother. She prayed for Hank, that he would come back safely to her, that he would be able to help her get home, and that he would be trustworthy.

Finally, exhaustion overcame Deedee, and she slipped into a sound sleep, her chin resting on her knees, the stick falling from her hand. She slept so soundly that she didn't even awaken when Hank returned, nor did she stir as he spread a blanket over her to protect her from the chill of the coming Caribbean dawn.

\* \* \*

The fire flared up momentarily then died down again as Enos stood near the edge of the harbor watching and waiting. He needed the help of the police, but they were busy with the burning boats. He'd been here for an hour already, and he was tense and jittery. He'd driven by Rapper's house, and as he'd suspected, there were no cops outside on surveillance. They'd left their posts to come here where the action was. Enos was tempted to go in and search the house, but he needed the superintendent to help him if that was to happen.

"Evening, Detective Fauler."

Enos jumped. He'd been so absorbed in his thoughts that he'd failed to hear Superintendent Brown approach. Sheepishly but with relief, he turned. "Hello, Superintendent," he said. "I've been waiting for you."

"I see. Enjoying the fire?" the superintendent asked.

*What a strange question,* Enos thought. "No, but I guess I'm not really thinking about it. I came down here hoping to find you but was told I'd have to wait, that you were busy."

"Very busy, Detective," the superintendent said flatly. "This is going to cost someone, insurance companies I suppose, a lot of money."

"Yeah, looks like several boats have been destroyed. What a terrible waste. But the reason I needed to talk to you has nothing to do with the explosion or the fire. Rapper has taken Meredith, Superintendent, and I need help—" he began.

The superintendent cut him off sharply. "Funny you should mention Rapper. A little yacht of his is where the explosion took place. Quite an expensive vessel."

"Probably stolen, if the truth were known, and that really is a strange coincidence," Enos said. "But I really don't have time to worry about Rapper's boat. He's got—"

Superintendent Brown cut him off again. "You got any idea who'd want to do this to Rapper's yacht?" the superintendent asked.

Enos looked at him warily. The lights of the harbor were dim, and it was hard to see the features of his dark face, but he could certainly hear the tone of his voice, and he didn't like it. "I have no idea," he said. "What makes you think—"

For the third time, the superintendent cut him off. "We have a witness, Detective. He described you, says he saw you down here earlier. He says you were on that yacht."

"What!" Enos exclaimed. "I didn't even know there was a yacht."

"Maybe, maybe not," the superintendent said coldly. "I gotta get back to work. See you around."

"Yeah," Enos said, still taken aback by the superintendent's veiled accusation.

The superintendent took a couple of steps, stopped and turned back. "Oh, and Detective, stay on the island. Understood?"

"I have no plans to leave until I finish what I came here to do," Enos said angrily.

"You can leave when I say," the superintendent retorted, then he walked back toward Enos. "I'll need your firearm, please," he said.

Enos reached inside his jacket and handed over the pistol. "Thanks, I'll take good care of it," the superintendent promised. Enos watched in shock as he strolled away.

Enos suddenly knew he had seriously underestimated Rapper, and he suddenly felt as though he had a noose around his neck. But he had work to do, and apparently he'd have to do it without the help of the cops. He hurried back to his car, figuring that maybe it was good they were busy because now he could take another look inside Rapper's house. It was against the law, and under ordinary circumstances, doing such a thing would never even cross his mind. But these were far from ordinary circumstances.

# CHAPTER 14

The road was as rough as any Meredith had ever been on. She could see that it had once been paved, but now there were deep ruts of varying sizes, the largest as wide and long as the Jeep Rapper was driving, the smallest the size of a basketball or perhaps a little smaller. Rapper swerved continuously to miss them, but at times, he'd simply slow a little and bump through them.

Tall pine trees grew thick to the very edge of the road, making it impossible to steer a vehicle off the road to miss the roughness. Once a wild boar streaked across the road through the beam of the headlights, and Meredith wondered what other creatures might live in this forest. Not that she cared to find out. Another time, the twisted and rusted frame of a crashed airplane appeared in the headlights as it lay mangled and forgotten in the trees and shrubbery. Rapper made no comment, nor did she.

Rapper, for his part, was almost acting like a gentleman, which was quite amazing, considering the way he'd held a gun to her head as she lay in her bed. He'd entered the motel room almost soundlessly. She had no idea how he'd done it, but she guessed that it was something he had experience at. She'd been unaware of his presence until the cold steel had touched her forehead and woke her from a deep sleep. She'd opened her eyes to see a shadowy figure leaning over her.

"Make a single peep, Counselor, and it'll be your last," a heartless whispering voice that sounded frighteningly familiar had said.

In that moment, Meredith remembered where she'd met Rapper before—and she knew he was a dangerous man. She dared not breathe. A moment had passed before he'd said, "You're coming with me, Counselor. After you and your cop friends left my house, I got to work and did what they couldn't do."

She tried to think of a way she could defend herself, but absolutely nothing came to mind. She shivered involuntarily, and he spoke again.

"I located your daughter, and it's my intention to get her back for you," he told her. "But I'm only doing it because you once did a favor for me."

"H—how can you get her back?" she'd asked in a doubtful whisper.

"You were right about who she's with. I'd never met the guy before, but someone who called himself Stu Chandler did come to my house looking for a place to stay."

*That's a lie,* Meredith thought to herself. She now recalled only too vividly the thumbs-up Stu had given this same man two years before. "He told me that the young woman with him was his wife. She looks older than she is, doesn't she?" Rapper had asked suddenly.

"Yes," Meredith said, and she knew that Rapper was not referring to that time two years ago in the courtroom in Duchesne.

"Get up and get dressed," he'd commanded softly.

"Where are they?" she'd asked.

"Stu and Deedee? Not at my place, as you saw for yourself," he reminded her. "I turned them away. I'm a law-abiding man, and I don't need trouble."

"This isn't exactly lawful, what you're doing right now," Meredith had been unable to keep herself from saying.

"Can't be helped. You're my lawyer, but I was afraid you wouldn't trust me and allow me to help you any other way. Please forgive me, Counselor, but I had no choice if you were to get your daughter back," he'd said. "Now, get dressed—but no lights."

Meredith didn't bother to remind him that their professional relationship had ended when he'd left court that day. Instead, she'd slipped out of her bed, grabbed the pants and blouse she'd worn the day before, and entered the bathroom. As she began to shut the door, he slipped his foot in front of it and said, "Leave it open, Counselor. I'll stand out of the way and give you your privacy, but I don't want you tapping any signals to your cop friend next door. He can't be involved in this or Stu and Deedee will never agree to meet you."

Without protest, she did as he ordered, and he stood well out of view with his small flashlight turned off. When she was done, she hung her bedclothes on a hook in the bathroom and rejoined Rapper.

"Good," he'd said as she slipped on a pair of tennis shoes. "Now, there is one more thing you'll do before we leave. Write a note to your cop friend. We'll leave it on his windshield. I'll tell you what to write."

The second he'd said that, she thought of a way to tip Enos off as to who'd taken her. It would be taking a chance, but she really didn't figure Rapper would know how to spell names of people he didn't even know. In the dim light, he probably wouldn't be able to see the note well anyway. It was a chance she felt she had to take, and she only hoped Enos would recognize the bad spelling and figure out what she was trying to tell him. Even now, as she and Rapper made their way down the long, abandoned road, she prayed that when Enos got up the next morning, he would decipher her message and know that she hadn't willingly gone off with anyone, leaving him out of what she was doing.

There had been only a little conversation as she rode with Rapper southward along the only road on the island, a two-lane paved highway that spanned its entire length. He'd told her that he was taking her to a place where Deedee would be brought to join her. "I'm risking my own reputation for you," he said, "by getting the girl back. You must promise to do exactly as I say, or I won't be able to make it happen."

Confused, she asked, "I don't get it. Why couldn't you just bring her to me at the motel?"

He'd said nothing more at that time, but now, as they proceeded quite slowly along the old road, he finally told her more. "Ms. Marchant, Stu Chandler is not a good man. To even be seen with him would harm my reputation, and I pride myself on being an honest and upright citizen. I've been accused of wrongdoing in the past, but as you know, others only tried to make me look guilty of something I'd never think of doing."

After he had literally taken her captive at gunpoint, his words were both hypocritical and self-serving, but she kept her thoughts to herself. She didn't trust him, but somehow, if there was any shred of truth to what he said he'd do for her, she had to appear as though she believed and trusted him. For one thing was true—she'd helped this man maintain his freedom two years before. That single fact gave her hope.

Rapper went on now, his voice almost melancholy. "I'm taking you to an old lighthouse, Counselor, one built early in the eighteen hundreds. As you can see from the road, it's not a place people go anymore, and it will be a nice, private place where your daughter can meet you and where we can work out the terms of her release. We must make them such that Stu is given a safe way out of what he did by helping your daughter to run away, something he assures me was the girl's idea and not his."

"I'm not interested in Stu," she said. "All I want is my daughter back."

"That's good," Rapper said, "because that's what I want for you. But Stu will need some money to make a new life for himself after this. After all, your daughter caused him to be in such a predicament. He probably deserves a little something, and money will make it easier for me to get his cooperation. You understand that I'm simply trying to help you here, don't you?"

"I understand," she said, thinking what a horrible man Rapper was. But the hope remained that perhaps he really did intend to help her. She forced herself to give a little chuckle before adding, "You picked a rather unconventional method of doing so, but I will be forever indebted to you for getting my daughter back for me. And the money doesn't matter. Deedee is what is important to me."

"We'll discuss money later—and you must understand that the money is for Stu, not me," he said with a sober face. "All I ask in payment is that you tell no one who helped you find her. Do I have your word?" he asked.

"You do," she promised, feeling ever stronger that what was happening was very different from what he wanted her to think. She'd gladly pay to get Deedee back, but somehow she had the feeling that it was not going to be that simple. Again she prayed that Enos, a man she'd come to trust like none she'd ever known, would somehow be able to help her.

"Good," Rapper said, and then he lapsed into silence again, concentrating on missing as many of the bone-jarring potholes as he could.

The road, after several miles, became better in some ways but worse in others. The pavement had ended and there were no more huge potholes, but it had also narrowed to the point that no car could turn around here or anywhere that she'd seen for miles. In fact, she realized, bringing a sedan down this road would be almost impossible because of the rocks that formed a literal ridge down the center of the roadway.

Reminding herself of Deedee as a young girl, Meredith asked, "How much farther is it to this lighthouse?"

"I'm not sure," Rapper said, "but it's a ways yet."

When he volunteered nothing further, she decided that it was no use talking more, and despite the tension in her gut, she was terribly tired. She closed her eyes and attempted to sleep.

\* \* \*

As Enos had suspected, neither Rapper nor his Jeep were at home. Wearing a pair of surgical gloves as a precaution, he had forced entry through a first-floor window. Knowing that he was already being suspected of a crime he didn't commit, he certainly didn't want to be accused of one he did. And he especially didn't want to leave evidence of his actions.

Enos hurried, aware that the longer he was in Rapper's house, the more chance there was he'd be caught. The first place he examined after entering the window was the garage. Seeing that the red Jeep was missing, he now knew for certain that Rapper had taken Meredith, and he was terribly afraid for her.

Enos needed to check one more thing before he left Rapper's house. He remembered seeing some cabinets in Rapper's bedroom the first time he'd been here, and he hurried to that room. After a quick search, he found what he was looking for. Large and funny shaped, the cabinets looked somewhat odd, and inside of one was a virtual armory, containing over three dozen firearms. There were several rifles, a couple of fully automatic weapons, an array of handguns, and hundreds of rounds of ammunition. There were also several dozen pairs of handcuffs.

Enos knew that unless he armed himself, he might never be able to rescue either Meredith or her daughter—if he could even find them.

So, feeling increasingly guilty but placing the life of those innocent people ahead of the guilt, Enos selected a pistol that was a different caliber but about the same size as the one the superintendent had taken from him earlier. He loaded it and slipped it into the holster he wore concealed beneath his jacket. After pocketing several rounds of spare ammunition and a pair of handcuffs, he closed the cabinet door.

He had intended to leave then but recalled the explosion on Rapper's yacht. He felt compelled, even if it took a few extra minutes, to look for explosives. He found none, but in the final cabinet he searched, he discovered a large number of items that appeared to be military in nature. Probably stolen, he told himself, but none of them had anything to do with explosives. Then his eyes fell on a Gerber knife with a five-inch serrated blade. After examining it briefly, he put it in its leather sheath and shoved it in his right boot. He was about to close the closet when he also spotted a small nylon case.

For a reason he couldn't fully explain, he felt compelled to pick it up. It weighed about a pound, and upon opening it, he discovered that it contained a small nightscope. He took the scope from the case, turned it on, and determined that the batteries were good. That probably meant Rapper put it to use on different occasions, he decided. He couldn't help but wonder what those occasions might be.

Enos shut off his little flashlight and peered into the eyepiece of the scope. Everything in the room was suddenly very clear and very close, and took on a greenish hue. Thrusting guilt aside and feeling that he was doing what had to be done, he held onto the scope, closed the cabinet, and headed for the window through which he'd entered the house a half hour or longer before.

He stood beside the window, then cautiously tilted his head just far enough to look out. It was a dark, overcast night, and only the outline of shadowy trees and shrubbery could be discerned by the naked eye. So he knelt down below the window, removed the scope from its case and, lifting his head just high enough to see over the windowsill, painstakingly began to search the backyard through it. His heart jumped when he spotted a man, partially hidden behind a large palm tree at the far end of Rapper's backyard.

Who was it? Regardless, Enos couldn't just climb out the window and hike the three or four blocks to where he'd left his car. He ducked below the window and took several deep breaths, then stretched up, this time looking without the aid of the nightscope. He could barely make out the outline of the trees. He again lifted the scope and peered through it. The man was still there.

For thirty minutes Enos waited, hoping whoever was there would leave. When he didn't, Enos moved to the front of the house and looked out. It only took a minute to find another man, partially secluded in some shrubbery. This time the fellow moved, and Enos could see that he was a uniformed police officer. The superintendent must have sent the officers here after he'd entered the house, Enos thought, or they would have come in after him.

Enos knew he was in trouble.

But he wasn't in as much trouble as Meredith—who was in the hands of Rapper, a depraved, dangerous, and possibly desperate man—and Deedee, who was most likely being held somewhere by Rapper too. He silently prayed for inspiration, and an idea came to his mind. Once again, Enos went to the back of the house, entered the garage, and examined the cars there. As he'd hoped, Rapper had left the keys in the white van. He climbed in, stored the nightscope on the seat beside him, located the garage door opener, then paused.

Enos knew if he were to accomplish his daring designs, he had to somehow make the officers outside think he was Rapper and that he was going out for some reason. He returned to the main house and found his way to Rapper's bedroom. He flipped on the light, waited a couple of minutes, then turned it off, turning on one in the hallway. He did this all the way back to the garage and even left on the garage lights when he climbed into the van, hoping his ruse would work. Afraid that he might lose his nerve if he hesitated too long, Enos quickly started the van, pushed the button on the garage door opener, and backed out, making sure the door closed behind him.

He glanced only briefly in the direction of the officer hidden beyond the back lawn. Then he gunned the van and shot from the driveway to the street, watching his mirrors, expecting to see lights behind him. There were none. After winding his way through a series of streets, he suddenly turned off his lights, drove into the driveway of what he concluded was an empty house, then pulled the van out of sight into the backyard. Satisfied that it could not easily be seen either from the street or a neighbor's yard, he grabbed his nightscope and leaped out, running quickly into some nearby trees. He prayed that the van wouldn't be discovered for some time.

Enos hurried the five or six blocks toward his car, only allowing himself to be visible on the streets when it couldn't be avoided. When he got close to the car, he hid in some bushes and pulled out the nightscope. He slowly and methodically searched the area, and when he was sure he was not being observed, he scrambled from the bushes, jumped into his car, and drove away.

When the sun began to rise a short time later, Enos was secluded only a couple of miles from Marsh Harbor on an old logging road that cut through the island's large pine forest. He realized suddenly that he was all alone, and he himself was a fugitive. And somewhere, Meredith needed his help. Her daughter needed his help.

Enos needed help himself, and he knew to what source he must turn.

* * *

Rapper had punctured a tire on the Jeep and spent half an hour changing it. He didn't seem to be very handy with manual labor, but he also didn't appear to be in any hurry. At any rate, the delay, as well as the extra caution he'd taken the rest of the way, put them into the early hour of dawn. Meredith had caught glimpses of the tall red lighthouse along their trip, and she'd also seen the sign pointing to a place called Hole in the Rock. Then they turned the opposite way and began climbing up a road almost overgrown with trees and shrubs. The Jeep literally pushed its way through the heavy foliage, bumping along the grassy yet rocky road that almost wasn't a road at all.

Finally, Rapper pulled the Jeep out of the tunnel of trees they'd been in for the past half mile and parked in front of the lighthouse and the abandoned buildings that adjoined it. "Get out," he said sharply. Since changing the flat tire, Rapper had been in a foul mood. Sensing that he could be dangerous like this, Meredith obeyed him without protest. "Throw your shoes and socks in here," he ordered.

She didn't want to do that, but she knew his gun was somewhere close. After she'd tossed her shoes on the floor in the back of his

Jeep, he said curtly, "You'll wait here while I go get Stu and your daughter."

"How do I know—" she began, feeling helpless and near panic all of a sudden.

"You'll just have to trust me, Counselor. I owe you one, remember? Here, in case you get thirsty or hungry," he said, and threw her two cans of warm 7-Up and a candy bar. "That'll hold you until I return. Oh, and if you think you can walk out of here, just remember the rocks, large and small, that we've driven over. You can't find a path without them on this island, but they would cut your feet to shreds if you were to try walking out of here. Stay put, and I'll return with your girl. If you try to leave anyway, you'll never see her again."

She watched in dismay as Rapper drove back onto the jungle road and disappeared into the thick, green foliage. Moments later, the nearby sound of huge waves crashing into the mountainous rocks thundered in her ears, and she sank to her knees in despair and bowed her head.

# CHAPTER 15

Deedee awoke to much less of a stench than what she'd gone to sleep enduring. The smell was now of rotted leaves, rust, and who knew what else, but at least it was no longer the horrible odor of pigs. She wasn't cold anymore, and it was not as dark as it had been. It was most likely light outside now, and Deedee moved her stiff arms, realizing she was covered with a blanket. She looked around quickly for Hank but couldn't see him. She assumed he had returned and covered her with the blanket, then left again. As her stomach cried out in hunger, she remembered he'd promised to bring food.

The warm morning sunlight flooded in welcome rays through the opening Hank had helped her through the night before. She slowly got to her feet, and as she did, she realized she was only wearing one shoe. That was strange. Where was the other one? She was sure she'd been wearing two when she and Hank had arrived at this frightening place.

Puzzled, she stretched, trying to work out the kinks out of her body. She was soon feeling more limber, but she wasn't in much less pain. She couldn't get rid of the stiff neck, bruised knees, and other bumps and scrapes, but she didn't dwell on her pain, for she wanted out of this place. She slowly worked her way around to the opening of the tank and looked out. Seeing nothing but the jungle, she hoisted herself up, pushed her way through, and jumped to the ground outside.

She walked a short distance from the tank, looking for Hank, and after a moment she began to panic. Maybe he'd come, covered her with the blanket, and left, deciding that she'd already caused him more trouble than she was worth. She headed toward the sound of the nearby ocean and could soon see the gentle waves lapping against the rusted steel of the ancient dock. The dead leaves were slightly damp, and her right sock was soon soaked through. She walked downhill for a while, looking fearfully about her for whatever creatures this place might be home to. It was not as frightening now as it had been in the dark, but it was still an eerie place.

She soon came to a short, steep hill, and she struggled as she worked her way through the dense trees and up the incline to the top. Once there, she discovered that it was only a short distance down a steep slope before she'd be out of the trees. From there, the ocean was only a few yards away beyond a trail of crumbling, broken concrete.

"Hey, you need to keep out of sight. We don't want somebody to see you, do we?" someone shouted.

Deedee jumped in surprise at the welcome sound of her new friend's voice. She turned to see him emerging from the trees near the end of the dock. He was grinning, his white teeth a sharp contrast to his dark face. She couldn't help but grin in return. As he got closer, she realized he was carrying something. A second later she recognized what it was.

"Hey, what are you doing with my shoe?" she asked when he'd reached her.

He grinned again, and it dawned on her that Hank was really a good-looking young man. "I washed it for you," he said. "I couldn't stand the smell of the wild boar dung. I don't know how you could sleep with it. Why you—"

Deedee interrupted him in alarm. "Wild boar? Where did I get it from?"

"I told you that they were around here, Deedee. I'm sorry if I frightened you by telling you about them, but I had to be sure you wouldn't try to leave here by yourself." He grinned again. "You must have stepped in some when we where going to the tank last night," he said. "Your shoe is wet now, but at least it's clean. You can put it on if you want."

"But now my sock's dirty," she complained lightly.

"Well then, hand it over," Hank said in mock disgust. "I'll wash that too, but you've got stay right here and wait for me while I go do it, okay? The tide's out, and the water's too low to wash it from the dock." Hank looked closely at her as she took her shoe from him and handed over the very dirty sock. "You hungry?" he asked.

"I'm starved," she told him.

"I'll hurry and clean this, then we'll fix something to eat," he promised.

Deedee stepped closer to the edge of the dock and peered over. The water was indeed much lower than it had been when they'd arrived during the night and clambered onto the dock from the boat. The water was so low that such a thing would be impossible now. She couldn't see Hank's boat. He could apparently tell what she was wondering. "The boat, it's over there," he said, pointing beyond where she'd first seen him come from the trees. "I hid it in the cove over there. I don't want to attract any attention to us here."

Deedee nodded in understanding.

"I brought enough food to last us for three or four days," he said.

"Three or four days," she said in dismay. "But you said—"

Hank touched her arm tenderly. "I know what I said," he told her gently. "But there's new trouble in Marsh Harbor, and—"

"Trouble?" she asked in alarm.

"It's okay, Deedee," Hank said reassuringly. "I don't know what's happened for sure, but I know that a boat got blown up in one of the harbors there, and the fire from it destroyed some other ones. I talked to a couple of guys who watched them burn. They say it was Rapper's yacht that exploded."

"Good," she said firmly. "I'm glad that yacht is gone. It was nothing but a horrible floating dungeon."

Hank looked puzzled. "What do you mean?"

"Did you look for me on the yacht?" she asked.

"Yes, I did, but I couldn't find you," he told her.

"That's because I was in a dungeon." She went on to explain in more detail, and Hank looked horrified.

"Why would he have such a place?" he asked.

"I don't know, but I'm glad he doesn't anymore," Deedee said in relief. "He won't be able to use it to find us now."

"That's not exactly true, Deedee," Hank said. "They tell me he has another boat. And the police are all over the place." He looked worried as he continued. "If anybody saw me on his boat or if they saw me taking you away from the bungalow, they might think I blew up his boat. Then the police would be looking for me."

"Oh, Hank, I'm sorry," Deedee said. "I've gotten you into trouble."

"No, I don't think anybody saw us, but if I'm wrong, then I'm to blame, not you. I'll go back tonight and try to find out what's going on if I can, okay?"

"Don't let anyone catch you," Deedee cried. "I don't want you to get in trouble, and I want to go home."

"I want to help you do that," he said. "You trust me, don't you?"

Deedee nodded as her eyes filled with tears. "You're risking your life for me," she said. "You got me out of that place Rapper locked me in—and you didn't have to do it. Of course I trust you."

"Good. I'll clean your sock, then we can eat. And while we eat, I'll tell you what we need to do," he said.

"Thank you," Deedee said, and impulsively she threw her arms around him and kissed him lightly on the cheek. "You're the best friend I have in the world."

"Well," he began as he awkwardly pulled away from her, "I don't think so, but I am glad I'm your friend."

"It's true," she said. "No one else ever risked their life to save me. Why did you do it anyway?"

Hank's grin broadened. "You're the prettiest white girl I've ever seen," he said, lowering his eyes shyly. "And I knew that Rapper was going to do something bad to you. I couldn't let that happen, could I?" His grin faded, and a faraway look came into his eyes. "I hate men who hurt women," he said after a long pause, and Deedee was taken aback by the intensity of his voice as he spoke and the angry flashes in his eyes.

She sensed there was something more he could tell her, a reason he despised men like that, but he only turned and walked away, the dirty sock dangling in his hand. "Will you tell me about it some-time?" she called out.

He turned back. "You're not only the prettiest white girl I've ever seen, you're the smartest too." The look returned to his eyes. "Maybe sometime I'll tell you about my mama and the terrible things my papa did to her. Maybe sometime," he said. "But now, you watch out there," he said, waving toward the open sea. "If you see a boat, even a long way off, you hide yourself, okay?"

She looked back up the steep incline. "No, you don't need to climb up there," he said. "You can just hide behind chunks of this concrete." He gestured, then jogged away.

Deedee started after him, but her bare foot was tender and she didn't want to put the shoe on without the sock. She sat down on the edge of a large chunk of cement that had somehow been broken from its place and thrust upright. From that perch, she watched Hank disappear into the jungle and silently thanked God for him.

When Hank got back, he handed the wet but surprisingly clean sock to her and said, "Get it on and we'll get off this old dock. We don't want anybody to see you."

She followed him, glad to be going farther away from the tank. However safe it may have been, she didn't want to spend another night there. When he finally led her into a small clearing several hundred yards into the dense forest, it was both quiet and not a place someone would likely stumble onto, although not as secure a hiding place as the tank. Hank had already hauled up a cooler and a large box from the cove where he'd moored his boat. When he opened the top of the cooler, he said, "I got some food for us. I hope there's something in here you'd like for breakfast."

She eagerly began to pull out milk and juice from the box while Hank got some bread and cold cereal. She ate ravenously and caught him smiling at her several times, once commenting, "You really were hungry, weren't you?"

When they'd finished eating, Deedee asked, "So what do we do now?"

"We'll wait until dark," he said. "Then I'll go to Marsh Harbor and try to call your mama in the states."

Deedee was suddenly depressed, and Hank noticed the change in her demeanor. "What's the matter, Deedee?" he asked. "You want to let your mama know you're safe now, don't you? And I'm sure you want to go home as soon as you can."

Deedee hung her head in shame. "I do," she said. "But I'm not sure my mother wants me."

"Of course she wants you," Hank said in total surprise. "What mama wouldn't want a girl as nice as you are?"

"I haven't told you everything," Deedee admitted. "I'm not sure she wants me to come home."

Hank rose to his feet and nervously circled the small clearing, wondering what he'd gotten himself into. What had this girl not told him? Finally, he returned and sat beside her. "Okay, Deedee, I'll listen while you talk, okay?" he urged. "Tell me all your troubles."

As Deedee spoke, she tried to be honest, but she didn't ever tell Hank that she was really younger than most people thought. She figured he just knew that, and it didn't seem relevant to the story. After she'd finished, Hank put an arm around her shoulder and pulled her close to him. "I'm so sorry about all your troubles, Deedee," he said.

She pulled away from him and got to her feet. "It's my fault," she said angrily. "I should have listened to Mom all along. I can't believe I even thought Stu was a nice guy. He was just so much older than me, and I guess I was flattered that he would be interested in someone as young as I am."

"As young as you?" Hank asked as he stood. "How old is Stu?"

"He's twenty-four," she said.

"Oh, and you're what, maybe nineteen?" he asked.

"No, I'm not as old as you think, Hank," Deedee said, realizing he, too, thought she was older.

"How old are you then, Deedee?"

She dropped her eyes. "I'm fifteen," she said. "But I'll be sixteen in just a few months."

Hank was stunned. "You're only fifteen, and Stu took you from your country? What was he thinking?" Then he stopped and looked suspiciously at Deedee for a moment. "Or did he think you were older too?"

Deedee quickly shook her head. "Oh, no, he knew. The first time we met he didn't, but I told him. He only seemed to want me to go out with him more after that."

"The creep," Hank said. "I'm not a mean guy, but if I see him again . . ."

"I hope you never see him again, Hank," Deedee said honestly. "Stu's involved in drugs and who knows what else."

Hank had heard enough of Stu. In his culture, fifteen was not too young to date, but even so, he was shocked that a man Stu's age would intentionally press a girl as young as Deedee to go out, and even worse, to help her run away.

"Let's sit down, Deedee," Hank said, suddenly feeling more mature and very protective of his young companion. "We need to think about things and see if we can decide what to do."

She sat beside him on a fallen tree trunk and they talked. Finally, he persuaded her to give him her mother's phone number so he could call her that night when he got back to Marsh Harbor. "She'll be glad to find that you're okay, and she'll be wanting to see you soon. I think she'll do anything to get you back."

"I hope you're right. But you won't take any chances, will you, Hank?" she pleaded. "I'd feel terrible if anything happened to you."

"I'll be okay," he said, but he shivered with fear, wondering what dangers lay ahead. He'd dreamed at times of being a hero, but now he didn't feel like a hero at all. He was just a frightened young man who had started something he had to finish.

# CHAPTER 16

The main question in Meredith's mind was no longer whether Rapper would bring Deedee to her. She was fairly certain he would, for he was after money. But what would happen after they made whatever arrangement he insisted on to get the money to him? As the day had worn on, she'd become increasingly uneasy about what he'd do to both of them. Bringing her to such a secluded spot seemed odd. A closer, more convenient, and yet reasonably private place could have been found for a secret meeting and exchange of money. But the fact that Rapper had actually left her a candy bar and some pop gave her hope he would return.

The burning question was what would happen when he did. Somehow she felt that what he had in mind wasn't a happy reunion between mother and daughter. Meredith knew that just because she was willing to give him money and promise not to tell anyone what he'd done did not mean that she and Deedee would be allowed to live. Growing more worried, Meredith wondered what she might do to save her life and that of her daughter when Rapper and Stu showed up with her. And she also wondered what she could do if he happened to come back alone.

Being without shoes limited her options considerably. She'd soon realized that walking barefoot the many miles back to the highway would be impossible. Rapper was right about the rocky ground, which included what Meredith knew was plater rock, more commonly called flint rock. Extremely sharp and jagged, it could cut a person's feet to shreds in just a few steps. Of course, there were also spots of soft leaves or rotting wood, but it was impossible to go very far without having to walk through large areas of plater rock.

She'd tried a few steps and already had terribly painful feet. Then she'd tried tying thick leaves from some of the trees to her feet with a vine. After failing in that attempt, Meredith had climbed the long, winding stairs to the top of the ancient lighthouse. From there she could see a good distance away. Certainly no one could approach the lighthouse without her knowing it if she was very watchful. From her lofty perch she could see that either landing or launching a boat anywhere nearby would be impossible. Sheer cliffs met huge waves that crashed wickedly against the rock. In the distance, she could see the water as it sprayed in intermittent columns, driven with tremendous force through the cliff in what she thought must be the geological aberration known as Hole in the Rock. In the other direction there was a long wall of sheer rock cliffs as far as she could see. The lighthouse sat on one point at the end of a peninsula, and Hole in the Rock was near the other point. She was surrounded by dangerous seas on three sides and dense, rocky jungle on the fourth.

The terrain was fascinating but offered neither an easy way to escape nor safety if she stayed. The fact that she could see someone approaching from the lighthouse was no comfort, for when they came, she'd be trapped there.

Meredith next explored the surrounding outbuildings, again concluding if she tried to hide there, she'd only imprison herself. Finally, in desperation, she searched until she found a couple of somewhat suitable pieces of wood from which she fashioned makeshift sandals. She secured the wood to the soles of her feet with some tough vine, using leaves to separate the wirelike vine from her tender flesh.

Once she had them on, she couldn't walk very well, as they forced her to move awkwardly and slowly. But at least she could walk, and since that was her only choice, Meredith decided to travel right down the tunnel-like road that Rapper had driven in on, hoping she could hear him coming long before he got to her, thus giving herself plenty of time to conceal herself in the foliage. Then she could make sure Deedee was with him before revealing herself. Her plan went only that far, for if Deedee was with him, she wasn't at all sure how she'd proceed. If he was alone, with Stu, or strangers, she'd do her best to avoid detection.

She started on her way, carrying both cans of the 7-Up Rapper had left her, her candy bar shoved into a pocket of her pants. So far she'd avoided eating or drinking, but she knew that wouldn't last long. She hadn't walked far from the clearing that surrounded the lighthouse before she spotted an ancient four-wheel-drive vehicle of some type that had been driven over a low embankment and left to be overgrown with vines and bushes. She forced herself closer and leaned in, hoping she wouldn't encounter any snakes or other terrifying creatures of the wild in the dense jungle.

The old vehicle had little left of anything that would deteriorate when exposed to the elements. The seats were but bare and rusted springs, the tires flat and split open. The steering wheel was badly cracked, and what had been a canvas top was now shreds of brittle string. In the back were some rusty tools, and Meredith picked up an old hammer, thinking it might be used as a weapon if she grew desperate. She took it, shoved it into the waistband of her pants, then clambered back to the road, eating a couple of bites of the candy bar and taking a drink of warm pop.

She had proceeded for several hundred yards before noticing a crude wooden sign that indicated there was a cave somewhere in the jungle to her right. Just then, she heard the sound of an approaching car. She darted into the brush, her heart pounding wildly.

The Jeep, if indeed it was Rapper, was still some distance away, and Meredith was grateful for the time she had to force her way through the vines and branches. She secluded herself where she could peer through the leaves and hopefully get a look at the Jeep when it passed.

A few minutes later, the Jeep approached, traveling slowly, which was really the only way on this primitive road. Meredith wasn't sure whether she wanted to see Deedee in the Jeep or if she wanted Rapper to be alone. However, when the Jeep finally passed in front of her, she felt a great sense of relief wash over her when she saw that he had no passengers. Something told her that an encounter with him right now was not a desirable thing, and she shrunk back from the road and began to work her way up the trail as quickly as she could.

A few minutes later, she heard an angry voice shouting but couldn't make out what Rapper was yelling. She figured it would only frighten her more if she knew what he was trying to say, so she didn't even try to listen any closer.

She reached the end of the trail where it entered the mouth of a cave and started to enter, then thought better of it. If by some chance she'd left evidence that might help Rapper figure out where she'd gone, the cave, like the lighthouse, would only be a trap. So she bypassed the cave and found herself literally forcing her way through more thick branches and vines where there was no trail. She finally drank the can of pop she'd opened, tossed the can out of sight in the thick vegetation, and continued on with one free hand. Meredith hadn't gone far before she realized with a shiver of terror that she was leaving behind her the clear sign of her passing. Torn leaves, broken branches, and tromped vines littered the way she'd come.

But since there was nothing she could do about it, she prayed and worked her way onward. Then she heard the Jeep as it bounced down the road from the lighthouse. She stopped and held her breath, hoping to hear it pass by, but her worst fears were realized when she heard it pause, and then the engine died at what she calculated was about the point where the cave's trail led away from the road and into the jungle.

She could hear Rapper shouting again, but this time he was closer, and his voice carried much more clearly. "Counselor," she heard him shout, "I know you're heading for the cave. It's no use. Without shoes you must already be almost beyond walking. Give yourself up to me and I'll still work with you in getting Deedee back."

There was a long pause. She didn't dare move for fear he'd hear the sound and know where she was. A moment later, he said, "Shout back, and I'll come help you. I'll even bring your shoes. I only want to help."

The tone of his enraged voice didn't in any way mesh with the words she was hearing. There was no mention of money, meaning something had likely changed. He had no intention of helping her, she thought fearfully. Again he shouted, "You're making me angry. If I have to come find you, I'll make you wish you'd cooperated." There was another break, then he added loudly, "I know you're in the cave, and I'll find you there. You better give up now."

Meredith knew she had to do something, but moving ahead and breaking branches didn't seem like such a good idea. She considered her options, then moved back the way she'd come, finding it easier going where she'd already broken a path. She hoped he'd take a little time in the cave, but not knowing its dimensions, she had no idea how long he might be in there. She climbed about a hundred feet before dropping to her stomach and crawling into the bushes at the side of the trail, wriggling around until she again faced the way she'd just come, the way Rapper might pass if he followed her clumsy trail into the jungle. She pulled the hammer from her waistband, sat her pop on the ground, and mentally prepared herself for a wait. She hoped he'd pass by and that she'd be able to hurry back down to the Jeep and drive away. She didn't want to have to fight him, for a hammer wasn't much of a weapon against a pistol, and she knew he'd still have one of those.

The wait seemed endless. She knew when Rapper entered the cave because he shouted from the entrance. Then just a few moments later she heard his muffled voice from somewhere inside. She wondered for a minute if there might be time for her to hurry back to the Jeep now, if he might have gone far enough into the cave that he wouldn't hear her pass by. But she didn't dare try it, so she lay where she was, figuring that either he'd come after her and pass by, making it possible for her to get back to the Jeep before him, or he would give up and drive off, leaving her there.

A few more tense minutes passed. A slight rustling in the bushes beside her caused her to turn ever so slightly and gasp. A creature she had only seen in horror movies was inches from her face. Tiny, dark black eyes squinted at her, and a long, pointed tongue darted from its mouth. The creature was tan colored, scaly, and seemed to be several feet in length. It was all Meredith could do to keep from screaming. She gripped the hammer tightly, figuring that if the large, lizardlike animal attacked her, she'd only have one swing, and she had to make it count.

She also knew that a big noise could bring Rapper straight to her, so she prayed silently and stared the animal down. For at least a minute, maybe longer, it studied her, then, to her relief, it decided she either wasn't a meal worth having or she didn't present a danger to it. It moved silently when it left, and after a moment, all was calm again.

Several minutes passed before she again heard Rapper, but this time he wasn't shouting. He was breaking sticks as he followed the path she'd made into the jungle. His progress was slow, and every so often she'd hear him stop, as if searching the surrounding bushes for her. Then he'd continue. Soon she could actually hear his coarse breathing and knew that he was close.

Then he was only a few feet away, and she actually saw his feet, stopping right at the point where she'd crawled from the trail. Could he tell where she'd gone? If he were to drop down and look into the bushes at ground level, he'd spot her and she'd be forced to take desperate measures.

Rapper didn't kneel or stoop, but he did stand in that spot for what seemed like an eternity. And he was so still that she scarcely dared to breathe for fear he'd hear her. Finally, to her relief, he moved on. She waited until she could no longer hear his breathing before she slid out of her hiding place and started as quietly as she could down the trail. She hoped beyond hope that he'd keep going until he came to the point where she'd turned around. By then, she should have a good lead on him and with a little luck could be to the Jeep in time to drive away before he could fire a shot at her.

If the keys were in the Jeep.

The possibility that they weren't nearly paralyzed her, but she forced herself to believe they were. Why wouldn't they be? Unless he was smart enough to realize she might attempt exactly what she was trying. Discouraged, but not defeated, Meredith hurried on as quickly and as silently as she could. The makeshift shoes were falling off, and Meredith realized her real shoes were more than likely still in the Jeep. She could go barefoot that far, she decided, and hurriedly removed the encumbrances from her feet.

She had only picked her way back the way she'd come for another fifty feet or so when she heard Rapper screaming and crashing through the bushes, cursing as he ran. Judging from the sound of his voice, he was going the other way, so she used his distraction to hurry faster. He cursed again, then she heard a single shot. "That'll teach you, you stupid iguana," he laughed.

A moment later, Meredith was back on the trail that led away from cave. If Rapper, despite the providential delay caused by what she now knew was an iguana, had reached the end of the path she'd blazed, he'd be on his way back—and he'd know she was ahead of him.

She was out of breath and gulping for air by the time she reached the Jeep. Both feet were cut and bleeding, but she didn't give them a second thought when she climbed in the door and saw the keys. She waited to shut the door until she fired the engine up, then slammed it, shoved the Jeep into gear, and sped away.

She realized Rapper was closer than she'd thought when she heard the whine of a bullet. She ducked instinctively as the second one hit somewhere in the back of the Jeep, and she began swerving crazily to make herself a difficult target. She didn't dare look back. Another bullet whined past, then several more were fired, but she knew she must be out of sight because none of them hit the Jeep.

When she finally emerged from the jungle road into more open forest, she was at the intersection of the main road and the road that led to Hole in the Rock. She turned right and headed for the highway, more miles away than she cared to think about.

She drove far faster than was safe, but every yard took her farther from Rapper. If he were to somehow catch her now, he would kill her—of that she was certain.

She watched the odometer, willing it to rack up the miles. She'd only gone about three miles from where the road had split when she felt the Jeep pulling heavily to one side. Her stomach turned, and she stopped and jumped out. The right rear tire was very low, so she checked the spare. Rapper hadn't bothered to get it fixed.

She jumped back into the Jeep, gunned it, and traveled another mile before the tire went clear flat. Driving on the rim, she kept going for more than another mile before a front tire blew out. Still, she didn't stop, not until the front rim was so badly banged up that she could no longer steer. She came to a stop and looked at the odometer. She'd left Rapper at least six miles back. She had no idea how far the highway was from here, but she certainly had the advantage now.

All she needed was to put on her own shoes and run, but to her dismay, her shoes and socks were not in the Jeep. That fact alone was all the evidence Meredith needed to convince her that Rapper had returned to the lighthouse without any intention of allowing her to live.

She wondered if he'd already done something horrible to her daughter. She could only pray that he had not, that Deedee was still alive, and that she and Enos could find her before Rapper walked out of the forest.

In searching for the shoes, Meredith found four items that she could use. There was a knife, very sharp and fairly long, lying in his glove compartment. She wished it had been a gun, but it was better than the hammer, which she tossed into the trees before slipping the knife into her waistband. Then she found a bottle of water. She'd left her 7-Up in her haste to get to the Jeep, so she was doubly glad for the water. She also found a dirty T-shirt, which she cut in two, tying a half to each foot. It wasn't much of a shoe, but it was better than nothing. After searching a moment longer, she found a detailed map of Abaco.

A quick study of it revealed she was still about eight miles from the highway that would take her back to Marsh Harbor. She felt like crying, but instead she left the Jeep and started hiking, her feet already sore. Thoughts of her daughter and Enos helped her to move along quickly, ignoring the burning pain and hunger.

# CHAPTER 17

Ordinarily a man of action, Enos had never felt so helpless in his life. The woman he'd come to consider a very close friend was in the hands of a vicious man, as was her daughter, while he was sitting in a rental car in a desolate forest doing absolutely nothing! Yet he was also a practical man, and he knew that if the police in Marsh Harbor saw him, he could well end up in their little jail, and then he would really be helpless.

The only way he could work now was under cover of darkness, and that meant waiting and trying to sleep during the hot daytime hours. But sleep proved to be difficult as he worried so much about those he was trying to protect.

The hours dragged on, and Enos became hungry and thirsty and tired. Sleep only came in short snatches, not restful hours as he needed. When it was finally dark, he drove back to town to the service station where he'd rented the car. He was taking a risk, he knew, but it was riskier to chance the police seeing him in it. "I need something with less mileage," Enos told the attendant. "I'll be doing a lot of driving in the next few days, and I get nervous every time I see how many miles this poor thing has gone."

The fellow didn't question his motives at all, and within a few minutes Enos found himself in a tan Buick with only 88,559 miles on the odometer, half what the one he'd been driving had. As a precaution, he quietly slipped the knife, the pistol, and the nightscope into the spare-tire well. He wasn't sure what he'd do next, and he felt that he could retrieve those items if he decided to leave the car at some point. As he drove away from the station, Enos decided that he would first drive by Rapper's house to see if he was at home.

As he pulled to a stop at a nearby intersection, he suddenly found himself between two police cars, and his heart sank. If only they understood what was really going on.

The superintendent met Enos at the jail, and no amount of talking could convince the man to either help Enos or to release him. "You have overstepped your bounds," the superintendent said sternly. "We have a witness who saw you carrying something onto Rapper's yacht, and he saw you leave without it. A very short time later, the boat exploded. I would suggest that you come clean with us, Detective Fauler. We want to help you and the lady lawyer, but we can't allow you to break the law."

"You really don't know what you're up against here," Enos said emphatically, anger in his voice. "Your witness is working for Rapper, and he's lying to you. Rapper is in the business of stealing women and young girls and selling them into slavery in third world countries— and I'm not the only one who knows it. You're playing right into his hands and risking the lives of innocent people."

Superintendent Brown leaned across the table that separated the two men. "Rapper has lived quite peacefully on our island for several years. Not once has he created a problem for us. It's only when you came that crimes started happening. You are in much trouble, Detective, and I have no choice but to put you in jail where you can't create any more disturbances while we sort this thing out."

"Think," Enos pleaded. "Why would Rapper have that room in his house designed to lock people in?"

"That's not proof of anything. You have taken matters into your own hands, and that just can't be allowed."

"Call my boss in Utah. He'll vouch for me. I don't know the first thing about explosives. I swear, I didn't blow anything up." Enos was growing impatient.

"Give me your boss's number," the superintendent said.

After supplying it, Enos said, "Maybe Rapper had the boat blown up himself. Maybe there's evidence in it he didn't want found. Or . . ." Enos stopped, unable to go on.

"Or what?" Superintendent Brown pressed.

Enos dropped his head into his hands as tears stung his eyes. Finally, he choked out, "What if Deedee and Meredith were in it?"

"I hadn't thought of that," the superintendent admitted. "We'll look into it."

"I could help," Enos offered.

"No, I can't let you. But I will investigate," the superintendent said in a kind but firm voice.

"What about my rental car?"

"I'll keep it safe enough," the superintendent assured him. He smiled and then added, "You underrate us, Detective Fauler. I suspected you might be wanting to get a different car. You walked right into my trap."

"I've got to give you credit for that," Enos said, and he wondered if they had discovered his little cache of stolen goods in the spare-tire well—not that it mattered at this point. "But you're expending all your energies making problems worse and not solving anything," he continued. "You've have made yourself responsible for the lives of Meredith and Deedee, and you're making a grave mistake by ignoring that, Superintendent."

Superintendent Brown squirmed visibly, and for a moment, he appeared to waver in his resolve. Enos pressed what he saw as a tiny advantage. "Superintendent, I'll not leave your side, I promise, if you'll just help me find out if they're still alive. Please, sir, Rapper is a dangerous man."

The superintendent could see that Enos was quite serious, but then there was the witness, who'd also been serious. He knew he couldn't let people go running around his jurisdiction blowing up boats and not do anything about it. To be seen with this man at his side as if nothing had happened would be viewed as irresponsible by the people, especially his officers. "No, Enos, I'll have to put you in my jail while we try to find out what's really happening. There is nothing else I can do," he said.

"Or that you *will* do," Enos added angrily. "I'm holding you personally responsible for the lives of Meredith and Deedee Marchant. Believe me, I'll make trouble for you that you can never put to rest if you don't help me find them. You've let yourself be taken in by a master criminal. Eventually that will be proven."

The superintendent seemed shaken, but he stood firm. "You have been accused of a serious crime, Detective. I will keep you posted on the progress of our investigation."

* * *

Hank listened with waning hope to the recording. He had called Deedee's home hoping to find her mother there, but after several tries and no answer, he wasn't certain what he'd tell the girl when he returned. His own mother was wringing her hands with worry over Hank's unusual behavior. She was a tiny black woman who'd never been close to crime once her brutally abusive husband had died when Hank was just a little boy. She lived in a humble home in the poor part of Marsh Harbor, and since becoming a widow, she'd worked hard to raise her children. Hank was the youngest, and it appeared now that he was in some kind of trouble.

Hank hung up the phone and stared into space, wondering what he could possibly do to help Deedee find her mother. Then an idea came to him, something he didn't want to do, but he didn't know what other options he had. Several minutes later, he dialed another number.

As the phone on the other end began to ring, Hank's mother spoke up. "Hank, who is going to pay for all these phone calls?"

"I will, Mama, so quit worrying," he said. "I need you to go in the other room. I can't have you hear what I'm saying. Please, I can't put you in danger too."

As his mother left the room, the phone was answered at the other end, and Hank felt his mouth go dry. Calling the police was something he'd never done before, and he thought about hanging up. However, the image of Deedee's innocent face came to his mind, and he forced himself to speak. "I'm trying to find a woman from Duchesne, Utah. Her name is Meredith Marchant."

"Who is this calling?" the dispatcher asked eagerly.

"I'm a friend of Deedee Marchant," Hank said, struggling to keep the quiver from his voice.

"I see, and where are you calling from?" the dispatcher asked calmly.

"I'm not in America," Hank said. "Please, I tried to call her home, but I got only a recording."

"Yes, Ms. Marchant is away from home right now. What do you need to talk to her about?"

"Her daughter, Deedee."

"I see." There was a pause. Then the dispatcher said to Hank, "Would you stay on the line please? I'm going to try to connect you with someone who can help you get in touch with Ms. Marchant."

"I'll do that, but please hurry. This is costing me money I don't have," Hank said nervously.

"I understand," she replied. "Oh, and in case we somehow get cut off, can you give me the number you're calling from?"

"I'm not sure it—" Hank began hesitantly.

"Please," the dispatcher said. "This could be very important."

"I don't dare," Hank said honestly. "Please, I just need to find Deedee's mama."

The dispatcher sounded frantic to keep him on the line. "I never did catch your name," she said. "We'll need that for our records here."

"Hank," he said. "When will you find someone I can talk to?"

"Someone is working on that," he was told. "So your name's Hank. Is there a last name?" she asked, stalling so she didn't lose the call. She anxiously watched the other dispatcher, hoping she could find Sheriff Robinson quickly. The young man she was talking to was clearly frightened of something.

"I don't think I should tell you what it is," Hank responded.

"I've got the sheriff on the line," the second dispatcher whispered.

"Hank, we've got the other party on another line now. Hang on just a moment longer and I'll connect the two of you."

Hank again thought about hanging up, but once more, the innocence of the young girl he'd literally risked his life to save filled his mind, and he decided he'd better stay on. After all, he'd promised Deedee he'd find her mother, and he couldn't bear to let her down.

"Hank," a deep voice suddenly said, "I'm Sheriff Robinson, a friend of Meredith Marchant. I can get you in touch with her if you need to talk to her."

"I do," Hank said, intimidated by the ring of authority in the voice at the other end.

"What do you need to talk to her about?"

"Deedee. She wants to talk to her mama and tell her she's sorry. She wants to go home."

The sheriff's heart began to race. "Is Deedee okay?" he asked.

"She's fine now, but she was not so good when I found her," Hank said.

"Is she there with you? I'd like to talk to her if she is," the sheriff said.

"She's not here, but I know where she's hiding."

"Where's that?"

"I don't think I should tell anyone. I don't want to take a chance that she gets hurt," Hank replied. "There's a very bad man who will hurt her, and he will kill me if he thinks I took her from him and hid her."

"Is the man Stu Chandler?" the sheriff asked.

"No, Stu's gone. A very bad man took her from Stu," Hank said earnestly.

The sheriff was convinced that this was no prank call, and he knew he had to find out where the young man was calling from.

"Okay, Hank, let's talk about this for a minute. Deedee's mother is my friend, and she's with a policeman, a detective of mine. His name is Detective Enos Fauler. They're in a town called Marsh Harbor in Abaco. That's in the—"

"The Bahamas!" Hank finished excitedly. "That's my home." The relief was almost overwhelming. He couldn't believe that Deedee's mother was right here in Marsh Harbor.

"This is good news. Now I need to help you get in touch with them, and they'll help you once you meet them," the sheriff assured him. "They're staying in a motel there." He gave the name of the motel to Hank, then said, "They're working with the local police. They believe that a man by the name of Rapper is holding Deedee."

"Yes, that's his name, but he doesn't have her now. I took her from him," Hank said. "I hid her somewhere. He'll kill me if he finds us."

"Can you give me the phone number where I can call the police? I'll tell them what's going on. In the meantime, if you'll go to the motel and see if Enos and Meredith are there, I'd appreciate it," the sheriff said. "And then call me back if you need to. Please, Hank, don't worry about the cost. I'll see that you're reimbursed for every cent you spend to help us. Be very careful."

"I'm being careful," Hank assured the sheriff.

"When you get to the motel, call me back or have Detective Fauler or Ms. Marchant call me as soon as you find them." Sheriff Robinson then gave his phone numbers to Hank, and Hank gave him the number of the local police.

Hank drove straight to the motel in his mother's car and knocked on both the rooms the sheriff had told him they were in. There was no answer, so he went to the manager's office and asked if Mr. Fauler and Ms. Marchant were still staying there. The look on the manager's face frightened Hank. "Why you want to know?" he growled.

"I need to talk to them," Hank said, his voice breaking.

"They're not here anymore," the fellow said. "Sit down. I'll get somebody who can tell you what's happened."

Hank bolted. He didn't want to see anyone who would tell him what was happening. He only wanted to see the detective or Deedee's mother. He rushed back to his home and called Sheriff Robinson in Utah. The sheriff answered on the first ring. "Sheriff, there's something very wrong," he began.

"I've discovered that," the sheriff said. "I just got off the phone with Superintendent Brown. This Rapper character is very dangerous, and it seems like he has the police believing everything he wants. Here's what I need for you to do."

"I'm not sure if I dare do anything now," Hank said.

"Please, I need your help, Hank. Call Superintendent Brown. You don't have to tell him where you're calling from. Tell him what you've done and ask him to at least let you talk to Enos Fauler on the phone. Then call me back," the sheriff instructed. "You've done a brave thing, Hank, in getting Deedee away from Rapper. But the superintendent won't let me talk to Enos. Maybe he'll let you."

Sheriff Robinson was boiling inside, but he knew he had to hide his anger from Hank. The superintendent had admitted that he had no idea where Meredith was but that Enos was under suspicion of blowing up a yacht! The sheriff assured him this couldn't be true, but when Superintendent Brown told him the boat belonged to Rapper, the very man Enos believed was holding Deedee, the sheriff knew that things were deteriorating badly in Abaco. He needed to get there himself, but that would take many hours—hours Meredith and Deedee probably didn't have.

Hank was his only hope. "Please, Hank, make the call and call me back. We've got to convince the superintendent to let Detective Fauler go."

Hank agreed to try. He called, and the superintendent answered. Hank didn't identify himself, but he did say, "Rapper was holding a girl by the name of Deedee Marchant in a bungalow in Hope Town. He took her there in his yacht, where he had her locked in a secret dungeon below the lower deck. I got her away from him, but Rapper will kill me if he finds out I helped her. Please, I need talk to Mr. Fauler. I need his help."

"Come down here," Superintendent Brown said, "and you and I will talk. Maybe I can help you out here. We've been looking for the girl you're talking about."

Hank knew he could never go down there. If they'd throw a cop from the states in jail because Rapper orchestrated it, he was convinced they'd do the same to him. "Please, sir, I gotta talk to the American officer," Hank begged.

"Where is the girl?" the superintendent demanded. "You could be in a lot of trouble if you don't tell me."

"I know that, sir, but I'm afraid to tell anyone where she's at. But she's safe now," Hank insisted. "I promised her I'd talk to her mama if I can find her. Do you know where she is, sir?"

"You let me worry about that, young man. If you know where Deedee Marchant is, you better come tell me. Then I'll handle things from there."

Hank didn't like where this conversation was headed, so he quietly hung up the phone. His mother was sitting in her bedroom when Hank spoke to her a moment later. "Mama," he said, "I've got to go now. Please, if anyone asks you, don't tell them I was here."

"Son, if you're in trouble, I'll help—"

"I'm not breaking the law. I can't explain right now, but someone needs my help. Please, if somebody asks, say you haven't seen me."

Hank's mother nodded, and he kissed her on the cheek. "I'm on my way, Mama. I love you," he said, and ran the two blocks to the little harbor where he'd left his boat. He untied it from the dock and climbed in. Dark as the evening was, Hank wasn't worried. He knew the sea like he knew his own home. He had to get back to Deedee, and together they'd decide what to do. He was so shaken that he forgot all about calling Sheriff Robinson back.

* * *

Superintendent Brown wasn't used to dealing with serious crimes. He was in over his head, and he knew it. He also knew that he'd made Sheriff Robinson very angry, and he was especially concerned that the man had promised to place a call to the governor-general of the Bahamas. He really didn't want to be attracting the attention of the leader of his country—or even the man's staff—especially when he wasn't that sure of himself. He knew that the sheriff might just have been bluffing, and he also wasn't sure if the governor-general would even talk to the sheriff, but someone on his staff might! He decided, in the interest of self-preservation, to talk to Enos Fauler again. Or better yet, maybe he should talk to his informant once more. If it turned out the man was lying and an innocent cop from the states was in jail, he really could be in a mess.

Finding the informant turned out to not be an easy thing. Even though it was late at night, he wasn't at the address he'd given Superintendent Brown. With the help of a couple of his officers, the superintendent visited all the bars and restaurants in town, even checking over in Hope Town. But he wasn't to be found.

There was also the matter of the young man who had called him earlier. He had no idea who he was or where to find him. Finally, depressed and very worried, Superintendent Brown returned to his little jail and had Enos Fauler brought out to talk with him.

* * *

"Did you talk to her?" Deedee asked the moment Hank walked into their little camp.

"No, she wasn't there," Hank said. "But I talked to the sheriff in Duchesne, Sheriff Robinson."

"He's my mother's friend," Deedee said brightly. "Did he know where she was?"

"She came here with a detective," Hank said.

"Here!" Deedee exclaimed. "To Abaco?"

"Yes, but I couldn't find her," Hank added hastily.

"Is she looking for me?"

"Of course she is, Deedee," Hank said.

"Then she can't be far. Let's go and we'll find her somewhere," Deedee suggested, excited to know that her mother was so close by. If she'd come all the way to the Bahamas, she must want her back after all, Deedee decided hopefully.

Hank said nothing, and she looked closely at him from across their little fire. "Hank, what's wrong?" she asked, the hope she'd just found dissipating rapidly.

"The police here don't know Rapper very well, and they believe whatever he wants them to believe," he stated simply.

Deedee thought she was hearing wrong. She knew Sheriff Robinson and some of his deputies, and the thought that they would believe someone as hideous as Rapper was ridiculous. Surely the police here were no different. "What do you mean, Hank? Police aren't on the side of people like Rapper."

"These policemen are," Hank said bitterly. "They put the detective your mother was with in jail, and they say they don't know where she's at now. I don't believe them."

Tears welled in Deedee's eyes. For a moment she'd thought she'd soon be back with her mother. Now this. Hank moved across the little clearing and put an arm around her shoulders, and she dropped her head against him. There they sat, neither knowing what to say or do.

# CHAPTER 18

Never in her entire life had Meredith's feet hurt like they did now. She'd walked several miles, but she was nowhere near getting back to the main highway. She'd cut her pants off below the knees and added that material to the now-ragged cloth around her feet, but they were cut, bleeding, and excruciatingly painful. She was certain an infection was setting in.

To further complicate matters, she kept stumbling in the darkness, and her shins and hands were bruised and bloody. The chocolate bar and most of her water were gone. What little strength she had left wouldn't last long, and she felt an overwhelming desire to simply lie down at the side of the road and sleep. Only the thought of her daughter kept her plodding painfully on.

She wondered how far back Rapper was. He had shoes that fit, and he was in very good physical condition. He was probably making triple the time she was. If that was the case, despite the lead she'd built before the Jeep quit, he could be approaching fairly soon, which frightened her. She wondered if it would be better to get off the road and hide in the forest until morning.

With that thought on her mind, the sound of an approaching vehicle didn't register on Meredith's numbed brain. Only when she saw lights flashing through the trees did she realize a car was coming from the direction of the main highway. Her first thought was that Enos was coming to find her, and she stumbled ahead with renewed vigor.

Then she realized that was unlikely, since he had no way of knowing where she was. Maybe it was an islander just out for a drive—but that also seemed odd. This road was practically unused, and at this hour . . .

Then it hit her. What if someone knew Rapper was overdue and was looking for him? In a sudden panic she limped into the trees only moments before the headlights of the approaching car swung around and lit the very spot she'd just vacated. The car was going slowly, swerving to miss as many of the potholes as it could. She hunched down behind a tree several feet from the road and watched the vehicle pass. It was too dark to see the driver well, but the car was a four-wheel-drive vehicle of some kind with high clearance. Whoever it was knew the kind of vehicle needed to travel on this road. She watched as it continued on and eventually disappeared from view.

Meredith tried to get to her feet but found it very difficult and painful. That short time on her knees had allowed her muscles to bind up, and it was all she could do to make them work. The pain was excruciating, but she knew she had to get to the highway and flag down a ride. But then she wondered if there would even be any traffic on the highway at this time of night.

Meredith fought to clear her thinking. She had to be rational, had to do the right thing. What would be best right now? And then she knew. She had to work her way deeper into the forest and spend the rest of the night there. She couldn't physically continue without rest, and if the car looking for Rapper came back soon and she was on the road . . .

She forced herself to stumble several hundred feet into the dense forest, tripping several times in the darkness. She finally felt the softness of rotted leaves beneath her feet and sank to the ground.

Meredith sat with her back to the trunk of a pine tree and closed her eyes—then opened them with a start. The vehicle was coming back, its headlights filtering through the trees. She knew she was too far to ever be spotted, but she instinctively slid down until she was stretched out on her back. With her eyes open wide and her ears tuned to the approaching car, she waited. As it passed by she heard voices, and somehow she knew that Rapper was on his way back to Marsh Harbor. It brought tears to her eyes. Meredith lifted a feeble hand to her face, wiped the tears away, and within seconds fell asleep.

* * *

Enos had finally fallen asleep when an officer shook him by the shoulder. "The superintendent wants to talk to you," he was told. "Wake up and come with me."

What the superintendent wanted now, in the middle of the night, was a mystery, but Enos could only hope the man had experienced a change of heart. He was sitting at the same table he'd been behind when they'd talked earlier. He looked tired, and waved Enos to a chair. "I talked to your boss in Utah." The superintendent didn't mention that it was Sheriff Robinson who had called him and not the other way around.

"Do you believe me now?" Enos asked eagerly.

"I don't know what to believe," Superintendent Brown said evasively. "But he persuaded me to help you. He speaks very highly of you and denies that you'd ever do something like blow up a boat." He wasn't about to tell Enos that he'd refused to let the sheriff talk to him.

"Well, time will prove it all. Why don't we begin by finding that informant of yours? Believe me, Superintendent, he doesn't know me—I doubt he's ever even seen me. He has to be working for Rapper. You do know where he lives, don't you?"

Superintendent Brown nodded. "I've been there already. He's not home."

"Does anyone know where he went?" Enos asked.

"No one was there to ask."

"I see. Well, maybe he's at a bar or something, if there are any open this time of night."

"We've already checked. We can't find him," Superintendent Brown said.

"Do you have any idea what he drives?"

"Actually, no. I never saw him with his car, if he has one," the superintendent admitted.

"Where does he work?" Enos pressed.

"I'm not sure of that," Superintendent Brown said.

Enos sat back, exasperated. "You don't know anything about him, do you, Superintendent?"

"His name is Carlton Sebastian. Goes by Carl, he told us."

"Describe him," Enos requested.

"A little over six feet, I'd say, and maybe weighs two hundred pounds. White man, blue eyes, long graying brown hair. Wears it in a ponytail."

"Okay, so you do know a little about him. Now, will you help me?"

Before the superintendent could respond, his phone rang. He answered, listened for a minute, then said, "I see. Thanks, Inspector." Then he turned to Enos. "They succeeded in pulling up the remains of the yacht from the bottom of the harbor."

"And did they find anything?" Enos hardly dared to ask.

"The little girl wasn't in it, nor was her mother, but they did find something most unusual. Beneath the main deck of the boat was another space, and there is still evidence that there were chains bolted to the walls. Each chain had a handcuff attached to the end of it."

"I was right!" Enos exclaimed. "Rapper is—"

"Yes, it looks like he's been taking people somewhere in that yacht, and very much against their will," the superintendent said.

"We've got to find him, and we've got to find Deedee and Meredith." Enos's voice rose in urgency.

"I don't know where else to look," the superintendent said. "But I'll give you back your gun for now and you can go."

"Thank you," Enos said sincerely. "But there is something you could do, if you don't mind."

"What's that?"

"Watch Rapper's house again—and his other boat. I'm certain that he's taken Ms. Marchant somewhere, and if he comes back, I'd like to talk to him."

"I'll arrange that," the superintendent promised.

A few minutes later, Superintendent Brown walked Enos to his car, then said, "Detective Fauler, I think it would be best if you don't break into Rapper's house again. We know you were there."

Enos neither confirmed nor denied it, but he did say, "Do you really think I'd ask you to keep it under surveillance and then break in?"

He unlocked his car and opened the door just as the superintendent spoke. "There is one more thing. We got a call, probably a prank, but some kid claims he knows where Deedee Marchant is."

Enos whirled around. "When did he call?"

"After you went to jail. He wouldn't tell us anything except that he had somehow taken her from Rapper," the superintendent said. "Maybe this Stu fellow she came here with is trying to get us to drop the whole thing."

"Thanks for telling me about it, Superintendent," Enos said. "Let me know if this kid calls again, will you? I'll keep in touch."

Enos drove back to his room, thinking about all that the superintendent had told him, and wondering what it was that the superintendent had kept to himself, for he was sure the man hadn't told him everything. And who was the anonymous caller? Did the young man tell the superintendent more than the superintendent cared to tell Enos? Was Deedee really safe now?

He looked at his watch as he parked in front of the motel. It was three o'clock in the morning. It would be five in Duchesne—much too early to call in to the office. But he had to talk to Sheriff Robinson soon.

He opened the door to Meredith's room on the outside chance that she might have returned, but she wasn't there. He entered her room, turned on the light, and called Sheriff Robinson.

"Enos, that you?" Sheriff Robinson asked when Enos said hello to him.

"Of course it's me," Enos said as he turned off the light in Meredith's room, unsure of why he did. "Who else would be calling you at this hour?" he asked.

"Are you out of jail?" the sheriff asked.

"Finally. What time did the superintendent call you?" Enos asked.

"I called him after a young man named Hank called me. It wasn't late then, but I didn't look at my watch. Superintendent Brown doesn't seem to trust you, and he wouldn't let me talk to you when I called, so I'm surprised he let you out of jail after being so stubborn earlier. Maybe it's because I threatened to call the governor-general."

"Slow down, Sheriff. You mean *you* called the superintendent? Who's Hank?"

"He's a young man who says he knows where Deedee is, and he was supposed to call Superintendent Brown and ask to talk to you, then call me back. He never did, but I believe the young man does know where Deedee is. He claims he got her away from Rapper and has her hidden somewhere. He was supposed to—"

"Call the superintendent, but when he did, the superintendent thought it was a prank—right?" Enos continued without waiting. "When he talked to you, did he give you any idea who he was or where I might find him?" Enos asked.

"All he said was that his name is Hank. He called here looking for Meredith. He said Deedee wants to go home, and when I told him Meredith was with you in Abaco he got real excited until he found out you were in jail. Then he got scared he might end up in jail too," the sheriff said. "I think he's afraid the police are corrupt."

"They aren't corrupt," Enos said. "They're just in over their heads and don't know how to handle it."

"Where's Meredith?" the sheriff asked.

"I'd like to know," Enos said. "I think Rapper took her."

"Oh, no, Enos. That could be serious."

"I know. Believe me, Rapper is one bad actor. They pulled the remains of his yacht from the bottom of the harbor and found evidence that he's been transporting people in a lower deck, people who are handcuffed to the walls."

"What the police in Los Angeles think might be true." The sheriff sounded sober.

After discussing the situation awhile longer, Enos finally said, "Call me if you hear from this Hank fellow again. If I'm not at the motel, leave a message with the police. I don't think they'll mess around with us again."

Enos had just hung the phone up when he heard a car drive up outside. He stepped to the window and parted the curtain ever so slightly. Two men were getting out of a gray SUV, and as they walked beneath the streetlight, Enos gasped. The smaller of the two men was Rapper.

Enos slipped his gun from its holster and waited near the door.

To his dismay, Rapper returned to the car, but the other man strode confidently toward the very room where Enos waited. The man didn't knock, and it only took him a moment to pick the lock on the door. When he stepped inside, Enos didn't hesitate. He brought his pistol down on the back of the man's head and sent him reeling to the floor.

Enos made sure he was unconscious, then hurried back to the door. To his dismay, Rapper was already driving off. He lifted his gun, considered firing a shot, then thought better of it. He didn't need more trouble with the local police. Instead, he studied the vehicle as it sped away, then shut the door, turned on the light, and stepped over to the unconscious intruder, turning him over.

He'd never seen his face before. Enos pulled out the handcuffs he'd taken from Rapper's collection and cuffed the man's hands behind his back. Next he tied his feet together with a pillowcase that he ripped in two. That ought to make the manager angry, he thought to himself.

He pulled the fellow's wallet out and found both a New York driver's license and one issued in the Bahamas. The pictures on each looked like the man on the floor, and the name was the same on both—Carlton N. Sebastian.

Bingo. Enos had found Superintendent Brown's "missing informant."

Enos got a glass of water from the bathroom and dumped it on the intruder's face. The man spluttered and awoke cursing. When he struggled to get up, Enos put a foot firmly on his chest. The man's eyes grew wide. "Who are you?"

"Does it matter?" Enos asked. "It seems I can do about what I want with you now."

Fear crossed over the man's face, and he cursed again.

"Watch the language," Enos said. "I've been known to kick men's teeth out for less. Mind telling me what you're doing breaking into this room, Carl?" he asked.

"None of your business," the man said, and Enos could tell that the use of his name had surprised him.

"Yes, I know your name, Carlton N. Sebastian. And I know something about you. It's very much my business what you're doing here."

"It's not your room," Carl insisted, struggling against his restraints.

"You're right, it's not," Enos agreed. "But I have permission to be here. The woman asked me to keep an eye on things for her."

"She can't have, she's . . ." Carl began, then stopped.

"You were about to tell me where she is?" Enos raised his eyebrows.

"I don't know what you're talking about."

"Don't give me that. Rapper knows, and you know too. And you *are* going to tell me."

Carl clamped his mouth shut, and Enos suddenly swung a big, booted foot hard near the man's head. He intentionally missed, but Carl jerked away nonetheless.

"Next time, I won't miss," Enos said. "Now, you were saying?"

"Don't know," Carl insisted.

"Then tell me where you keep your explosives. I already know you're an expert with them," Enos said.

The sudden change in questioning threw Carl off guard. "I could blow you clear off the face of the earth if I wanted to."

"Just like you did Rapper's boat. How much did he give you for that little job, anyway?"

Carl didn't answer for a few moments, then he said, "I don't know what you're talking about."

"Of course you do. Superintendent Brown's been looking for you. Seems you not only did the dirty work for Rapper, but you lied to the superintendent. He's not going to be happy with you."

"Superintendent knows who done it. He said the man was going to jail."

"Know who I am?" Enos asked.

"Never seen you before in my life. Now get these cuffs off me and let me go."

"Name's Enos Fauler," Enos said softly. "Detective Enos Fauler. But I have no authority as a police officer in Abaco, so I can kick you all I want to, or break your fingers, or whatever else I decide to do if you don't tell me where Meredith Marchant is. And if you think Rapper's going to help you, just give a thought to Stu Chandler."

"Who's Stu Chandler?" Carl asked.

"Partner of Rapper's," he said. It was a guess—but he was almost positive it was right. "Stu brought a girl here. I think you know about the girl, but where do you suppose Stu is now?"

"Have no idea what you're talking about," Carl insisted.

Enos bent over and gave Carl's face a resounding blow with his open palm. The man cried out in pain. "That's nothing compared to what Rapper's going to do to you for letting me catch you—if he ever sees you again. Which he won't if you don't tell me where Ms. Marchant is at."

Carl was silent for a moment, and he appeared to be considering his options. Finally he said, "I don't know exactly where she is. She gave Rapper the slip out at the Hole in the Wall Lighthouse. Might be dead, for all I know."

Enos grabbed the phone and dialed the home of the superintendent. A woman answered. "I need to talk to Superintendent Brown," he said. "It's important."

The superintendent came on a moment later. "Superintendent, Enos Fauler. Got a man here who claims he doesn't know me. Goes by Carl. Claims Rapper took Meredith to the Hole in the Wall Lighthouse. I'm headed out there."

"Enos, I'm coming right over. That road's a bad one. Take a car on it and you'll never make it. I'll bring something with higher clearance."

"Fine, but hurry."

"Where are you?" the superintendent asked.

"At the motel. Mr. Sebastian made the mistake of breaking in on me. Seems he wanted something of Meredith's, but he isn't willing to say what. Oh, and he claims to be an explosives expert," Enos added. "Got paid to blow up Rapper's boat for him."

# CHAPTER 19

The vehicle Superintendent Brown brought for Enos was an old Isuzu Trooper. "I'd go with you, but it looks like I've got all I can handle here," the superintendent told him. "But I'll send one of my men to help you look for her. You'll like Manny."

Carl clammed up and wouldn't admit to anything once the superintendent arrived, but the superintendent was now convinced Enos had been right all along. While Enos and Manny looked for Meredith, the superintendent and more of his officers planned to look for Carl's vehicle and for Rapper, as well as get a warrant to search Carl's property. All Enos wanted was to find Meredith, and he hoped that while he was doing that, the young man named Hank would keep Deedee safely hidden from Rapper.

The sun was up and shining brightly by the time Enos and the middle-aged officer known as Manny Younger had turned onto the road to the lighthouse. Manny was around forty, with light brown hair but a dark tan. As they rode together, Manny driving, Enos learned that the man had only been an officer for five years. Born in Abaco, he'd spent his growing up years both there and in Miami. He'd spent most of his life fishing for a living but had given it up when he'd gotten the chance to go to work for the police department. "I just needed a change," he told Enos, who immediately took a liking to him. Only about 5'8" and weighing maybe 140 pounds, Manny didn't look like much. His skin was leathery and weathered from his years on the ocean, but he was wiry and strong, had a keen sense of humor, and seemed to know what he was about.

Manny was also familiar with the road they were now driving on. "We have occasional tourists get themselves in trouble out here," he chuckled. "I don't know why the maps don't show it as an unpassable road. You look at a map and it indicates it's a simple dirt road leading to the lighthouse. It can be very deceiving."

Enos had never been on a road with such terrible chuckholes, so he could see why the superintendent had warned him not to head out here in a sedan. "How far is it in to the lighthouse?" Enos asked after they'd gone maybe a few miles.

"Oh, as I recall, it's fourteen, fifteen, maybe even sixteen miles."

Enos groaned. "At this rate, it'll take us over an hour to get in there. Is the road this bad all the way?"

"No, actually, it gets worse," Manny said with a chuckle.

"I suppose she could be walking out," Enos observed after another mile.

"Let's hope so," Manny agreed. "But then again, she might be hiding out in the lighthouse or one of the outbuildings there."

Enos thought otherwise. "If she gave Rapper the slip, as Carl indicated, she probably wouldn't want to be seen or allow herself to get trapped in case he came back. The fact that they were breaking into her room makes me think they were after something of hers and planned to come back and find her," Enos reasoned.

Manny nodded. "Keep an eye off to the side just in case she's staying in the trees a little bit. I can't imagine her walking out there for long, though. It's rough hiking, what with the sharp rocks and all. A pair of tennis shoes wouldn't last long out there."

Nor would a person without water, Enos thought soberly, knowing it was very likely Meredith would be without water, and it was going to be a hot day. He closed his eyes and for the hundredth time asked the Lord to watch over Meredith.

* * *

Meredith could hear the vehicle coming long before it reached her. She'd been walking, if it could be called that, for a half hour already. She'd never known such pain, but despite her bleeding and blistered feet, she'd made herself move, afraid Rapper would come back looking for her. She'd worked her way back to the road and was walking on it because the forest floor was just too difficult. Sharp rocks jutted up everywhere, and just as frequently there were jagged holes, concealed with rotting foliage and creeping vines.

She'd tripped six or eight times just getting back to the road, and her shins, knees, and hands were bleeding again. Her pant legs were ripped in three or four places, blood and dirt caked on them. Now, with a car coming, she had to go back into the forest. She cried as she left the road. She couldn't let Rapper find her. She fell again, only about thirty feet off the road, and could hear the car coming a little faster now. She concluded there must be a smoother stretch of road just ahead, remembering it from when Rapper had brought her in here.

There wasn't time to rise and move farther from the road, so Meredith simply wriggled behind a large bush and waited for the car to pass, allowing herself just a tiny peek through the trees. The vehicle had slowed again and was trying to navigate past a particularly nasty spot in the road. She recognized it as an Isuzu Trooper. Two men were in it. She didn't recognize the man who was driving, and the passenger she couldn't see plainly.

Meredith slipped farther behind the bush and waited for the sound of the Isuzu to fade. When it finally did, she rose to her feet and made her way very slowly and painfully back to the road. She took the one final swig of her water and even shook the bottle to coax the very last drop from it. Then she sank to the road and sobbed. Her throat was parched, and she was so very weak. She wasn't sure she could physically make it all the way to the main road.

But she had to. Deedee's life depended on her making it back to Marsh Harbor. With that thought, she forced herself to stand, and with her ears listening to the road behind her so she'd know when the Trooper was coming back, she forced herself to stumble forward.

Her empty water bottle lay in the center of the road where she'd dropped it. She didn't even know she'd let it fall. Not that it mattered; it was empty anyway.

\* \* \*

Enos recognized Rapper's red Jeep the moment he saw it on the road ahead. As they neared it, he leaped from the Isuzu and ran toward it. One front tire and rim were destroyed. A back one was nearly gone. Someone had apparently driven it until the Jeep would go no farther. He and Manny looked it over carefully. The keys were in the ignition, but there was nothing they could find that indicated who had abandoned it—unless the bullet hole in the back was a clue, Enos thought as he pointed it out to Manny. "This looks fresh," he said. "Meredith just might have been the last one to drive this."

Rapper might have been shooting at her, he thought, trembling with anguish.

The spare tire was flat, which explained why it had been driven as far as it had with two shredded tires. He had to wonder why Rapper would drive like that though, even though he obviously had the resources to get whatever he needed whenever he needed it. Enos felt the more likely scenario was that Meredith had driven as far as she could—while being shot at—then abandoned the Jeep.

Enos began a sweeping search of the area. "What are you looking for?" Manny asked. "We've got to get busy and move this thing if we're going to get past and look for Ms. Marchant."

Enos nodded. "And we'll have to move it quite a ways before we can find a place wide enough to pass. Do you have a chain?"

"I think there's a towrope in this outfit," Manny said. "You're looking for something, aren't you?"

"Yes, but I don't know what," Enos admitted. "I'd just like to look around before we do anything with the Jeep. You never know what we might find. It would be really helpful if we could be sure who was driving this Jeep."

"Do you think it was Ms. Marchant?" Manny asked with some surprise.

"I think it's quite likely," Enos said with conviction. "After seeing that bullet hole, I can't help but wonder if she somehow escaped from Rapper and took the Jeep. She's a bright and resourceful woman."

Manny joined in the search, and the two of them soon explored into the trees. Enos spotted an old and very rusty hammer. "I might have something here," he called to Manny.

A moment later, the officer joined him. "That could have been here for years," Manny remarked after a cursory glance. "As you can see, it's very rusty." He chuckled. "People here in Abaco have a tendency to just leave things lying around. Like that old airplane we passed a ways back—that's been there for years and nobody's ever bothered to try to move it."

Enos had remarked about the plane when they'd first passed it. It had obviously crashed into the trees at the side of the road many years ago, and now there was little left but rusted steel. Manny didn't seem to know when it had crashed there or the fate of those aboard; he hadn't even seemed very interested. Enos was fast learning that this was the way of many of the islanders. It seemed that when something had ceased to be useful, it was left there to return to the earth, even if it took several centuries.

But this hammer was different. Enos pointed at it and said, "You'll notice that there's the end of a small piece of that fern beneath the hammer. It didn't grow there."

Manny leaned over and squinted. "I think you're right."

"Someone's thrown it there recently," Enos concluded. "And considering how little use this road gets and the hammer's proximity to the Jeep, it would only seem logical that it was thrown here by whoever left the Jeep."

Manny agreed, adding his own thoughts. "Rapper wouldn't be carrying something like that, and if he was, he'd have no reason to throw it here."

"But Meredith might have carried it as a weapon to defend herself with," Enos said. "Maybe she found something more useful in the Jeep, like a gun or a knife of Rapper's."

"Could be, and then she might have just tossed this here when she got out of the Jeep to start walking," Manny guessed.

"Which means it's likely she was the one driving. And if that's the case, we'd be wasting our time moving this thing out of the road so we could go on. If Meredith was driving the Jeep when it stopped, she'd have continued on foot back toward the main road."

Enos picked up the hammer. "We must have passed her. Let's head back."

They had to back up for several hundred yards before they finally found a place wide enough to turn around, but after doing so they traveled as quickly as they could on the rough surface. After a couple of miles they slowed down, and every so often, one of them would call Meredith's name out the window.

Enos kept his eyes trained on the forest while Manny drove, and it was Manny, whose eyes were constantly watching the road, who spotted the water bottle. He slammed on the brakes. "What is it?" Enos asked hopefully.

Manny was already opening his door. "There's an empty bottle in the road. I know it wasn't there when we came by earlier."

Enos felt hope fill his heart as he knelt and studied the bottle. It was empty, but there was a bead of moisture clinging to the inside. He picked up the bottle, then began to scan the roadway. The surface was rough, the old pavement broken up badly, and the dark spots he noticed didn't look right.

Again he knelt, touching a finger lightly to the surface of the road. "Blood," he told Manny, who agreed after Enos showed him. They then began to search even more carefully, and Enos soon found where someone had come from the trees to the road. It didn't take long to find the very spot where they had lain while Enos and Manny drove past earlier. There were crushed leaves and more traces of blood there.

Tears filled his eyes knowing it was probably Meredith's, but hope filled his heart. Back on the road, he began to walk, trying to find tracks. But this wasn't a surface that lent itself to tracks. However, he did see more spots of blood. "Her shoes must be torn up and her feet bleeding," Enos concluded. "I'm going to walk for a while," he told Manny. "You follow in the car."

They continued for several hundred yards, but Enos couldn't find anything indicating whether or not Meredith was still on the road. He signaled for Manny to shut off the motor, then yelled Meredith's name. Manny joined in.

They listened.

Nothing.

Enos got back in the car. "Let's stop every hundred yards or so and shout," he suggested. "I can't imagine that she could be far."

"Unless Rapper's come back and found her," Manny suggested.

That was the last thing Enos wanted to hear or even think about, and yet he knew he couldn't discount the possibility.

\* \* \*

Meredith looked at her watch when she heard the Isuzu Trooper again. She'd been forcing one foot ahead of the other for nearly two hours since it had passed by earlier. In that two hours, she doubted she'd progressed much over a mile. She knew she had to hide again and continue on until she reached the highway—even if it took every ounce of strength she had. Surely someone on the highway would stop to give her a ride. The people who lived on this island were mostly good Christian folks who attended church weekly. Someone would help her—if she could just keep Rapper from finding her first.

The air was turning very hot and muggy, and Meredith looked up as she turned toward the side of the road. Thick black clouds were gathering overhead, giving the appearance of rain. She wasn't sure if that was good or bad. Good, she hoped as she forced herself off the road. Maybe a few drops would ease the terrible burning in her mouth.

Meredith stepped over a large rock, around another, then stumbled over a smaller one and fell to her knees. She tried to get up, but it was just too painful, so she crawled desperately, ignoring the cutting and tearing and bleeding. She looked over her shoulder, noting with alarm that Rapper would see her if she didn't get farther into the woods. Then she realized that the sound of the approaching vehicle had stopped.

She strained to listen. Maybe they'd turned back again. Maybe she should go back to the road. Then she heard a voice shouting—two voices! They were looking for her, calling for her. She had to get away!

Meredith finally managed to get to her feet, and, using the trees to help keep her upright, she slowly moved deeper into the forest. The car started up again, coming closer. Certain it would stop when it neared her, she hurried to create more distance between her and the road.

The next time Meredith looked back, she could no longer see the road at all through the foliage. That was good, but still, she moved on. She had gone maybe another hundred feet when she heard the car stop. She tried to rush ahead, to gain just a little more distance.

A foot caught a root, and she lost her balance and fell forward. The last thing she heard before her head struck a stump was someone calling her name—it had sounded like Enos. But that thought had barely registered before she fell unconscious.

* * *

"Maybe she made it to the highway and caught a ride to town," Manny suggested.

He and Enos were standing beside the highway, trying to decide what to do next. Enos was terribly discouraged, and he wondered if somehow Rapper had gone back and found Meredith while he and Manny were at the abandoned Jeep.

If only he knew whether she was still back along that road somewhere, hiding, afraid to answer his calls, or too far from the road to even hear them. "How about if we go back to Marsh Harbor and see if by any chance she's returned?" Manny suggested.

"Sure," Enos said. "Maybe we'll find that they've caught up with Rapper."

"I can radio in from here and ask that," Manny reminded him. Enos nodded.

The rain started to fall hard as they pulled onto the highway.

# CHAPTER 20

Rapper threw the door against the wall with all his strength. Even though he had already discovered that someone had removed its hinges and carried Deedee away, he was angry all over again. He knew the cops hadn't found her, as he'd first suspected, or they wouldn't still be searching the way they were. He hadn't even been able to return to his own home—they were watching it every minute. But they weren't watching this place, which meant they likely didn't know about it. Someone else knew about it and had taken the girl, and he couldn't imagine who it would be or why they'd done it.

His first reaction after finding her missing had been to return to the lighthouse and take out his anger on that attorney woman, the girl's mother. He'd left her there, planning to somehow take Deedee to join her, then gain access to her money. After that, he planned to either dispose of the woman and her daughter, or, if he thought he could pull it off without the use of the destroyed yacht, he'd take the girl away from here in his fishing boat.

That had all changed when he found Deedee missing. But he hadn't expected her mother to cause him any problems when he returned. He figured he'd find her slowly walking up the road toward the highway, her feet bleeding perhaps, but with her making progress nonetheless. He'd badly underestimated her, and he cursed as he recalled the way she'd turned the tables on him, leaving him on foot out at the lighthouse. He wished he'd figured out a way to get her money earlier and taken care of her permanently then. He'd made a mistake, something he seldom did.

That mistake had mushroomed. He'd walked several miles before he finally decided to call Carl on his satellite cell phone and ask for the man's help. Now Carl knew far more than Rapper wanted him to.

Rapper had also thought he'd figured out a way to both distract the police and rid himself of that pesky detective from Utah. He'd sacrificed his yacht only to discover that somehow, Detective Fauler had avoided jail. Now both he and Meredith Marchant were loose ends that he had to take care of. He'd gone back to Meredith's room, planning to have Carl remove everything the woman owned. Then he was going to pay Carl to add to his story about Enos being in the yacht, claiming he now remembered a woman going into the yacht with the detective but not coming back out. Enos would be held for murder as well as blowing up the yacht.

Then he and Carl had unwittingly walked straight into the detective. Rapper felt fortunate to have gotten away, but Carl, who knew way too much already, appeared to be in custody.

Things were not going well, which was galling to Rapper. He was used to planning jobs and having everything fall neatly into place—and that wasn't happening now. Meredith Marchant was out there someplace, and there wasn't a thing he could do about her until he could get a car that no one would recognize and go back out and look for her.

He brought his thoughts back to his immediate concern—where the girl was. He'd been so angry when he first discovered her missing that he'd driven straight back to the lighthouse, bent on revenge instead of looking for clues as to where the girl might have been taken. He'd assumed the police had taken her, but as he calmed himself, he assumed nothing. Someone had taken the girl, and it was very likely they still had her.

Rapper began to canvas the neighborhood, reasonably certain no one had seen him when he brought the girl in. But what about when she was taken out?

He began to ask if anyone had seen any suspicious activity the past couple of days. "I was asked to keep an eye on the place while the owner's gone," he told one person after another. "Now I see that someone's been in there. They did some damage and might have taken some of his valuables."

After about twenty minutes of asking around the neighborhood, Rapper found someone with information. "Yes, I saw a couple of kids coming out of there late at night," an elderly lady said. "I probably wouldn't have thought anything about it if it hadn't been that I know the black boy, but I'd never seen the pretty white girl he was with before."

"So you know the man's name?" Rapper asked, trying not to show his elation.

"Course I do. He does odd jobs around here from time to time. He's just a young fellow from over in Marsh Harbor. Comes by boat and works," she finished.

"What's his name?" Rapper asked. "Maybe I'd know him."

"Hank's his name. His mother's a widow, Alice Prentice. Hardworking lady. She comes over here sometimes too."

Rapper congratulated himself. He knew Hank, all right, but he didn't let the woman know that. He'd take care of Hank, he promised himself. There would be no more mistakes, no more trying to avoid doing what had to be done.

"What about the girl?" Rapper asked, even though he was certain of who it was. He didn't want the lady getting suspicious.

"Seemed right pretty, although I didn't get a real clear look at her. Her hair was long and sort of a dark reddish-brown color," the lady said. "I don't know what they might have been doing in there, but they seemed friendly like."

"What do you mean?" Rapper asked.

"Well, you know, they were holding hands and all when they left, and they were sneaking around like they didn't want anyone to see them together. I can't imagine why."

"Well, you never know about kids these days," Rapper said with a disarming smile. "Did you see them when they went in?"

"No, sir, only saw them leaving, but like I said, they were being really sneaky. You know, slipping behind bushes every little while, waiting, then running quickly and hiding again. Hank probably doesn't want his mother knowing he's got a girlfriend," she said.

"Where did they go?" Rapper asked.

"It was dark, but I think they were headed for the little dock where Hank always ties up his boat when he's over here," she said. "Sometimes he comes by ferry, but when the weather's good, he comes over in his own boat."

"So they left in his boat, did they?"

"I'm sure they did. Must have come the same way. I know I've never seen the girl around the island before."

It had suddenly begun to rain, but Rapper was ready to go anyway. He thanked the woman for her help, then returned to his boat, drenched by the time he got to it. As he climbed aboard, he realized a few things that made him stop and think. The cops were looking for him, and they might know by now that he had a fishing boat in addition to the yacht. Once they discovered where he kept it moored, they'd be watching for it, and he didn't need that. Rapper knew his time in Abaco was coming to a close—his identity was surfacing too quickly. First he had to tie up a few loose ends, and they included the Utah cop, Meredith Marchant, her daughter, Hank Prentice, and Carl. Once they were all taken care of, he'd leave here for good, assuming another identity along with a well-padded bank account. Disappearing was not a difficult thing for Rapper.

While he admitted in the back of his mind that loose ends were not that important, Rapper was a proud man and felt compelled to even the score. He also believed he could safely do that, get away from here soon, and set up a new base of operations somewhere else. Maybe Jamaica, he thought with a grim smile. It wouldn't be as convenient as the Bahamas, but he could make it work.

Rapper made another short visit to the bungalow, stowing some extra clothes in a bag and carrying them out with him. The rain had quit while he was in the house. He didn't try to be sneaky and even waved at the neighbor lady who was watching as he left. "I'll be checking back with you," he shouted. "Keep an eye on things, will you?"

"I'll watch closely," she called back to him.

He changed into the clothes when he arrived at the boat and left his own wet clothes there. He tucked his pistol securely out of sight, then, for the sake of his own security, left his boat, probably for the last time. Rapper slipped away in another boat his friend who lived in the bungalow owned and that he kept tied up nearby. When he approached Marsh Harbor, he tied up at a run-down, dirty commercial dock near an older residential area. Many of the poorer residents of Marsh Harbor lived here, and he had a feeling he might be able to find Alice Prentice close by.

Rapper knocked at a door and made some inquiries. A young woman with several kids clamored around her told him what he needed to know. "Everybody knows Alice and Hank," she said. "Hank's done a little work for me. He's a hardworking boy."

"He did a little work for me too," Rapper said, not telling her that it had been many months ago. "I was in the states when he finished the job. I just got in this morning and wanted to square it with him, but I lost his address."

Within minutes Rapper was hurrying through the rain that was once more falling hard. He found Alice Prentice's house just a few blocks away. He smiled to himself as he knocked at the door and introduced himself as a friend of Hank's.

* * *

Alice Prentice was not at all happy to see the man who stepped inside and stood in front of her. His demeanor had changed the instant she'd shut the door behind him. He was evidently not in a good mood and had immediately unleashed his anger on her. "Your boy Hank took something that doesn't belong to him," Rapper said. "I aim to get it back."

"I don't know what you're talking about," Alice said, her voice trembling and her body shaking slightly. Hank had been acting very strange lately, and she knew that he was up to something. She would never have believed that he would steal anything, but this man who refused to give his name was certain that he had. She was frightened for both Hank and herself.

"Maybe I'll just stay until he comes home," the man suggested.

"No, you don't need to do that," Alice pleaded, afraid he'd hurt Hank.

"Maybe you could tell me where to find him, then," he suggested next.

"I haven't seen him for a long time," she stammered. "I don't know where he is." That was the truth, and she was glad she didn't know where he'd gone because she'd hate to be forced to tell this man and have him go looking for Hank.

"If you'll give me a phone number where Hank can call you when he comes home, I'll see that he does," Alice suggested. She had no intention of doing any such thing, not unless Hank were to admit he'd done something wrong and that calling this man would make everything okay again. Somehow, she just didn't think it would all be solved that easily.

\* \* \*

Rapper intended to find Hank. He was his first and most aggravating loose end. He would just wait for a few minutes, he decided as he calmly tied Alice Prentice up in her bedroom and made himself at home while he waited. Not many minutes had passed before he became anxious to be up and doing something. He could be patient when he had to, but that was when he was planning and carrying out profitable jobs. What he had to do now was both unprofitable and unnecessary—Stu shouldn't have brought the girl to the island in the first place. Rapper finally couldn't stand to wait anymore. He entered Alice's bedroom. "I'll need to borrow your car. I have some other things to do, and I'm on foot. Where are your keys?"

She told him where they were, but before he went to the kitchen to retrieve them, he said, "Now listen, lady, I'm going to put a gag in your mouth. I can't have you making any noise while I'm gone. I don't plan to hurt your boy, only to get back what's mine." That was a lie, but telling lies was the least of Rapper's many sins. "If you try to do anything to attract the cops or to tip Hank off if he gets back before I do, then I'll hurt him, and I'll hurt him real bad." He was quite certain that Alice would cooperate because she clearly feared for her son.

Rapper found the keys and slipped out into the rain. This car wasn't the best for driving on the road to the lighthouse, but it was something, and he didn't care if it got damaged. By now, Meredith was probably getting close to the highway, if she hadn't already made it into town. He'd check the motel if he could do so safely, and if she wasn't there, he'd head south again and make one more attempt to get rid of her permanently.

\* \* \*

Meredith awoke with a terrible headache. She was drenched to the skin, and it was still raining. It took her a couple of minutes to figure out where she was, and she groaned when she remembered Enos's voice calling out to her as she fell. Now he was gone. The thought was almost more than she could bear.

She rolled painfully onto her back and let the pouring rain enter her mouth. It wasn't much, but it felt good. She lay there for a long time, hoping she could get a little of her strength back and continue her arduous journey. By the time she finally rolled back onto her stomach and began the painful process of getting to her feet, the rain had stopped. She felt marginally stronger, but her head pounded unmercifully from the blow she'd received when she fell. Once back on her feet, she wasn't at all sure she could finish the long walk back to the main highway.

Meredith had never been a quitter, though, so she awkwardly worked her way back toward the road. She'd only covered half the distance when she heard a car coming. "Enos," she cried weakly when it passed slowly by. She couldn't see it, which meant that he couldn't see her either. "Help me, Enos," she called out again. Her parched throat was only a tiny bit better as a result of the rain she'd let fall into her mouth. She could only pray that he'd hear her.

The car stopped, and someone got out. She opened her mouth to shout again, but suddenly her throat closed up tightly. She cried inwardly for help and opened her mouth again, but once more, nothing came out.

Then the man searching for her called for her. "Counselor."

She leaned against the nearest tree and fought the panic that suddenly clutched at her chest. The only person on Abaco who called her that was Rapper!

"Counselor, if you can hear me, shout. I'll come help you if you're hurt or anything. I'm the only one who can help you now."

No help was better than anything Rapper might give her. Meredith stayed as still as she could. Once again Rapper called to her, and his words chipped away at her resolve. "Your good friend Enos Fauler is in jail, and he won't be getting out. There's no one but me to help you get your girl back."

Enos in jail? But he was here not that long ago. She almost gave up and might have done so if Rapper hadn't said what he did next. "He was arrested for blowing up my yacht. He'll be in jail for a long, long time."

That was a lie. She'd heard Enos's voice—she was sure of it. She clung to the tree, motionless.

Rapper waited, then she heard him get back into the car. It started up and moved a short distance, then she could again hear his voice calling out. He was too far away now for her to make out the words, but she was sure he was repeating what he'd just said. She made no effort to move from her spot until the car had driven on. Then she backtracked and found a reasonably comfortable place to sit and wait. She dared not go back to the road again.

Eventually she heard the car pass once more. It was dark now, and she decided to wait a little longer to continue her arduous trek.

* * *

Hank and Deedee were talking, as they had been most of the day. Hank had stretched a tarp between four trees, and they had managed to stay dry during the hard rainstorm. Now the air smelled fresh and clean, and Deedee breathed deeply. The storm and listening to Hank talk were both refreshing to her. She drew strength from him as he conversed in the Bahamian dialect that she was beginning to understand better and enjoy more. He'd told her a lot about the island and about the work he did, acknowledging it wasn't very glamorous but that there weren't really any glamorous jobs on this island, unless maybe the men who took people out fishing in the ocean.

Later, as they'd watched the sparkling drops of water drip from the tarp and the nearby leaves, he'd told her about the church he went to, and she'd told him about hers. "If I ever get home, there's a book I want to send you, but you have to promise to read it."

"I'm not a very good reader," Hank admitted sheepishly.

"But you can read?" she pressed.

"Yes, I read the Bible."

"Good, then I'm going to see that you get a copy of the Book of Mormon. It's about the people that lived in America many centuries ago. Jesus appeared to them, and it tells about that."

Hank was suddenly interested. He had grown up on stories of Jesus from the New Testament. "I'd like that," he said. "And I promise I'll read it."

"Good," Deedee said with a grin. "You'll like it. It makes a lot of things clear that are confusing in the Bible."

Hank was thoughtful for a minute, then said, "If there's one thing I'd like to be made clear, it's where the black hole came from."

"The black hole?" Deedee asked. "Isn't that something way out in space?"

"Maybe, but there's a place here on this island we call the black hole. It's deep and round, a scary hole in the forest between Marsh Harbor and Treasure Cay," he said. "I've only seen the black hole one time. It must have been made by a meteor or something. It's the scariest place I've ever seen."

"Why's it scary?" Deedee asked as she suddenly recalled Rapper making reference to a place he called the black hole when she protested being locked in the room at the bungalow. He'd said something about her being better off in that room than in the black hole. It hadn't made sense to her then, but now it was beginning to. If it was the same place, it must be really terrible.

As Hank went on to describe it, she tried to create a mental picture. He explained that it had a huge round rim and that it was a long ways down when someone looked over the edge. He trembled a little as he spoke, especially when he mentioned that all a person could see down inside the hole was black water, black as anything he'd ever seen. He described in some detail the trees, bushes, and vines that were so thick on most of the rim that they prevented a person from walking all the way around. His eyes grew larger when he told her that from what it looked like, a piece of the rim could break off and drop a person in the water if they went out too far. She could tell he was convinced that if anyone ever fell in, they'd die.

"There's no way out of there," he said, his voice thick with fear. "The sides of the hole, they're like a cone turned upside down." This gave her the impression that the rim was a lot smaller in circumference than the inside of the hole where the water was. Hank went on to describe things that sounded like giant icicles that hung from the rim but didn't actually reach the water surface deep down inside the hole. He explained that it was a very dangerous place and that the water was very deep. "It's bottomless," he said.

When she expressed skepticism at that, he told her that some guys he knew had put a weight on the end of some fishing line and kept letting it go deeper and deeper. He swore it never did reach the bottom.

Deedee was beginning to share Hank's concern now. His eyes kept getting bigger the more he talked about it. "Do people go there a lot?" she asked as he began the task of building a fire from the dry wood he'd stacked beneath the tarp before the storm.

"Oh no, Deedee. Not many people have seen it." It was hard to find, he explained, and had only been discovered a few years back when a white man was hunting wild boars. The hunter's dog had apparently been chasing a boar through the forest, and as he followed them, he suddenly came out of the trees and almost fell right into the hole. Hank told her the man was lucky to be alive, lucky that he didn't tumble in and die right there. He again stressed how thick the trees and foliage in the area were. Deedee pictured a jungle thicker than the one where they were hidden near the molasses tanks. As the fire began to blaze and Hank once again sat down beside her, he swore that a person couldn't see the hole until they were right on the edge of the rim.

"So not many people go there?" she pressed.

"Oh, no, the trail's very bad," he said, then told her about a short but very poor length of road that a person could drive on for about a half mile after leaving the highway. From there, it was a difficult hike for the next few hundred yards. Hank emphasized to Deedee that even when a person was looking for the hole and expecting it, it would always catch them by surprise when they first saw it. It was a frightening place, he told her so convincingly that she found she didn't care to ever go there despite the curiosity he'd created in her mind.

"It must be awful if you're scared of it, Hank," she said. "You're the bravest guy I know."

He grinned at her and ducked his head, encouraged to tell her a little more about the hole. He said some men once lowered a cup down into the water and actually pulled up some of the black liquid, but the surprising thing was that it wasn't black at all in their cup. She could tell from his expression that he didn't believe it was really clear water either.

"Wow," Deedee said. "It must be a horrible place."

"It is," he said, shivering. Then Hank looked around. It was almost dark, and the fire was burning brightly. "I better go, Deedee," he said.

"Hank, do you have to go?" Deedee pled when he prepared to return to his boat. His story had frightened her, and she didn't want to be alone now.

"We can't wait here forever," he said. "You stay, and I'll go into town again. Maybe this time I can find your mama or that Detective Fauler. Maybe I'll call Sheriff Robinson again. He'll tell me what to do."

Deedee felt tears well in her eyes. She stood and wrapped her arms around Hank. "I'm so afraid for you when you go. Maybe I should come with you."

"No!" he said gruffly. "That's a bad idea. Nobody knows I brought you here; if Rapper sees you, he will take you away, and you would never see your mama again."

Deedee knew he was right, so she slowly released her hold. "Don't be long," she begged.

"You sleep, then the time will pass more quickly," he promised. "I'll come back soon. You'll be surprised when I get back so quickly."

"Please be careful, Hank," she pleaded.

"Of course," he promised as he faded into the dark beyond the fire.

# CHAPTER 21

"I'm going back out to the lighthouse road," Enos said to Superintendent Brown. "Meredith must be hurt or she'd have shown up by now. Do you have a light I can use?"

"Of course," Superintendent Brown said. Then he turned to Officer Younger. "Can you go with Detective Fauler and help him? I know you both must be worn out."

Manny chuckled. "And you aren't? Of course I'll go."

Rapper seemed to have vanished. The police had been searching for him throughout Marsh Harbor. Carl's vehicle had been located near one of the docks, and they'd learned that Rapper's other boat, a small fishing vessel, was missing. The superintendent was now arranging for several men to sail over to Hope Town and search for his boat in the docks there. He'd offered to let Enos go, but Enos was interested only in continuing his search for Meredith. Even though it was dark, he and Manny, armed with two strong search lights, started southward again.

* * *

Rapper checked at the Prentice house as soon as he got back in Marsh Harbor and found Alice still lying on the bed right where he'd left her, the gag securely in her mouth. He reminded her that he'd be back again and to make sure Hank stayed there if he came. "If he cuts you loose, you better stay put, and you better make sure he does too. You can't run far enough to get away from me."

Alice nodded. She had lived a quiet and peaceful life on this island since the death of her abusive husband many years ago. While she knew of fear, it had become so foreign to her since his death that she trembled at its suddenly familiarity. She wondered what her precious Hank had taken that could cause a man to be so angry.

Rapper checked to make sure she couldn't move off the bed, and after shutting off all her lights, he drove away in the old car. While he was waiting for Hank to come back from wherever he was hiding Deedee, perhaps he could go see to the problem of Carl. He checked his gun. The jail was small, and it was unlikely there would be more than one officer on duty there. He was confident he could get Carl out, then decide what to do about him. Maybe he could actually be of help to Rapper for a little while before Rapper would send him to see Stu Chandler.

* * *

It was unusual for Hank's mother to be out at night, but when Hank walked up from the harbor and saw that the lights were out in the house and the car was gone, he guessed she must have had some-place she needed to go. *They must be doing something over at the church,* he thought. That would be the only place she would go, and at this time of night, it didn't seem very likely. He wasn't sure he wanted to call Sheriff Robinson yet, so he decided not to go in and use the phone. He knew his strange behavior had worried his mother, but he promised himself he'd stop back later and reassure her when she was home.

He'd hoped to use the car, but since his mother had taken it, he chose to ride his bike. He pedaled fast, knowing how worried Deedee was to be left alone. He felt responsible for her well-being. A few minutes later, he swung in at the motel. There were no lights in either room where Ms. Marchant and Detective Fauler had been staying. Hank wondered if the manager had told him the truth before, that they were no longer guests at the motel. Maybe Detective Fauler was still in jail.

He decided to go to the motel office again and try to find out if they were really gone or if they still had their rooms. He just didn't believe they'd leave Abaco while Deedee was still not back with them. He also couldn't believe the detective would still be in jail.

He went to the office and rang the bell. When the manager came out, Hank asked him if Mr. Fauler or Ms. Marchant were still checked in at the motel.

"I'm not sure that's your business." The manager eyed him.

"Please," Hank begged. "I need to find them."

The manager seemed suspicious. "Are you a friend of theirs?" he asked.

"No, but I need to talk to them. I have some important information I need to give them. They still have their rooms, don't they?" he asked.

The manager frowned. "They still have the rooms, but I haven't seen the woman for two days. The other guy, the cop from the states, he comes sometimes, but he never sleeps." The manager also mentioned that Enos had told him the lady was missing and that would explain why she was never in her room.

Hank listened with worry building. He asked if he could leave a message for Meredith or Enos, and the manager promised to see that it was delivered if he saw either of them.

That wasn't good enough for Hank. He wasn't sure the manager would remember or if he'd even be on duty when someone came. He asked for a couple of pieces of paper, explaining that he'd slip them beneath the doors of their rooms. The manager nodded his approval.

Hank wrote the same message twice. Somewhat self-conscious about his writing, Hank slipped a note beneath each door explaining that he was Deedee's friend and that she was fine and needed to talk to them. He wanted to tell them where he was hiding Deedee, but he didn't dare. In fact he didn't dare even sign his name. What if Rapper or one of his friends were to get their hands on one of the notes?

Discouraged, he jumped on his bike and headed for home, afraid that neither note would be read in time to help. He hadn't made his mind up whether or not to bother the sheriff in Utah yet. When he pedaled up to the house, it was still dark. He pushed his bike around back, planning to put it in the shed, then decided not to, thinking he could put it in the boat and take it to the hideout with him when he returned. It would give him another way to get around besides his boat if he needed it.

\* \* \*

Rapper was so angry he could barely speak. He'd taken the officer at the jail at gunpoint and ordered him to turn over his prisoner only to learn there was no prisoner. Rapper hadn't believed him at first and had forced the man to take him back to the tiny cells.

The officer had not lied. Carl was not there, nor was anyone else. "Where have they taken Carlton Sebastian? I need to talk to him."

"They took him in a plane to Nassau," the frightened officer said.

"Idiots!" Rapper shouted. "They shouldn't have done that."

When he left the jail a few minutes later, the little building was no longer without a prisoner. The officer was sitting alone in the very same cell Detective Fauler had occupied earlier. But he wasn't complaining; he was just glad to be alive.

\* \* \*

Hank entered the house through the back door and flipped on a light. He couldn't imagine where his mother might be, but he figured she'd be home soon. He went into the kitchen and fixed himself a sandwich, then decided to call the sheriff in Duchesne. It would feel good just to talk to someone friendly. He placed the call, and within minutes he had the sheriff on the line.

"Have they found Deedee's mother yet?" the sheriff asked, and Hank could hear the worry in his voice.

"I'm not sure what you're talking about," Hank said as he remembered what the motel manager had told him about her not being in her room for a couple of days.

"You don't know she's missing?" the sheriff asked.

"I haven't been hanging around," Hank said. "I've been watching out for Deedee. And I'm sorry I forgot to call you back. I was scared."

"You should be," the sheriff said. "You be really careful. Have you been back to the motel to see if Detective Fauler is there? We did manage to get him out of jail, and the police are helping him now."

"That's good," Hank said with considerable relief. "I just came from the motel. They're not there. Is Deedee's mama in trouble?"

"I'm afraid so," Sheriff Robinson said. "Rapper took her."

Hank felt a chill descending upon him. He knew Deedee would be devastated if anything happened to her mother. She already felt so terrible for running away. Hank wasn't sure he could tell her this latest news. She'd blame herself, and then she'd probably want to go back to Marsh Harbor. He couldn't let her do that. No, he decided, Deedee didn't need to know that her mother had been taken by Rapper.

"They think Ms. Marchant got away from Rapper," the sheriff continued. "But the last I heard, they hadn't been able to find her. They're not sure Rapper hasn't caught up with her again. They also have reason to believe she might be hurt."

"This is terrible," Hank moaned.

"Hank, I think it's time you told us where Deedee's at," the sheriff said, and it didn't sound like a suggestion. "Tell me where Deedee is and where you are. I'll call the police in Marsh Harbor and get someone there right away. Once they have her back, then they can concentrate on finding her mother."

Hank took a deep breath. He hadn't dared to write Deedee's hiding place on the notes he left, but surely he could trust this man. He had to trust someone—the burden was becoming much to heavy for him alone. He slowly exhaled and then said, "I'm at my mama's house." He told the sheriff what the address was, then said, "Deedee's out by the old molasses tanks. I'm going there now so she won't be alone when they come for her."

"No, you wait there, Hank. I'll have Enos meet you," the sheriff urged.

But Hank didn't want to leave Deedee alone any longer than he had to. He could be there in his boat fairly soon, but who knew how long it might take the sheriff to locate his detective? "She's scared," Hank said. "She needs me. I'm going there right now. I'll watch for them to come. The police will know where I mean when you tell them we're at the molasses tanks."

After hanging up, Hank wondered again about his mother. It was getting really late, and he had been sure she would be home by now. Maybe he could ride his bike over to the church, just to let her know he was okay. If she was there, he'd tell her not to worry about him and that he would explain everything very soon. Then he could go straight to the harbor, throw his bike in the boat, and hurry back to Deedee.

\* \* \*

Alice could hear Hank moving around the house, talking on the telephone and rummaging in the cupboards. As she moved the little bit she could, she came dangerously close to the edge of her bed, and if Hank had stayed a moment longer, he may have heard the bump from the bedroom.

\* \* \*

Hank shut the lights off again, jumped on his bike, and began peddling toward the church. He'd only gone a couple of blocks when he noticed a car behind him. He swerved to the side of the road so it could pass, but when it got close behind him it slowed down and stayed there. He looked over his shoulder, and even with the headlights glaring at him, he could see that it was his mother's rusty Chevrolet. She must have been driving up to the house when he started out and saw him leaving, he thought with a sigh of relief. He hopped off his bike and ran back to the car.

The black barrel of a pistol greeted Hank when he looked in the window.

"Get in, Hank," Rapper ordered.

What was Rapper doing with his mother's car? Hank began to shake with fear. And where was his mother?

"I've got to—" he began as he took a step backward, away from the car.

"You can get in or I'll shoot you," Rapper said calmly.

Hank thought of his mother and Deedee. He even thought of Deedee's mother, whom he'd never met. He was very afraid for all of them. But right now, he was the one facing a gun.

He got in the car with Rapper.

His bike lay at the side of the road, and Rapper almost ran over it as he peeled out. He didn't speak until they were out of town, then he slowed down, pulled to the side of the road, and said, "You've stuck your nose in where it doesn't belong. I'm not a patient man, Hank. Tell me where the girl is."

Hank couldn't do that. He'd die before he told Rapper where Deedee was. The cops would soon find her, and she'd be okay then. If he told Rapper now, it would all be over for both him and Deedee. He said nothing to Rapper.

"Hank, I'm not kidding with you. Tell me where she is or you'll wish you had," Rapper threatened.

"I won't," Hank said.

Rapper's hand moved swiftly, and his fist caught Hank right on the chin. The young man's head snapped and hit the glass of the passenger window. *This is it,* he thought to himself, sure he was going to die. He felt like crying, but then he remembered what Deedee had said that very evening. She'd told him that he was the bravest person she knew.

Hank straightened up in his seat. "Speak up, Hank," Rapper ordered. "I'm out of patience."

But Hank wasn't going to say any more. He wanted to ask Rapper what he'd done to his mother, but there was nothing he could do to help her now. He wished she hadn't gotten involved.

"Hank, do you think I'm bluffing?" Rapper snarled.

Hank remained silent.

"I'm not," Rapper continued as he raised the gun and pointed it at Hank's face. It was dark in the car, but not so dark that Hank couldn't see the barrel.

"Then shoot me," Hank said bravely. All he could do now was die. He waited for the gun to fire, hoping it wouldn't hurt for long.

There was no shot. "You are a meddling little rat," Rapper told him. "Shooting you would be too easy. Ever hear of the black hole?"

If there was anything that Hank feared more than death, it was the black hole.

"Scares you, doesn't it?" Rapper said.

Hank didn't answer.

"Well, it should," Rapper said coldly. "Because unless you tell me where you've taken my girl, you're going to find yourself treading that putrid black water in the black hole."

Hank couldn't subdue the fright in his eyes.

Rapper laughed and started the car. "You don't *have* to go to the black hole," he said. "Tell me where you took the girl, and I'll let you out right here."

Hank didn't believe that for a minute, but despite the terror Rapper had managed to strike in his heart, he wasn't going to give in. Maybe Rapper was just bluffing, he thought. Not many people actually knew where the black hole was. Surely Rapper didn't. He could only hope that was the case.

"Hank, you're making a big mistake," Rapper hissed. "Talk now, or you're going for a dark, deep, cold swim. And it will be your last."

Hank said nothing. He remained quiet both because he was committed to keeping Deedee's location from Rapper and because he knew that if he opened his mouth, he'd cry out in fear.

"Then it's off to the black hole," Rapper said angrily, and he gunned the car.

Hank thought desperately for a moment, then he knew what he had to do. He had to open the door and jump out. If it killed him, he would be no worse off. If it didn't, maybe he could make a dash for the trees and get away. "Don't think of jumping out," Rapper said as if he could read Hank's mind. He slammed on the brakes.

Hank smashed into the windshield, then fell back into the seat again, dazed. Rapper then reached across and slammed the barrel of his gun against Hank's temple. The brave young man was knocked out instantly. Rapper pushed on the gas pedal again. Hank would regain consciousness, and when he did, he would have one last chance to tell Rapper what he knew. Then he'd go into the black hole. Rapper smiled to himself, remembering.

* * *

Superintendent Brown called Officer Manny Younger on the radio. "Sheriff Robinson just called. He talked to Hank a few minutes ago. Hank told him where the girl is." Manny and Enos had just arrived again at the intersection of the highway and the road to the lighthouse. They were prepared for an all-night search for Meredith.

"Ask him where Hank is," Enos said quickly.

"The sheriff told me that he was calling from his mama's house but was planning on going back to where he had Deedee hidden," the superintendent answered.

"Where's that?" Manny asked.

"She's hiding out at the molasses tanks," the superintendent said.

Enos turned to Manny. "Do you know where the molasses tanks are?" he asked.

"Sure do."

"Are we close?"

"As close as anyone," Manny said.

Enos considered their options. He wanted so desperately to search for and find Meredith, but he knew she'd want him to take care of her daughter first. "Let's head there; as soon as we find her, we'll come back here."

Manny relayed their intentions to the superintendent, who said, "Good, but hurry. I'm on my way to Hank's house. I hope to get there before he leaves. If I find him, I'll drive out that way too. She may be hard to find if she's hiding from everyone but Hank. It will be easier if he's with us."

Manny turned the Trooper and headed north. Enos sat back in his seat. Never had he wanted to be able to be in two places at once as badly as he did now. Yet as much as he hated leaving the area where he thought Meredith might be, he knew he was doing what she would want.

# CHAPTER 22

Consciousness came slowly for Hank. He opened his eyes, felt the throbbing of his head, and was aware that he was in a car but couldn't remember how he got there. A minute or two passed before he made the connection that it was his mother's old Chevy. Then he looked over at the driver, expecting to see his mother, and he was thrown into total consciousness when he recognized Rapper's profile.

Fear tore through him as he remembered the threats Rapper had made earlier. He tried to grab the door handle only to discover that his hands were tied behind his back. "You'll get out when I tell you to," Rapper said with a sinister chuckle, "not before."

The car was going very fast, but Hank recognized the area they were passing through. The black hole was only a short distance away, but he wasn't sure exactly where the turnoff was.

Rapper suddenly slowed and pulled the old car off the highway, steering it slowly up the little side road, which was almost invisible if a person didn't know what they were looking for. Rapper clearly had been here before, and that thought froze the blood in Hank's veins.

Tree branches slapped the windshield and screeched against the sides of the car. Rocks tore at the undercarriage. Rapper swore and finally stopped the car. "Piece of junk your mom drives," he said to Hank. "Guess we walk from here, unless of course, you're ready to tell me where my girl is."

Hank didn't think he was nearly as brave as Deedee did, but he was a man of honor, and even though he knew that he faced a certain terrifying death if he didn't tell Rapper where he'd hidden her, he kept his mouth closed.

"Fine, have it your way," Rapper said. He forced Hank to get out of the car. "Is there a flashlight in here?" he demanded.

"No, Mama doesn't drive at night much," Hank said. The darkness gave him a little hope. Maybe Rapper couldn't find his way to the black hole if he couldn't see.

But the darkness didn't appear to deter Rapper very much. "Move along," he warned, prodding Hank with his pistol. "I ain't got all night."

It was slow going, for the road was rough and the stars cast a faint light in the blackness of the night. When they reached the end of the road, the trail led over fallen trees, through low-hanging branches, and across rocky areas. Hank kept stumbling, and every time he did, he received more bruises. With his hands secured behind his back, there was no way for him to break his fall.

Hank kept veering from the trail, and when he did Rapper would grab his shirt and jerk him back onto it. He figured they'd been walking about fifteen minutes when the moon began to rise. The little bit of extra light made the going slightly less difficult, and Rapper prodded him on a little faster.

Hank thought about trying to escape, figuring if his hands weren't tied behind his back he could maybe dive into the heavy foliage and crawl away from Rapper. But without his hands free, that would be impossible. And even if he could try it, Rapper had but to pull the trigger of his gun and Hank would die. There was always the slim chance that something else would happen to save him, although he couldn't think what that might be.

As the moon rose higher, it became light enough for Hank to see the rim of the black hole as he climbed the last steep incline and stepped out of the bushes. He stopped, fear pounding in his temples. This place had frightened him the first time he'd been here, and that was in the middle of a sunny day. Now, in darkness, with the newly risen half-moon casting long shadows over the area, it was beyond frightening.

"You have one last chance," Rapper said coldly. "Where is the girl?"

Hank couldn't have told him even if he'd wanted to. Fear had literally seized his voice. In a sudden, frenzied act of sheer terror, he spun on his heels and charged away from the rim, right into Rapper. Cursing, Rapper fell backward, sprawling in a large bush. His gun rattled on the rocks, then slid into a crevice. As Rapper clawed his way out of the bush, attempting to get his feet under him, Hank plunged down the trail.

Had his hands not been tied behind him he might have gotten away, but he'd only gone about thirty feet when he tripped, falling forward, the full force of his speed and weight slamming him against the ground. Dazed, it took him a moment to get his bearings—and that was a moment he couldn't afford.

Rapper was on him, slamming a fist into his already-battered face. Hank slumped, and Rapper dragged him back up to the rim of the black hole. Hank didn't have the strength to offer any significant resistance, and though he did wiggle back and forth, he was helpless with his hands tied. Rapper, breathing hard from dragging Hank up the steep trail, dropped him facedown on the rim when they finally got back up there and bent over, breathing heavily.

A minute later, Hank closed his eyes as Rapper struggled to shove him forward. Rapper stopped after a moment, breathing deeply again from the exertion. Hank opened his eyes and gasped. His head was at the very edge of the rim! He could see the reflection of the stars shining up at him from the surface of the black water far below. He couldn't bear to look, and he shut his eyes again.

Rapper was grasping Hank's hands now, doing something with the belt he'd tied them together with. Hank didn't think it could possibly be pulled tighter, but that wasn't what Rapper was doing. A moment later, the belt came free. Hank pulled his hands forward until they were even with his shoulders. They were stiff, and even as he thought about trying to shove his way backward, Hank discovered that he didn't have the strength.

"Wonder why I cut your hands free?" Rapper asked.

Hank did wonder, but he remained silent.

"Don't want you to drown too quickly," Rapper said with a hoarse laugh. "You can tread water for a while and think about how you might have saved your own worthless life."

Hank felt Rapper grab him by the seat of his pants and shove him forward again. He had to do something. In a few seconds, he'd plunge over the edge and into whatever that black liquid was that awaited him so far below. Hank prepared himself to hang on with every ounce of strength he had left. He began to struggle as the strength slowly returned to his arms.

"Last chance," Rapper hissed. "Where is she?"

Hank suddenly twisted with energy he didn't think he had, strength gained from the surge of adrenaline that flowed through his body. He managed to break Rapper's grip on his pants and to turn from his belly to his back and sit up, facing away from the hole. Rapper, caught off guard by the sudden show of strength, slipped on the rock surface and slid backward. Hank managed in that brief moment to get his feet beneath him, but Rapper also came to his feet, and when Hank made another desperate attempt to ram Rapper and rush past, Rapper's fist came around hard, connecting with Hank's chin.

The force of the blow made Hank step backward to maintain his balance. Rapper swung again, and Hank ducked to miss the blow. He felt his right foot slip as it came to the very edge of the black hole. He tried desperately to lunge forward, throwing his weight onto his left foot. But once again, Rapper's fist caught Hank in the chest, and the force of the blow was all it took to carry him over the edge of the precipice.

Hank turned over in a backward somersault as he fell, and he entered the water headfirst. For what seemed like an eternity, he sliced downward through the water. Then finally, he stopped and began to swim upward. When his head finally broke through the surface, he sucked in a great lungful of air.

"Have a good swim," Rapper called down from above. He laughed, and the horrible sound echoed about the chamber for several seconds. Then it was silent.

The water was not thick like Hank had expected, and although it was slightly cool, it wasn't cold. The smell from the surface of the water was bad but not nearly as terrible as he would have expected it to be. He began to tread water and wondered how long he could keep that up. No one would ever find him here, so he'd simply tread until he couldn't do it anymore, then he'd face death as bravely as he could. The terror he'd felt before his plunge into this dark hole in the earth had vanished. A melancholy acceptance of his fate settled over him. He'd be brave like Deedee would expect him to be. And he'd pray.

\* \* \*

Deedee was getting scared again. Being alone in this jungle was not a pleasant thing. Even though Hank had assured her that there weren't snakes that could hurt her or other creatures that were likely to, she couldn't stop herself from worrying. She wished Hank would get back, and she prayed that when he did, he'd have good news for her. Maybe he'd even bring her mother with him.

That thought was comforting, and for a few minutes she was able to relax beside her fire. Then she heard a sound from the direction of the ocean, and she smiled to herself. *It must be Hank,* she thought. But then the sound vanished and it was quiet for a minute or two. She wondered what Hank was doing, so she picked up the little flashlight he'd brought for her and stepped away from the fire. She hesitated at the edge of the trees and heard what sounded like steps again, so she clicked on the light and walked a few steps into the darkness. "Hank," she called out, "what's taking you so long?"

She heard a movement again and hoped Hank was near. *It couldn't be anyone else,* she reasoned. "Hank, where are you?"

There was a loud grunt, and a large figure rushed past her. It was only in the beam of her light for a second, but she knew what she'd just seen was a huge wild boar. Her heart began to pound, and she knew it would turn and come back, that it meant to hurt her. She panicked, and in her panic, she began to run back to the fire where Hank said no wild animals would come. But she'd strayed farther than she'd thought from the fire, and when she couldn't see it, she became disoriented, and continued to run. She stumbled frequently but picked herself up and continued on, finding that the farther she went, the less dense the forest became and the faster she could go.

When she finally gained control of her fear and stopped, she found she'd gone quite a long ways. Exhausted and totally out of breath, she had no idea where her camp was. She listened fearfully for the grunt of the hog as she caught her breath, flashing her light all about her, but when she saw and heard nothing but trees and bushes, she felt safe enough to sit down and rest.

As her strength returned, Deedee became angry with herself for panicking. When Hank got back, he'd wonder where she'd gone, and he'd be worried. He'd have no idea where to look for her, and he might even think she'd given up on him.

She tried not to cry, but she couldn't help herself. She had only made things worse. She should never have left the fire, she realized. Hank had told her to stay right there, that she could get lost if she wandered. Well, she was lost all right, and she had no idea what to do now. She sat on the ground, wishing it was light, and wishing, she realized, that she had her Book of Mormon. She recited the handful of scriptures she'd memorized in seminary, and she felt a measure of peace settle over her.

\* \* \*

Manny parked the Trooper near the end of the road overlooking the sea, and he and Enos got out. They shined their lights around. "This is the old molasses shipping point," Manny said. "The question now is where those two kids are hiding."

"If Hank's expecting us, maybe he'll come out and meet us if we honk the horn," Enos suggested hopefully.

Manny stepped back to the vehicle and blew the horn. It echoed through the forest for several seconds before he stopped. Then they waited, hoping that Hank and Deedee would come. After several minutes, no one had appeared. Manny hit the horn again with no success, so they took their large flashlights and worked their way into the jungle with its tangled mass of trees and vines. For nearly an hour they searched.

It was Manny who smelled the smoke. "Enos," he called out, "come over here."

"What is it?" Enos asked. "Did you see something.?"

"No, but I caught a whiff of smoke," he said. "Maybe they have a campfire."

A slight breeze blowing in from the ocean kept shifting, so the two officers stood patiently. Finally Enos said, "There, I can smell it."

He licked a finger and held it up for a moment. "The breeze is coming from that direction," he said, pointing beyond where the ancient wharf and the forest met. "It's got to be their campfire."

Slowly, the two men hiked into the trees, every now and then catching a whiff of the smoke. Ten minutes later, they stepped into the little campsite. "The fire's burned down, but it can't have been much over an hour ago when they left," Manny concluded.

"But there's still food, water, and bedding here," Enos noted. There was also a small tarp that had been hung as a shelter between four trees. "Why would they have left?"

"Afraid, maybe," Manny said. "They can't be sure it's us and not Rapper, I suppose. The poor kids have probably been very frightened out here."

Enos agreed. "Maybe they're still nearby," he said. Then he shouted, "Deedee, it's Detective Fauler. I've come to take you home."

Nothing but the breeze stirring the leaves and the nearby thrashing of waves on the beach made a sound. "Hank, Sheriff Robinson said you'd meet us here," Enos called out.

Still no one responded, so the two men went in opposite directions, away from the fire, each calling out every minute or so. After thirty minutes they'd had no results, and they met again to reconsider their plans. They decided to go back to the road and drive up it a ways. "Maybe they didn't hear us come in and are walking out to meet us," Manny suggested.

Enos agreed. When they reached their vehicle again, they honked the horn and waited, then drove slowly back out toward the highway. Enos was feeling increasingly desperate. Meredith was also still in trouble, and the longer it took here, the longer it would be before they could resume searching for her.

"You're worried about Ms. Marchant," Manny said after a couple of minutes. He was driving very slowly, hoping the kids would see them and come out of the trees if they happened to be nearby.

"I am worried. Meredith must be hurt or she'd have found her way out by now," Enos said.

"We need some help," Manny suggested. "There are a lot of good people on this island who would be willing to assist us. I think we'd better go into Marsh Harbor and find someone. Then we can do a

proper search for both Ms. Marchant and her daughter. Should we
head back?"

Enos hated to leave without Deedee, but it seemed like the only
thing to do. "Yes, let's go get some help," he agreed.

* * *

Deedee had heard the honking. She'd been frightened at first, but
as she thought about it, she decided that if it was Rapper coming for
her, he'd come quietly, trying not to attract attention. She really didn't
think it would be him, though, since it was unlikely he would have
figured out where she was. Then she had an encouraging thought.
Maybe Hank had located her mother. If he had, it would only make
sense that they would drive here. After all, the ocean route was a lot
longer distance, according to Hank, than the road.

She began to walk as quickly as she could in the direction the
honking had come from. A long time passed before she heard the
horn again, but when she did it was closer, and she hurried on,
excited to see her mother, certain this nightmare she'd gotten herself
into was about to end.

The lights of a car passed just a short distance ahead of her as she
neared the edge of the trees, and Deedee ran again, shouting for it to
stop. She ran from the trees and onto a dirt road. She could still see
the taillights in the distance, and even though she screamed and
waved her flashlight, the taillights disappeared around a curve.

* * *

"Manny," Enos said, "did you see a flash of light in the mirror?"

"No, I didn't see anything," he replied.

"I just happened to glance past my mirror, and I'd swear there
was a light," Enos said. "It was only there for a second, and I can't be
sure of what I really saw, but maybe if we could just back up for a
moment . . ."

* * *

Deedee sat right down in the middle of the road and bawled like a baby. So close, she thought, and now if it was her mother and Detective Fauler, she'd missed them. It dawned on her that Hank would probably be with them, and that he would have gone right to the fire and found her missing, and . . . she couldn't bear to think about it. Why had she ever run away? She had asked herself that question a thousand times these past few days. Would she never cease to pay for her childish behavior?

Then Deedee heard the crunch of tires on gravel and the whining of an engine. She looked up and saw the taillights that had vanished only moments before coming toward her. She jumped to her feet and started running. The car stopped, and someone got out. "Deedee, is that you?" a man called out. "I'm Detective Fauler."

"Yes, it's me," she cried with joy and ran into his arms.

While Deedee sobbed against his shoulder, Enos held her tight. "It's all right now, Deedee," he soothed. "You're safe now."

As he held this beautiful girl, Enos thought of her mother. How he wanted to hold the two of them and then see them hold each other. "Deedee," he said. "Let's get in the car. We need to get back to Marsh Harbor."

"Where's Mom?" she asked. "And where's my friend Hank?"

"Get in the car with us, and I'll explain while we drive," Enos said. How he hated to have to tell her that he didn't know where her mother was. When he did, he feared he'd destroy all the happiness she'd just found.

# CHAPTER 23

Deedee cried on the way to Marsh Harbor after hearing that her mother had been missing for a couple of days. Enos held her against him, trying to comfort her. "It's all my fault," she kept sobbing.

"No," he said firmly. "Much of this is because of Stu's actions. You didn't know he would use every power at his disposal to persuade you not to return to your mother."

"I should have just run away from him," she said.

"You tried, remember?"

The sobs let up for a moment, "How did you know?"

Enos allowed himself a chuckle before saying, "It's my job to know things, or at least to investigate until I get to know them. A kind woman by the name of Victoria Deveaux called your mother's office. She was telling her secretary that you were with her in the airport in Miami when she suddenly stopped speaking."

"Yes, she was calling, but then Stu came after us, and she gave in, and—" Deedee began.

"Deedee, she had a heart attack. But she was trying to help you, and it was because of her that we went to Miami and discovered that Stu had bought tickets to Abaco. So in a way, it's because of you seeking the lady's help that we came here when we did. If we'd have been even a day or two later coming here, it might have been too late for you."

"But now it might be too late for my mom," she said as her eyes filled with tears.

"We'll find your mother," Enos said with more optimism than he felt. Then he added, "We've got to find her. We've just got to."

Deedee, distraught as she was, heard something in Enos's voice and looked up. "I didn't know you were Mom's friend."

Enos was embarrassed, but he was honest with Deedee. "Your mother is a great person, Deedee, and we are very good friends."

Suddenly, something felt different about this big man whose arm was tight around her shoulders. He felt like more than just a cop who was helping her. He felt like someone she should care about, someone who cared about her. He was her friend as well as her mother's.

As they neared Marsh Harbor, Manny talked to Superintendent Brown on the radio. Deedee, whose thoughts were more on her mother than anything else, suddenly took interest in the radio conversation when Manny said, "She hasn't any idea where Hank went?"

"Hank?" Deedee asked Enos. "Where's Hank?"

"Just a minute," Enos said, for he too was interested in the radio conversation.

As soon as he finished speaking with the superintendent, Manny explained that they'd found Hank's mother bound and gagged on her bedroom floor. The distraught woman had told the superintendent that Hank was anxious to go somewhere but that he never did tell her what he was up to. Enos and Deedee both stiffened when the superintendent then told them about a man coming to Hank's home, threatening to harm Hank when he returned. Then he had tied up Hank's mother.

"Any idea who the man was?" Manny asked.

"He never told her who he was," Superintendent Brown answered. "But she says he had a shaved head and a beard."

"Rapper!" Deedee exclaimed in fright.

"The man, and I'm certain it was Rapper, said he wanted to see Hank. He stayed there for quite a while, then he asked her for her car keys and stole her car."

"Any idea where he went?" Manny asked.

"No," Superintendent Brown's voice was solemn.

"We'll meet you at Hank's home," Officer Younger said into his radio as Enos attempted to calm Deedee down.

They were there in a matter of minutes, and it didn't take long before they discovered Hank's bike missing. A check at the closest harbor turned up Hank's boat, and at that point there was only one conclusion that made any sense to the officers—Hank had been abducted by Rapper and driven away in Hank's mother's rusty old Chevrolet.

Deedee had finally calmed down, but other than spending a few minutes with Hank's mother, who helped the girl clean up a little, she wouldn't leave Enos's side. The superintendent offered to let her stay with his wife, and Manny Younger made the same offer, but Deedee felt safe with Enos, and she wanted to help hunt for Hank.

"Okay," Enos said after it had become apparent that Rapper had taken another victim, "we need to decide where the most likely places he might have taken Hank would be."

The superintendent reported that Rapper kept a small fishing boat at one of the harbors. However, he also noted that they'd checked earlier and the boat was gone, but he ordered two officers to go check again, just in case it was back.

"Where else?" Enos asked.

"Maybe the bungalow where he kept the girl," an officer suggested.

Deedee knew she was *the girl,* and it seemed strange to hear herself referred to in that manner. She felt an increased respect for Enos when he said, "Her name is Deedee."

Enos continued. "He'd need to go to Hope Town, and it doesn't seem likely that he'd use the ferry. It would be too risky for him, since Hank wouldn't very likely be cooperating."

"Maybe he has access to another boat," Manny suggested. "He seems to have friends around."

The superintendent dispatched a couple of officers to Hope Town, then said, "We still have an officer watching his house. If he shows up there, we'll know it at once."

"Where would he take Hank?" Enos persisted. "Manny mentioned that he might have other friends. Who besides the explosions expert do any of you know about on the island?"

One by one, the officers shook their heads until they came to Manny again. Manny had been thinking hard. "He wouldn't go to the jail to break Carl Sebastian out, would he?" he asked.

"We moved Sebastian for just that reason," the superintendent said as he called the jail. There was no response. "Get over there," he ordered two of his men, and like the earlier ones, they left in a hurry.

Deedee was thinking hard and praying silently that Hank and her mother would both be found. She liked Hank a lot. No boy had ever treated her with the courtesy, kindness, and respect that Hank had.

Just then, the thought came to her, and she began to tremble. "Mr. Fauler," she said timidly.

Enos looked at Deedee and moved toward her. "You can call me Enos," he said as he put a comforting arm around her shoulder.

She nodded, and he gave her a little squeeze. "You spent a lot of time with Hank," he said. "Do you have any idea where Rapper might have taken him?"

"The black hole," she said softly.

"Did you say the black hole?" Manny asked.

"Yes," she said. "Hank says it's a terrible place. And Rapper said something about it when he locked me in the place at Hope Town. He said I was better off locked in that room than I would be at the black hole. I thought he was referring to the dungeon in his yacht because it was so dark there, but now I don't think he was."

The superintendent suddenly looked very concerned. "The black hole is over between Marsh Harbor and Treasure Cay. It's a deep hole in the ground that's full of black water. I would guess that a large majority of the people of Abaco don't know about it, or if they've heard of it, they don't know where it is. Most of the people who do know are scared of it. I do know that if anyone were to be dropped into it, there would be no way out for them."

Enos was already heading toward the vehicle he and Manny were using, Deedee right beside him. Over his shoulder, he said, "Can you take us there, Superintendent?"

Before Superintendent Brown could answer, his radio crackled with a report from one of his men that they had found Hank's mother's car. An old man at the harbor where the men were had just told the officers that he saw a man leave the car and take off in a boat he'd never seen before.

The superintendent spoke into his radio and ordered an officer to get a description of the boat as well as to get the police boat ready to go. Then he turned to Manny Younger. "Do you know where the black hole is?" he asked.

"I know the general area," Manny answered. "I've never seen it though."

"It's between here and Treasure Cay," the superintendent said. "But I also don't know its exact location."

It seemed that none of the officers present knew where it was, and Enos was beginning to doubt its existence. But Manny said, "Hop in, Enos. It'll be light in a few minutes. We'll find it. It's as good a lead as we have right now."

"We'll catch Rapper," the superintendent said. "I'm taking the rest of these men with me."

Deedee and Enos crowded in beside Manny, and they shot up the street. When they hit the main highway, Manny stomped on the gas, and they raced up the long straight road.

"Rapper was at the jail," the superintendent's voice came over the radio. "But he was alone." He then explained that Rapper had locked the jailer in a cell there and left. He guessed that based on the amount of time that had passed since he'd been at the jail, he could easily have found Hank and taken him somewhere.

Deedee's tender stomach was already rolling from the ride, and when the superintendent said what he did, it almost made her throw up. But she squeezed Enos's hand, and he tightened his grip around her shoulder.

A few miles and several minutes later, a solid wall of trees streamed by on both sides of the highway. "It can't be too far off," Manny said. "The turnoff, I'm told, is on the right. And it will be hard to see."

It was almost fully daylight by now, and they were approaching a lonely business on the side of the road. A young man was sitting outside of it, his thumb out. Manny slowed down and pulled off behind another car that appeared to be offering the young man a ride. Enos could hear the young man say, as he sauntered over to the other car, "Hey, I gotta get to Coopers Town this morning. Going that far?"

Apparently getting a yes, the young man then circled around to the passenger side, where Manny called out, "Hey, kid, we're looking for a place referred to as the black hole. You wouldn't know where it is, would you?"

"Uh, I'm not sure. I've never actually been there, but I know where the road is that leads to it. I'll jump in here with these folks. Follow us."

Enos looked with dismay at Manny, who said, "He'll get us close or I miss my guess."

They pulled on the road behind the other car and followed at a painfully slow speed for a short distance up the highway. Suddenly, the other car pulled off to the right side of the road. The young man jumped out as Manny stopped behind them. "Should be along here," he said. "Kinda hard to spot. Trouble up there?"

"We don't know," Manny said.

"Well, good luck, man. They say that's a nasty place."

He returned to the car, and they pulled away. Manny was already looking for an opening in the trees.

"What if this isn't the right area?" Enos said.

"We're close. That young fellow would never have left if we weren't," Manny said.

He seemed very sure of himself, but Enos was not nearly so confident. "How do you know he was telling you the truth?"

"Most of the natives here are honest as the day is long," Manny told Enos and Deedee. "Ah, there it is." Manny pulled into a narrow opening in the trees. Low-hanging branches rubbed the top of the vehicle, and branches scraped the sides.

"Are you sure this is a road?" Enos asked in doubt.

"Not much of one," Manny agreed, "but yes, it's a road."

They couldn't go very fast because it was so rough and there was so much foliage, but after about a half mile or so, the road ended. There wasn't even a place to turn around. "This must not be it," Enos moaned. "We'd just as well start backing out."

"No, Enos, this is right," Deedee said excitedly. "Hank told me the road just ends and you have to walk for a ways."

"She's right," Manny said as he opened his door and got out. "See, there's a trail of sorts right up there."

It was a trail of sorts, all right, Enos thought to himself as he and Deedee followed the officer, climbing over fallen trees, pushing through thick branches, and constantly watching their footing. It went in a northerly direction for just a short distance, and then it turned and headed east.

"It's sure not used much," Enos observed.

"Not many people even know it's here," Manny explained. "And most of the natives rarely venture up here because they're scared of it."

"Hank was afraid of it," Deedee said. "It's a terrible place." She was already beginning to wish she didn't have to go there, but if by any chance Hank had come this way, she'd go. After all, she owed him her life, and if he could be brave, so could she.

After just a few hundred yards, the trail suddenly turned steeply upward for a short distance. Manny was in the lead, followed by Deedee. Enos brought up the rear. It was difficult walking, and every few feet they had to push branches back. Suddenly, Manny said, "Whoa, here it is!"

He stopped abruptly, and Deedee did the same even though she was several feet back and down a steep incline from him. She glanced to her left and let out a yelp. There was a brushy depression, and it was quite deep. As she looked into it, she involuntarily stepped to her right. All she could see was blackness at the end of it.

"That must go into the main hole or cavern, or whatever it is, through there," Enos said as he took her hand to help her up the last few yards.

But Deedee resisted. "Enos, what's that down there?"

"It's the water, I suppose," he said.

"No, it's metal. I think it's a gun."

Enos slipped around her and peered back into the depression, which dropped at about a sixty-degree angle for several yards until it ended in a hole. About six feet down there was indeed a pistol perched precariously against a stick. If bumped, it would slide the rest of the way and drop into the black hole.

"Manny," Enos called.

"Coming," the officer said as he approached them. "I don't think there's anyone in the water. I looked and can't see anything but black water down there," he said. "What are you two looking at?"

"There's a pistol down here," Enos said. "This is a stretch, but if it was only recently dropped in there, it could mean we will need to get divers up here and look for Hank's body in that hole. Here, take hold of my foot, and I'll see if I can reach it. Deedee, you help him. I don't want to slide in there."

Manny looked thoughtful for a moment. "Not many people here carry pistols," he said. "But we know Rapper does."

Enos agreed and quickly worked his way an uncomfortable distance into the depression. By the time he'd reached the pistol, only his legs from the knees up weren't in the steep, dangerous hole. Deedee and Manny held tightly to his ankles while he braced himself with his left hand. Then he stretched as far as he could and just managed to get the thumb and forefinger of his right hand on the pistol. He gripped it the best he could and said, "You two pull, but go slow. I don't have a very good grip on this gun."

They both tugged, and Enos used his left hand to push. In a minute he was back on the trail, examining the pistol. "It hasn't been down there long," Enos said. "There's no dust on it. Someone's been here recently."

"Do you think Rapper shot Hank?" Deedee asked in fear.

Enos was already inspecting the pistol. "There hasn't been a single round fired," he said. "The clip is fully loaded." He shoved the pistol in the waistband of his jeans and said, "Let's go on up."

Manny again led the way the last few yards while Enos helped Deedee up the steep incline.

"Ooh!" Deedee exclaimed as she found herself on a narrow strip of porous rock. Just a few feet ahead was the black hole, an impressive and terrifying sight. She forced herself to inch forward, clinging to Enos's hand. In a moment she was able to see over the edge. Far below them was the absolute blackness Hank had described, and Deedee suddenly got dizzy. She dropped to her knees.

The surface of the black water was quite smooth, with just the slightest ripple crossing the ebony surface. If Hank was in there, she feared she'd never see him again. But she called out anyway, "Hank? Hank, it's Deedee. Are you down there?"

"I don't see anyone," Manny said. "And I looked pretty carefully when I first came up here."

"Hank told me that it's shaped like an upside-down cone. It's wider down there than it is up here," she explained. "See how the other side is? He could be back under this side. I want to look there just to be sure."

"How do we do that?" Manny asked. "There's no way we can work our way to the other side with the growth so thick, and it would take too long to go around and force our way in from that side."

But Deedee was already inching forward on the rim. Enos reached down and gripped her hand tightly. "Not too far—this could break off under us."

"I've got to," she protested, and still on her knees, she began to move slowly forward again. She was very frightened, but she was also thinking of Hank. If he'd stumbled or been thrown into that hole . . .

The officers had decided to follow her lead, but none of them were yet where they could see beneath the ledge they were on. They would have to crawl out farther. "Hank," Deedee yelled. "Hank, answer me. It's Deedee."

# CHAPTER 24

The water hadn't seemed cold to Hank when he'd first been shoved into the black hole, but after several hours, it had become almost unbearable. His whole body was chilled, and the chill was affecting his ability to move his arms and legs, his ability to continue to tread water. Hank honestly didn't know how much longer he could survive. He prayed that someone would come soon, and yet he knew that was very unlikely. The will to live was all that kept his body functioning, and yet he knew he couldn't last much longer.

Had it not been for a scare he'd received about an hour ago, he might already have succumbed to the chill. Initially he'd spent most of his time treading water in the middle of the pool, but as he began to tire, he'd wondered if he could make it any easier on himself if he swam to the edge and tried to grasp the rough rock and hold himself up, perhaps give himself a break from the tiresome work of treading.

It had only taken a few moments to swim over to the far side of the pool, the side where he figured he could at least be seen from above if anyone happened to come. But what he'd encountered as he reached for the rock wall had nearly caused his heart to stop beating. His hand had touched something cold and slimy that moved when he touched it, and he'd recoiled with a shout of fear. He honestly hadn't considered there might be a creature of some sort that lived in here, one that could rise from the endless depths of this hole.

All Hank had been able to see as he swam away from whatever it was he'd touched was a dark form silently hovering just barely beneath the surface. He'd crossed the pool and rested at the far side beneath the huge overhang of rock above. There he trembled, gripped the rock wall, and wondered how long it would be before the creature came after him.

Within a few minutes, however, Hank recognized that his greatest danger lay in the inability of his body to adjust to the cool of the water. His limbs were becoming weak and immobile, and he could imagine himself sinking below the surface, his lungs sucking the black water in, smothering out his life. He admitted that perhaps it would not be long before that happened, and he was gradually coming to accept the fact that he was going to die. He grieved for his mother. He was the only family she had left, and he hated to think of her being alone.

Then he thought about Deedee. He wondered what she might be experiencing now. She had to be wondering what had happened to him, why the long night had passed without him returning. He prayed that the sheriff from Utah had let someone know that they'd been hiding near the tanks. If he had, perhaps they'd find her.

Even as he thought about his young friend, he heard a voice in his head repeating his name. It was an indistinct voice, and it seemed to bounce around. Hank was afraid he was becoming delusional. Other than his name, he couldn't tell what that voice was saying.

A short time passed. He slowly moved his feet, sending faint ripples across the inky water of the hole. Then, once again, he heard his name—only this time it was more distinct and seemed to be reverberating within the depths of the crater rather than inside his head. "Hank," he heard clearly this time. "Hank, it's me, Deedee."

It was coming from across the water, from over where the creature was waiting! Hank's heart began to pound. The voice echoed off the walls of the deep pit. He shut his eyes tightly and started to pray.

Hank opened his eyes, let go of the wall, and started vigorously treading water. The ripples he sent out were larger. They frightened him as he watched them roll across the surface of the pool because he imagined that they might not be the creation of his movements alone. The creature might be moving slowly now beneath the surface of the water, making the ripples larger. He watched, his eyes wide with fright, waiting for whatever was in the pool with him to rear its fearsome head. The instinct to fight for his life began to again pump adrenalin through his badly weakened body.

He heard the voice once more, and this time it sounded an awful lot like Deedee's. A terrible thought entered his sluggish mind. Had Rapper found her? Was she dead? Was she calling for him to join her?

"Look at the water, Enos," the voice said. "The ripples are getting bigger. He must be way back under this overhang."

Overhang. Hank tore his eyes from the surface of the water where he was watching for the creature and looked up to see a bright, almost blinding, light. He blinked several times and thought he saw a hand flash for a moment over the edge. Then it was gone. He forced himself to keep looking up until his eyes had adjusted to the brightness.

He saw the hand again. His feet moved more rapidly, and he kept staring up. Then he heard another voice, deep and strong. "Deedee, don't go any farther. You might fall over the edge."

"But he's down there, Enos, and he's alive! I just know he is."

The fog cleared from Hank's brain. Someone was up there! Deedee was up there! He twisted his body in the water and began to swim toward the center of the hole. Gone was the fear of the creature he'd touched. Gone was the thought of dying. Hank wanted to live.

He was very tired and moved slowly, but he was soon several yards from the rock wall. The voice above was shouting, "It's Hank! Enos, it's Hank." Then, "Hank, look up here. It's me, Deedee. We're going to get you out of there. Hang on, Hank."

He quit swimming and looked up. What he saw shot hope through him like nothing he'd ever experienced. He could see the auburn hair of Deedee hanging over the edge of the black hole. Then her hand swept the hair away, and he could see her sweet face. She was smiling, laughing, shouting gleefully.

"Hang in there, Hank," a male voice shouted so loudly that it literally bounded around the walls of the cavern. "We've got to get some rope."

Hank didn't have the energy to shout, but he lifted a hand momentarily from the water, a feeble gesture to let them know that he understood and that he would try his best to keep above the water until they could get something down to him.

* * *

"Keep talking to him, Deedee," Enos said. "Reassure him that we'll get him out. And come away from the edge. We don't have any idea how thick or stable this overhang might be."

As Deedee did so, Enos and Manny discussed what to do, both knowing that time was of the essence. "Do you have any rope in your car?" Enos asked.

"I don't know—it's not one I regularly drive," Manny said. "I'll run back to the car and see what's there," he volunteered.

"Hurry. I'll wait here with Deedee."

Several minutes later Manny returned, and when he did, he had bad news. "There's no rope in the car, Enos. I'm going to have to go to the nearest town and get some."

"I don't think Hank has that kind of time left," Enos said.

Deedee had crawled back from the edge and was listening with a worried look on her face. Then she looked around at the thick jungle vegetation. "Could we lift him out using some vines for rope?" she suggested.

"I don't know," Manny said. "I'm not sure they'd be strong enough. I'm afraid the rock would chew them in two when we began to pull him up."

Enos was thinking hard. Deedee's idea would at least buy them time. "Manny, you go for rope and more men if you can find any. It won't be easy pulling him up. Deedee and I will cut some vine and lower it down, and he can use it to keep himself from sinking. Then at least he won't be making himself weaker."

"Good idea," Manny said, and he disappeared down the trail that led through the jungle to his car.

"Deedee, you keep talking to Hank. I'll get the vine," Enos instructed.

The tension was building in Enos. They were so close to rescuing Hank, but what about Meredith? Every minute could be critical for her. He offered a silent prayer as he started back down the trail searching for vines. He must have uttered a hundred prayers over the past few hours, and he resolved to keep saying them until she was safe.

Enos finally found what looked like a long, strong vine snaking through the tall branches of a gnarled tree. He was sweating profusely before he finally managed to pull a long piece free. Then he pulled the knife from his boot and cut it off, hoping that it was long enough to do the job.

To Enos's dismay, the vine was too short. The hole was a lot deeper than he had estimated, and he had to make another mad dash down the trail to cut another length of vine. This time, after tying the two pieces together, there was enough slack left to tie one end of the vine to a stout tree a few feet back from the rim of the hole and still have enough for Hank to tie himself to below.

Hank was too exhausted to secure himself with the vine. His limbs were weak, and though he knew what Enos wanted him to do, he simply didn't have the strength. Deedee and Enos watched in concern as Hank wrestled weakly with the vine. Then it slipped from his hands, and they saw him disappear beneath the ebony surface of the water.

Deedee screamed. "He's drowning, Enos! He's dying!"

Enos had always considered himself a brave man, but what he was contemplating now as he swiftly removed his boots made him quiver inside. He laid his two guns and the knife on the rock beside his shoes, and before he could allow fear to slow him down, he stepped to the edge of the rim and dove toward the inky liquid below.

It seemed like a full minute before he entered the darkness of the water. Once he did, he thought he'd never stop slicing through it. At last he was able to twist his body, and with great strokes he worked his way back to the surface. Hank, still fighting for life, had managed to once again get his head above water. Before he could sink again, perhaps for the last time, Enos swam to him and grabbed ahold of his shirt. Almost instantly, Hank quit struggling. Enos had come to his rescue just in the nick of time.

"Hang in there, Hank," he said as he towed the young man back to where the vine hung over the rim of the cavern.

"Is he alive?" Deedee shouted down from above, her voice filled with fear.

"Yes," Enos called back up, his voice mixing with hers as the sound echoed for several seconds around the rock crater.

He grabbed the vine and hurriedly tied it around Hank's chest and under his arms, adjusting it until it held his head well above the water. By the time he'd finished and let go of Hank, he was exhausted himself, and he wondered how Hank had managed to survive all those hours down here alone.

Enos tried not to think about how putrid the water smelled or of what germs might be finding a new home. He was just thankful he'd made it in time. Now he hoped it didn't take Manny too long to get back—and he hoped he'd have some help when he did come. Enos was quite certain that with only Deedee's help, he couldn't pull Hank up, let alone himself.

After a few minutes, Hank began to mumble. Enos, holding the vine to keep himself from having to tread water, assured him that they were going to be okay.

"Thanks for coming to help me," Hank murmured. "I'm sorry I couldn't do it by myself."

"You did the best you could," Enos said. "You're an amazing young man. Not many people could have lasted in here as long as you have."

"I was worried about Deedee," he said. "I was afraid you wouldn't find her. I was afraid I had let her down."

"She owes you her life," Enos said. "Now relax and save your strength. They'll be here soon to pull us up out of this place."

What Hank said next sent shivers up Enos's spine. "If the creature doesn't get us first."

Enos looked around the pool very quickly, seeing nothing. Perhaps Hank had been hallucinating, which was entirely possible. But when Hank spoke again, he seemed quite lucid.

"It was over there," he said, pointing to the far side of the cavern. Enos remained silent, hoping that Hank would not dwell on whatever it was that seemed to have frightened him.

After a minute, as Hank's strength continued to return, the young man said, "I swam over there so they could see me if someone came."

"Which was a good idea," Enos said when Hank paused again. "We couldn't see you under this side." He pointed to the wall beneath where Deedee waited.

"I was very scared when I touched it. It must have gone back down again," Hank continued. "But it might come after us if we don't soon get out of here."

"I'm sure it wasn't anything dangerous," Enos assured him, but he was beginning to feel the slightest prick of concern himself.

"It was alive," Hank assured him, his eyes growing wide as he remembered. "It moved when I touched it. I'm lucky it didn't get me then. Maybe I startled it." He paused before speaking again. "You have a knife or a gun, don't you?" he finally asked.

"Not down here," Enos said. "I left them up there before I jumped in to help you."

"Then have Deedee throw one down," he said.

Hank was so serious that Enos decided it wouldn't hurt to humor him a little. And frankly, he admitted, he would feel a little more secure with a weapon in his hand. But if she were to drop either one of the pistols or the knife, he knew he'd have a hard time catching them. He couldn't tread water with only his legs, and he knew he'd never be able to catch them with just one hand. He decided there was no way.

"Please, sir," Hank begged. "She'll drop the gun if you ask her to. Deedee's a good girl."

"How about my knife?" Enos said. "A gun would be too heavy, and it would be awkward to use in the water."

"Okay, but she has to hurry," Hank insisted.

"I'll call up to her," Enos said. "Deedee, you saw where I laid my knife, didn't you?"

"It's right here," she shouted.

He waited until the echoes died out, then he called up again. "I need you to drop it to me, but not until I tell you how to do it." He paused. "Tie it to a big stick. Make sure it can't come loose. Then drop it where it won't hit us." He couldn't help but smile. This was all so absurd, but if it made Hank feel better, what would it hurt? After all, they had nothing but time on their hands right now.

Deedee took several minutes securing the knife to a stick. Finally, she appeared at the edge of the hole again. "I'm ready," she shouted.

"Good, have you got it tied tightly?" he called up to her.

"It's as tight as I can get it," she assured him.

"Okay, then toss it down."

The stick was large, much larger than needed, and Deedee had to give it a hard fling to clear the rim of the black hole. When it hit the water a few yards from Enos and Hank, it was moving fast. It splashed water on them and then scooted like a torpedo toward the far wall as the momentum from the long fall carried it forward.

"I'll go get it, Hank," Enos said as he let go of the vine and swam after the stick. He caught it near the center of the pool and had to smile when he saw how securely the knife was tied. Deedee had sacrificed the sleeves of her blouse, cutting them into strips and tying them together to make a small rope, wrapping them around the little log she'd used. Enos swam back to Hank with the stick, and with one hand holding the vine and Hank helping what little he could, Enos finally managed to free the knife.

He felt rather foolish as he held the vine with one hand and the knife in the other, but Hank appeared to be very relieved, and that made the effort worth it. Now all they had to do was wait for Manny.

Several minutes passed, then Deedee called from overhead, "Aren't you going to use it, Enos?"

He wasn't sure what to say to her. He didn't want to make Hank look foolish in Deedee's eyes, but he also didn't know what possible excuse he could make that would satisfy but not scare her.

"Do you need to cut the vine?" she called again, concern in her voice. "Is it too tight on Hank?"

Her words gave Enos the answer he needed. "When they get here with the rope, I'll have to tie it onto Hank. I'll need to cut the vine off of him then."

That apparently satisfied her, and Hank was glad for what he'd said as well. "Thank you, sir," Hank mumbled. "We don't want Deedee to worry about us, do we?"

"You can call me Enos, and you're absolutely right," Enos agreed.

As the two of them settled in to wait again, Enos looked around the huge interior of the cavern. The enormous stalactites that hung from the rim reminded him of giant icicles. He recalled from a geology class he'd taken in college that these were formed as a result of mineral-rich water dripping from the top of the cavern.

There was really nothing so mysterious about this place he was in. It was something he remembered being termed a *cenoti*. The water he was treading was fresh water, although it was certainly not *clean* water. He even remembered that the water in these types of formations was at sea level. Though he had to climb a short way to get to the rim, his dive in had compensated for every foot, he was sure.

However, knowing what he was in didn't make this experience any more enjoyable. He prayed that Manny would hurry.

# CHAPTER 25

The sun was steadily climbing, the intensity of its rays ruthless as they bore down through the high branches of the pines. Even the gentle breeze that rustled the leaves of the bushes near her offered no relief for her suffering. Meredith was a very sick woman. Her blistered, lacerated feet were infected, as were the cuts and abrasions in her hands and her knees. The days and hours seemed like decades to her, and she wondered in despair how long she would lie there before the relief of death finally came.

Meredith no longer worried about Rapper. He couldn't do anything more to her than what he, combined with the brutal forces of nature, had already done. She had no idea how far she was from any roads, nor did it matter anymore. What did matter, far more than her own suffering, was the welfare of her daughter.

Nothing else really mattered anymore except Deedee. Meredith thought of her girl constantly and hoped that somehow she had been able to break away from her captors. She also worried about Enos Fauler, a man who had recently become a very good friend. Maybe even more than a friend, she admitted to herself. She had developed feelings for him that went beyond friendship. But all that didn't matter now. Maybe, she thought hopefully, Enos had found Deedee now, and maybe he would see that she was cared for.

The sun continued to rise higher in the sky, and Meredith had to close her eyes to keep from being blinded. She found little relief, for they were so dry that when she closed them, it felt like her eyelids were lined with sandpaper. Maybe she could move one last time, she told herself. Maybe she could slide herself into the bushes and shade herself.

She first had to turn onto her stomach, and then she used her injured hands and knees to crawl. She cried out in pain, and her voice tore at her parched throat. But she persisted and finally rolled onto her back in the relative comfort of a thick bed of rotting leaves and pine needles beneath some fairly dense bushes.

The pain of moving had managed to bring a tear to each eye, providing just enough lubrication that she could close the lids with minimum pain. Maybe she could fall asleep, she thought, and not wake up again. That would be such a relief.

While sleep didn't come right away, something else did. She heard footsteps approaching. They were moving slowly, but they couldn't be more than a hundred feet away. Meredith felt neither fear nor hope. She felt only a calmness settle over her, and a little of the loneliness lifted. She lay and listened quietly as she waited for death.

* * *

"Manny's coming," Deedee shouted into the cavern. "And he has somebody with him."

Enos glanced at his waterproof watch. It was working fine, and it informed him that the morning was passing rapidly. He wondered how long it would take to get them out of here so he could resume his search for Meredith.

A couple of minutes later, Manny Younger peered over the rim. "What are you doing down there, Enos?" he shouted.

Deedee answered. "Hank couldn't tie the vine around himself. He was drowning, so Enos dove in."

It all sounded very matter-of-fact as she related it, but Manny Younger's admiration for the big detective from Utah swelled to enormous proportions. The three young islanders whom he had recruited to assist him trembled at the very thought of what Enos had done. They all stayed a safe distance from the edge of the black hole, and had the officer not impressed upon them the fact that Hank had survived in the hole, he would probably have failed to get their cooperation.

As it was, all they intended to do was provide muscle, which they'd made clear as they walked up the trail behind Manny, who agreed to do the rest. "I'm lowering the rope down," he called to Enos.

"Okay, let it come," Enos said as he carefully pushed his knife into his jeans. When the end of the rope hit the water next to him, Enos snatched it and wasted no time tying it around Hank. When it was ready, he pulled out his knife, cut the vine, and then shouted. "Pull him up."

Hank had become very quiet the past fifteen minutes. Enos didn't doubt that the young man's body temperature had dropped dangerously. The warm sun on the rock above would do him good. In fact, it would do Enos himself a lot of good. He was getting chilled, and he'd only been in the water a fraction of the time Hank had.

As Hank slowly ascended from the black water of the cavern, Enos decided to try to warm himself up a little. After cutting the vine off Hank, Enos swam slowly toward the far wall, making certain his knife was secure. He glanced back frequently to see how they were coming with Hank. It was slow, but they worked steadily. To his surprise, Hank had managed to lift his arms, and he now had both hands gripped tightly to the rope.

When Enos reached the far side of the black hole, he touched the wall, turned, and worked his way slowly along it. He'd thought a lot about Hank's so-called creature the past few minutes, and he had become very curious. He'd only gone maybe twenty feet before his hand touched something that made him recoil. He'd found Hank's creature. Instead of swimming frantically away, however, Enos, ever the diligent detective, investigated closer. What he found caused him to almost retch. He had a feeling that if Hank had known what he'd touched, he would have panicked even worse than he did.

"Enos, we're ready for you," Manny called out.

Enos hadn't kept track of the effort above, and he realized he'd taken several minutes investigating his gruesome find. "There's something else here that you need to pull up," he shouted. "It could wait, but I'm not coming down in here again, and I don't think anyone else wants to either."

"What is it?" Manny called.

Enos avoided answering directly. "Deedee may want to go back to the car. I don't think this is something she needs to see."

"She's tending to Hank right now. I don't think she'll want to leave, but I'll check," Manny responded. He stepped out of Enos's line of sight for a moment, then came back to the rim. "She says she's not leaving Hank until he's ready to walk."

"Have your men help Hank back to the car, and make sure she goes with them. Then have them come back here. I want to get this over with and get out of here myself."

Manny again disappeared. When he returned to the rim, Enos was swimming back across the pool. "I'll need a short piece of rope," he called up. "Can you drop me one?"

Manny did as Enos requested, and Enos again began swimming to the far side of the cavern. He tied the rope around the object he'd found, then called back up, "Are they gone?"

"They are," Manny called down. "And they promised they'd hurry back as soon as they got Hank and Deedee in the car."

"Good, lower the rope then, and I'll start swimming."

By the time the three young islanders had returned to the rim, Enos was ready for them to begin their next task. When they found out what they had to do they balked, and only by getting angry did Manny convince them to start pulling their burden out of the cavern.

They had a more difficult time pulling Enos up. He was larger than Hank, and the men were getting tired. After a few very hard minutes, Enos finally was pulled to the surface. What he had suspected below was soon confirmed. "Stu Chandler won't be bringing any more runaway girls to your peaceful island," Enos said. "And I think you have some big questions now for Rapper."

"I don't think so," Manny said.

"Did he get away?" Enos asked. "I was hoping the superintendent and some of the other officers would catch him."

"I guess you could say they did, in a way. They intercepted the boat he'd taken, and when he tried to make a run for it, he got too close to shore and snagged some rocks below the surface. He went down with the boat."

Enos thought about that for a moment. "Are they sure?"

"Of what?" Manny asked.

"That he went down with the boat?"

"Well, the superintendent said that the boat sank, and no one saw Rapper come up," Manny explained.

"How far from shore were they when Rapper hit the rocks?"

"They were maybe five hundred feet or so from shore, a little close to be running a boat. It was going past the point of Hope Town and heading for the open sea. I don't know what he was thinking," Manny said. "He could never have outrun our boat."

"Maybe he knew that," Enos answered.

"What are you saying?" Manny looked intrigued.

"Maybe he intended to ditch it and swim to shore. If I were the superintendent, I'd check the sunken boat," Enos said, "just to be sure."

"I'll see that he does that," Manny agreed.

Enos took Deedee back to the motel after they'd dropped Hank off at his house. Hank was feeling a lot better and was anxious to have a shower and get something to eat.

"And get some rest, young man," Enos had told him.

He had the same advice for Deedee. He let her into her mother's room, explained that they'd gotten her suitcase from the airport, then said, "You'll want to clean up and get some rest. I'll arrange for someone to provide security and to bring you something to eat. I don't think it would be wise for you to be seen in town until it's confirmed that Rapper really went down with his boat."

"When are you going to go and look for Mom?" she asked.

"Just as soon as I can get a shower and change into some clean clothes," he said. "I may have spent over an hour in the water, but I've never felt so dirty in my life."

"Aren't you hungry?" she asked.

"I'm starved, but I'll grab something on my way out to search," he said.

"Are you going alone?" she wanted to know.

"No, Officer Younger is coming with me. And the superintendent is going to send some more people out later if he can."

"I want to come," Deedee said. "I'll shower fast."

"I don't think that's a good idea," he said.

"She's my mother," Deedee argued as tears filled her eyes. "And it's my fault she's lost. Please," she begged, "I want to help."

Enos thought about it for a second, then said, "Actually, I would feel better knowing you're with me. I'm really not convinced we're rid of Rapper."

"I'll hurry," she promised.

\* \* \*

Meredith awoke with a start. The last thing she remembered was listening to the sound of footsteps and thinking she was near death. She didn't know how long she'd listened to someone walking around before she'd fallen asleep. Whoever it had been apparently had not seen her, and that surprised her. She didn't think she'd crawled that far into the bushes. She was also surprised that she woke up. She'd fully expected to die in her sleep.

She thought about her loved ones and realized that she really didn't want to die. She was needed. Deedee needed a mother. She had to admit that Enos probably didn't need anyone, but she wanted to see him again, to get to really know him. She hoped he wanted to get to know her better.

There were footsteps again. Was someone doing some kind of work here in the forest? But that was absurd. What was there to do here? She had to find out.

Meredith wanted to live. She felt better than she had before she'd fallen asleep, and she now believed she just might make it if she could get someone's attention and get them to help her. She tried to cry out, but nothing much resulted from that effort. She turned on her side, and though it was difficult, it wasn't as painful as it had been earlier. She forced herself to sit up even though it hurt her hands to push. Once she was sitting up, she couldn't see anything but leaves. Meredith, as sick and injured as she was, found that she could actually smile at her own predicament. The rest must have done her a lot of good, she decided, not only physically, but psychologically as well.

The only way out of the bushes was to scoot forward. It was slow, and it hurt her hands and bare feet, but before she knew it she was almost free of the shrubbery. She heard a footstep very near, and since she still couldn't see clearly, she reached up and parted the branches. She found herself staring into a pair of large, glaring eyes.

\* \* \*

Enos had been quite surprised when he'd finished cleaning up and knocked on Deedee's door to find it answered by a grinning Hank. "Hey, you're supposed be resting," Enos scolded.

"While Deedee's mama is out there alone?" he said.

"But you can't possibly—" Enos began.

"I'm fine," Hank broke in. "I got out of the black hole alive. Deedee, she says she's going with you to find her mama. I'm going too."

"Okay, we can certainly use the help," Enos said. "But I'm not coming back again until she's found."

He'd stepped into the room as he was speaking. Deedee looked like she was about ready. She was just pulling on a pair of shoes over clean socks. Her freshly washed hair was still wet but it shone, and her face was radiant. Enos felt a pain in his heart. She looked so much like her mother, and he missed her mother a great deal. He had to find her.

"Are you ready?" Enos asked.

"Yes," she said. "And I know we're going to find Mom." Her face lost some of its glow when she added, "I just hope she's not hurt bad or something."

Manny pulled up out front just as they left Meredith's motel room. He had three other officers with him. "You may have to take your car as far as the turnoff," he said when he saw that Enos had help. "We can crowd up in here after that."

They stopped at a grocery store, stocked up on food, juice, and water, and then sped southward down the highway. Hank told them he had already eaten, and he looked tired. Enos was tired as well. In fact, he couldn't remember the last time he'd slept, but he had no time for that now. When they reached the turnoff to the lighthouse forty-five minutes later, Enos was anxious to get started, Deedee was very quiet, and Hank was asleep in the backseat.

Manny and the three officers were waiting at the intersection to the Hole in the Wall Lighthouse road. Manny quickly approached Enos as he got out of the car. "You were right," he said.

"About what?" Enos asked. Then it hit him. "Rapper's not with his sunken boat?"

"That's right," the officer admitted. "They've had divers there for quite a while. It's not very deep where it went down. I'm afraid Rapper has vanished. What made you think that might happen?"

"I'm getting to where I know the way his devious mind works. I'd guess that he probably dove off the far side before the boat actually hit the rock. And he was probably equipped to stay under the water all the way to shore," Enos suggested.

"That's exactly what the superintendent said," Manny admitted.

Enos shook his head. "I wonder what he plans to do now. I'm sure glad I brought Deedee out here with me," he said.

"Why are you glad I came?" the girl asked from behind Enos.

Enos turned around. Hank was standing beside Deedee. The nap in the car had done wonders for the young man. He looked as alert and bright as could be. Enos tried to flash Deedee a smile. "Because you're good company," he said.

"No, that's not what you meant," she said stubbornly. "So why are you glad I came with you?"

Enos decided this girl was as sharp as her mother, so there was no use trying to fool her. "Rapper apparently got out of his boat alive."

The look on her face and on Hank's told of their healthy fear of the man. "Do you think he'll try to come here?" Deedee asked, her eyes wide with concern.

"Only if he's a fool," Enos said. "Now let's get to work. We've got to locate your mother before dark."

# CHAPTER 26

After some discussion, it was determined that they would travel a short distance into the forest on the road to the lighthouse, and then Enos, Hank, and Deedee would begin to walk south, parallel to the road but through the forest to the east. The officers that came with Manny were assigned to walk in the same direction on the west side of the road, and Manny decided to drive south until he came to Rapper's abandoned red Jeep—unless he found Meredith before he got there.

Enos had Hank walk closest to the road, with Deedee next, and Enos walking the deepest route in the forest. They agreed to stay close enough to see and hear each other. It was very difficult hiking, but all three were determined. The officers on the other side of the road worked the same way. In addition, each team of searchers carried a handheld radio.

It took close to thirty minutes to walk the first mile, and Enos kept looking up nervously, knowing that the afternoon was growing late and that darkness was only a few hours off. They had covered another half mile or so when Enos noted what appeared to be tracks of several horses beneath his feet.

He shouted for Deedee and Hank to stop and join him for a minute. Then he radioed Manny, who was now approaching the abandoned Jeep. "Manny, would there be people riding horses in this area?"

"That's pretty unlikely," Manny responded. "There are hardly any horses on the island. There is a small band of wild mustangs, but the last I heard of them they were staying close to some agricultural property a few miles from here."

"Wild horses," Enos repeated in amazement. "So if I saw horse tracks, which I am in fact looking at right now, it's unlikely that there would be anyone riding them?"

"There would be no one riding horses, I can assure you of that," Manny said. "Abaco's famous wild mustangs must be down this way."

"Okay, thanks," Enos said. "I guess we'll keep looking. I guess you haven't seen any sign of Meredith."

"Nothing," Manny said. "And I'm just walking up to the Jeep now. Nothing seems to have been disturbed here. I'll start back in a minute, I guess."

Enos clipped his radio to his belt. "There are wild horses out here?" Deedee asked in awe. "I love horses. So does Mom."

"Really," Enos said as he continued to study the tracks. "Maybe you can come riding out at my place when we get back, you and your mother."

"We'd love that!" Deedee said, then she choked up. "If we find her."

"Stop that, Deedee," Hank said with uncharacteristic gruffness. "We'll find your mama. God saved me from the black hole. He'll save your mama too."

"I hope so," she sobbed.

"Yes, we'll find her," Enos agreed. He was stooped over, still studying the tracks. "There aren't any shoes on any of the horses that came through here," he observed. "They must have hooves like flint. You'd think this rock out here would tear their feet to pieces." He looked up. "They were traveling east, deeper into the forest. But that's beside the point. We don't have time to worry about a few head of wild horses."

Hank and Deedee had started back toward the road to resume their search when they both stopped in their tracks. A horse whinnied in the distance to the east. Enos turned toward the sound. A second horse whinnied. It sounded like they were only a few hundred feet away. "Something's startled them," Enos said. "I wonder . . ."

It seemed like a remote possibility, but something inside told Enos to follow his instincts, so he told Hank and Deedee, "Let's follow these tracks for a little ways. Be as quiet as you can."

For the next five minutes, the three of them moved as silently as possible through the woods, picking their path carefully. There was a slight breeze blowing toward them, making it unlikely that the horses would pick up their scent. Deedee stayed behind Enos, and Hank brought up the rear. Enos led them around a dense thicket, following the path the horses had taken, and came to an abrupt halt on the edge of a clearing.

What he saw before him took his breath away.

There were four head of small, sturdy horses milling about on the far side of the open space. A fifth horse was standing very still, the ragged, bloody figure of a trembling woman leaning against its front left shoulder. The woman's head was resting on the horse's neck, her long, red hair spread haphazardly across her shoulders and down onto the horse's mane.

In that first instant of seeing Meredith, Enos wanted to shout her name and dash across the clearing to her. But he recognized that if he did that, the horse would spook and she'd be sent sprawling to the ground. Enos turned and put a hand to his lips as Deedee approached him, followed closely by Hank. Deedee's mouth opened as if to shout in delight, and Enos said softly but firmly, "Shh."

Tears spilled from her eyes. Hank also spotted the tender scene before them, and he kept very silent. Both of the young people then looked to Enos for guidance on what to do next.

Enos reasoned that the best thing to do would be to stand there and let the horses discover them on their own. Then maybe Meredith would look over and see them. For two or three minutes, the three searchers stood very still. Enos suddenly realized that his radio would spook the horse if it came on, and he reached down to his belt and switched it off. The horses continued to mill about, all but the red roan acting as Meredith's support.

Meredith lifted her left hand, which, even from a hundred feet away, Enos could see was caked with blood. She gently and methodically stroked the roan's neck. Then she lifted her head and stood a little straighter. The horse quivered and turned its head toward her, and she gently placed her right hand on its back.

A gray mustang circled the roan and sniffed at Meredith, and its nose, pressed gently against the back of her neck, caused Meredith to again lean against the shoulder of the roan. After that, one by one, the other three horses crowded around, each in turn sniffing at the stranger. Enos kept praying that the horses wouldn't suddenly spook and send Meredith sprawling beneath their hooves.

Eventually the other mustangs moved away, their curiosity apparently satisfied, and began to graze on the short grass and bushes in the clearing. Only the roan still stood quietly, allowing Meredith to continue to pat its back and stroke its neck.

Enos, whose senses were at their keenest, noticed the direction of the breeze gradually shift until it finally carried their scent toward the horses. The gray one was the first to look up from its grazing and spot the three motionless searchers. It didn't seem unduly alarmed. Enos concluded that even though these mustangs might be considered wild, they were clearly used to people. As long as they did nothing to alarm them, their presence shouldn't send the horses racing away. A sorrel horse looked up next, and when it spotted Enos, Deedee, and Hank, it whinnied. That prompted the other two grazing mustangs to lift their heads and stare toward them.

The red roan was the last to turn its head and look. It shifted its feet slightly, and Meredith pushed herself free and stood alone on unsteady feet, one hand still petting the horse. When the roan moved a little more and snorted, she slowly turned her head as well.

Her right hand flew to her breast and her mouth fell open when she spotted what the horses had seen. The roan stepped away from her and joined his little band as all five of them began to drift eastward, away from the new strangers. Enos didn't wait any longer. He started a quick walk across the clearing, Deedee and Hank staying right with him.

Meredith began to sway, and Enos broke into a run, sending the five mustangs stampeding into the forest. He reached her as she began to topple forward and swept her into his arms. Weeping unashamedly, he knelt down and gently laid her on the ground, cradling her head in one arm.

Deedee dropped beside them, pressing her face against her mother's cheek. As she sobbed an apology, Enos pulled a bottle of water from a clip on his belt and began to moisten Meredith's lips and then to offer her little sips of water.

"Hank," he said after a couple of minutes, "pull this radio off my belt and let the others know we've found her."

Hank, grinning, his round, black eyes sparking, did as Enos asked. Enos couldn't help but smile as he listened to Hank say, "Manny, we've got Deedee's mama. Enos is holding her. She's gonna be okay. But she's got blood all over herself."

Hank then attempted to guide the others to their location. The three officers arrived within ten minutes. By then, Meredith had recovered her voice a little and had accepted a few bites of an orange that Deedee had carried in a small knapsack around her waist.

"I must look a sight," Meredith said to Enos in a weak, scratchy voice. "I'm sorry I look so awful."

Enos shook his head. "You really are a wonderful sight. I've been worried sick about you. I'm . . . we're so happy you're alive."

Deedee kept saying how sorry she was, and finally, Meredith took her hand and said, "Sweetheart, we're together again. That's what I've prayed for since you left. I love you, Deedee."

After they carried Meredith back to the car, they treated her numerous cuts, abrasions, bruises, and blisters. She was able to eat a little and gradually drank some more liquid. On the way back to Marsh Harbor, she gave them a brief account of what had happened to her. "I thought I was going to die today," she confessed. "I could hear these footsteps, but I didn't have the strength to call out. And it's good I didn't because it must have been the horses and I might have frightened them away. I fell asleep, and when I awoke, I felt stronger, and I heard the footsteps again."

"Was it the horses?" Deedee asked.

"Oh yes, but I didn't know that until I was trying to get out of the bushes where I'd fallen asleep and found the roan staring me in the eye," she said.

Deedee chuckled. "I told Enos you liked horses," she said.

"It's just good you didn't know they were supposed to be wild mustangs," Enos added. "You might not have tried to befriend them."

Meredith agreed. "The rest of them seemed wary of me, and the roan kept going off and grazing, but he'd always come back. He was standing there when I was finally able to get to my feet, and he let me lean against him. Something about him gave me energy and courage I didn't think I had left," she said.

"Mom, Enos promised we could ride his horses when we get home," Deedee said.

Meredith glanced at Enos, and he looked over at her. When their eyes met, he smiled. "I hope you will," he said shyly.

"I'd love to," she responded.

They followed Manny to the little medical facility where Meredith was given immediate and solicitous care. "You're badly dehydrated and have some infection, but other than that, your injuries are all superficial. We'll keep you here tonight, and tomorrow you should be able to leave," the doctor told her.

As he spoke, Meredith had been watching Enos closely. His eye sockets were sunken, his cheeks were sallow, and his head kept drooping. She turned to the doctor. "I think you better check Detective Fauler."

The doctor glanced at Enos for just a moment and then said, "All he needs is some sleep. I'd say he's been awake for two or three days."

"That's close," Enos agreed. "I'll be fine after I get some sleep. But tonight, I think I better stay right here with Meredith."

"You'll do nothing of the sort," she retorted. "They'll take good care of me."

"And I'm going to stay with her too," Deedee announced.

"Then I'm definitely staying," Enos declared.

"Enos, really," Meredith began. "Deedee and I could use some time alone together."

"I know that," Enos said as he stood up and approached her bed. "But Rapper is still on the loose, and I'm not taking any chances on either one of you getting hurt again."

"But we're safe now, Enos. Rapper has no reason to come after us again," Meredith insisted.

"You work with criminals for a living," Enos said. "In defending them, you must hear all their excuses for what they've done. Do their reasons always make sense? In fact, do they very often do things that are reasonable? They often do things out of hate, for revenge, or just for the morbid thrill of it, don't they?"

From the look on her face, Enos knew he'd made his point. "But he wouldn't dare," she said feebly. "Maybe he and Stu will just go off somewhere."

Enos tried to control the expression on his face, but he was so fatigued that he must have let something show when Meredith mentioned Stu. "Enos, there's something you aren't telling me," Meredith said sternly. "Please, after all we've been through these past few days, don't leave me out now."

Enos tried to avoid a discussion of Stu's fate by saying, "There's a lot we haven't told you yet. But there'll be time for all that. And you can tell us what you went through. I'd like to hear every bit of it, every minute of what you did after Rapper hauled you away. But it can wait, at least until tomorrow."

Deedee weighed in on the discussion, unwittingly coming to Enos's aid. "Yeah, we gotta tell you how Hank saved me from Rapper, and about the wild boar that chased me, and how Rapper threw Hank in the black hole, and how Enos jumped in and saved him."

Enos laughed. "Enough," he said. "We'll fill her in on all of that later. Right now, she needs rest."

"And so do you," Meredith said to Enos. "Go to the motel and sleep."

"I'll call you if we need you," Deedee promised.

Enos gave in at last, but not before he went in search of Superintendent Brown. Someone was going to keep an eye on Meredith and Deedee, and if the superintendent couldn't spare anyone, then Enos would sit in the car outside the little medical facility and do it himself.

Superintendent Brown committed the help, and Enos was asleep almost before his head hit the pillow.

* * *

Rapper had been watching when a couple of officers knocked on the door to his Hope Town bungalow. He'd seen them coming and slipped out the back door. They'd been here once before, just a few hours after he'd reached shore. That time he'd waited to enter the place until after they'd left empty-handed. He smiled to himself when they forced their way in this time only to come out a few minutes later, looking puzzled.

As soon as they'd gone, he went back in. He knew he needed to get away from this part of the Caribbean, but he had unfinished business first. People didn't mess with his perfectly organized life and get away with it. It was almost dark, and soon he would be on his way back to Marsh Harbor. He'd already scouted around the harbors in Hope Town and had a sleek, fast boat picked out.

In the short time between now and dark, Rapper stayed in the bungalow, changing into some of his friend's clothing, smiling as he did so.

He tried on two pair of dark glasses he found in a drawer and selected a pair with large lenses. They added a nice effect, he decided as he studied his image in the mirror. No one had ever seen him in glasses, not even dark ones, and he also never wore hats on his deeply tanned, shaved head—until tonight. He found one in the bungalow that put the perfect finishing touch to his disguise. He slipped a gun inside his pants. It was time to go back to Marsh Harbor.

Rapper slipped up to a dock in a small harbor and tied up without seeing a soul. Then he walked a few blocks into a residential area, where he had soon hot-wired a car, a sporty little Mazda. He began to cruise casually around town. There were still a lot of people on the streets. It was early yet.

He finally stopped and knocked on the door of a cheap, yellow house just a short distance from where Hank and his mother lived. "I'm having car trouble," he told the old gentleman who answered. "I need to call a friend and see if he can come tow me home."

The fellow showed him the phone, and Rapper dialed his own number, faking a conversation for the sake of the old man and his wife, who were listening. After hanging up, he said, "They'll be about ten minutes. Thanks for the use of the phone." He started for the door, then stopped. "I'm getting dense," he said with a chuckle. "I was just driving over to the police station to tell them that I heard someone talking about that girl and her mother who are missing. I forgot all about it after my car died. Maybe I could call the police from here. You folks heard about what happened, I suppose?" he said very calmly.

"Yes, it was a terrible thing," the man said. "We've lived right here since the day we got married. Nothing as terrible as this has ever happened. This is always such a peaceful place."

"We're so sad things are changing," his wife added.

"Yeah, well, I know how you feel, but I suspect it's just a one-time thing. After they find those people, things will calm down here again," he said.

"Oh, haven't you heard what's happened now?" the old fellow inquired with a raised eyebrow.

"Heard what?" Rapper asked, pleased that he might be getting some useful information. That was the entire reason he'd knocked on the door to this house. But he didn't expect to hear what he did.

"The women, they're both okay. They found them, both the girl and her mama." The old fellow went on to say that they had taken the woman to the medical facility to treat her for cuts, bruises, an infection, and serious dehydration. "She was out there by the road to the old lighthouse," the old man said. "She's lucky to be alive."

The man's wife then explained to Rapper that they were planning to keep the poor woman overnight at the medical facility. Then she added her own guess that they'd be leaving Abaco in a day or two. "But that terrible murder, that's what's really bad," she said, shaking her head.

"Murder, that sounds horrible," Rapper said with what he hoped was just the right touch of alarm. "Well, I guess what I had to tell the cops is old news now, so I'll be leaving. Who was murdered?" he asked as if he was just a little curious. "Anybody from Marsh Harbor?"

"Some poor guy. They're not saying his name, but they say he was found drowned out in that terrible black hole. It was the most horrible thing," the fellow said.

"I wonder how that happened," Rapper said, really wondering how they'd found Hank so fast.

He was really surprised by what the old man said next. "They're just lucky there weren't two dead men in there. Young Hank from down the street, he was alive when they found him. The white guy, he was dead." The old fellow then praised the detective from Utah who had come to Abaco looking for the girl, explaining that he had saved Hank's life. "Poor Hank," he said, shaking his head sadly.

Rapper had learned enough. He had more scores to settle tonight than he'd initially thought. Maybe he'd start with Hank again, and this time he'd make it fast and final. Then he'd deal with the cop from Utah. He'd save the medical facility until last. After he evened the score with the woman lawyer, then maybe he'd just take Deedee with him in the stolen speedboat.

# CHAPTER 27

After slipping from his bed and getting dressed, Hank checked on his mother. He was tired, but he'd had enough rest to keep him going for a few hours. He was still worried about Deedee, scared about what Rapper might do if he was, in fact, still alive. Somehow, Hank had the feeling that he was.

He went out the back door and jumped on his bike. He pedaled around the house, but before he came out of the shadows he saw a car coming very slowly up the street. He didn't recognize it, but just seeing it made him worry about his mother. He dropped his bike in the bushes, hurried inside, and woke his mother. "I don't mean to scare you, Mama, but we've got to get away from here. And we must not turn on the lights. I'm sure the house is being watched."

After all that had occurred, she didn't even bother to ask her son why he was so worried. She slipped from her bed and told Hank she'd hurry and dress. As she came out of her bedroom a couple minutes later, Hank heard the front doorknob being turned. It was just a slight sound, but it scared him, and he hurriedly rushed his mother out the back. Together, they crossed the yard to their neighbor's house, hunkering down beside a palm tree to watch their own back door.

Three or four minutes passed before a shadowy figure came out, entered the shed, then walked out of it and peered into their car. He slammed a fist against the car's door before walking around to the front of the house. "Stay here," Hank whispered to his mother. "I'll be right back."

He ran from the neighbor's yard and through his own before dropping to his knees beside the house. He crawled rapidly but as quietly as he could past his bike and peered into the street. Someone was just getting into a car, a blue Mazda—the same one he had seen just minutes ago. The driver had a hat on, a jaunty seaman's cap, and as he settled into the driver's seat of the car, he put on a pair of dark glasses.

Hank wasn't fooled. He ran swiftly back to his mom, and they returned to the house together. It was in shambles. In the short time Rapper had been in there, he'd torn, thrown, and kicked everything of value. Hank's mother wept as he grabbed the phone. He thought about calling the police first, but decided to instead call the motel where Enos was staying. He assumed that both Enos and Deedee would be asleep there right now. The manager wasn't happy about being disturbed, but Hank was frightened for Deedee, and he demanded to talk to Enos Fauler, the cop from Utah. "And be fast," he said to the manager. "If he doesn't answer his phone, bust down his door."

The manager protested strongly, but Hank was not about to accept anything short of speaking with Enos. He explained that a lot of trouble would happen and that the cops would be very angry if he didn't awaken Enos right then.

"Okay, okay," the manager grumbled.

Hank turned to his mother while he was waiting for Enos to answer. "Watch out the window, Mama. If that car comes again, we better get out of here fast."

* * *

Enos was sleeping lightly, tossing and turning, worried about Deedee and Meredith over at the little medical facility. When the phone began to ring, he was instantly started awake. His heart pounded wildly as he picked up the receiver. All the worst things that could have happened to Deedee and Meredith were rushing through his head.

"Hello, this is Enos," he answered, trying to be calm.

"Detective Fauler, this is Hank."

"What's happened Hank? Are you okay?"

"I'm all right," Hank said calmly. "But Rapper, he just left my mama's house after he busted everything we have. I saw him coming, so we got out before he could get us. But I think he's after Deedee again. We've got to stop him, sir."

"What's he driving?" Enos asked even as he parted the curtain slightly and peered outside.

"A blue Mazda," Hank said. "He was wearing a silly black hat that sticks up in the front and dark glasses. It doesn't look like Rapper, but it is."

"Thanks, Hank," Enos said, his mind racing. "Deedee isn't here. She stayed with her mother at the medical—"

Hank broke in. "Are the cops there?" he asked.

"Yes," Enos answered. "But I have a feeling Rapper will come here first. He probably thinks they're here. You stay put and take care of your mother. I'll call the police and have them alert the officer at the medical facility."

"I've got my mama's car," Hank said. "I'm going there."

"No, don't do that," Enos warned. "He wouldn't hesitate to hurt you. You stay put, Hank. I'll take care of things from here."

Enos had a feeling Hank would go anyway, but he figured there was nothing he could do about it. He called the superintendent at home, waking him up. The superintendent promised to alert his officers and then said, "I'll meet you at the motel, Enos."

Enos dressed rapidly, belted on a gun, shoved a knife in his boot, and eased his way out the door. After checking for the Mazda or a man with a black hat and seeing neither, he ran to the end of the motel and slipped around the edge of the building. He made it in the nick of time because just then, a little blue Mazda pulled up and parked in the empty spot beside Enos's rental car.

The man who got out of the car was wearing dark glasses, some baggy pants and a tropical-print shirt. His hat was black with the rim pushed up in front. Enos watched him slowly approach the motel, looking around as he walked. He never would have guessed it was Rapper if it hadn't been for Hank's description.

Enos expected the man to go to Meredith's room first, and he was surprised when he went straight to Enos's room instead. Enos had no doubt it was Rapper who once again looked about furtively before he slipped something into the lock. It had to be a lock pick, Enos thought. And Rapper was good with it. In seconds, the knob turned, and Rapper looked about once more as he put the pick in his pocket, pulled a knife from his belt, and gently pushed on the door.

Enos silently thanked the Lord for Hank's call, knowing the young man may very well have saved his life. He pulled his gun and hurried to the door, then stood beside it with his back to the wall and waited. He could hear Rapper moving about inside. There was a crash, and Enos had visions of his suitcase being upended. A car pulled up, and Enos recognized Superintendent Brown who leaped out and slipped silently up the stairs. When he joined Enos a moment later, he whispered, "Is Rapper in there?"

"He is," Enos said. "And it's his intent to do me harm."

The superintendent had a pistol in his hand. "Should we go in after him?" he asked.

Enos glanced at the superintendent. "No, let's wait for him to come out," he said.

"Good idea." The superintendent stood beside Enos as they waited. It didn't take Rapper long to check out the room. When he opened the door, he was cursing softly. The long blade of a knife gleamed in his grasp as he poked his head out—and looked straight at Enos. For a big man, Enos could move fast. Rapper tried to shut the door, but Enos brought his gun down with such force on Rapper's wrist that his hand flew open, and the knife clattered on the walk. Then Rapper stumbled backward, trying to shut the door as he moved.

Enos threw his weight against the door, and Rapper was thrown back against the bed. Enos moved swiftly, realizing that one of Rapper's hands wouldn't be of much use to him right now, but the other one was certainly pulling a gun. He leaped on Rapper, slapping his good hand as it came up with the gun, which flew to the floor. As Enos pulled Rapper to his feet by the neck of his shirt, Rapper tried to swing a fist at Enos's face, but Enos swung him around and threw him against the wall with such force that the wall shook. Superintendent Brown turned on the light as Rapper cried out in pain. He tried to kick Enos, but the detective was bigger and stronger and he slammed Rapper against the wall a second time. Superintendent Brown joined the fray and wrapped an arm around Rapper's neck. Rapper didn't stand a chance against the two officers, and though he continued to struggle and kick, he was soon facedown on the floor with handcuffs fastened behind his back. He howled, shouting that his wrist was broken, but Superintendent Brown wasn't sympathetic. "You've caused more trouble on my island than any ten men in the past ten years," he growled. "Keep yelling and I'll clamp them tighter."

Enos stood back, relief flooding over him. He offered a silent prayer of gratitude, then when more officers arrived, he headed for the medical facility. Enos found Hank and an officer talking beside the front door. Hank had a big grin on his face. "Superintendent Brown called. He says you got Rapper."

"Rapper will no longer be a problem," Enos agreed. "And it's thanks to you. In fact, I owe my life to you. He came to do me under."

Hank's grin grew wider. "Guess we're even then."

"Yes, we're even," Enos agreed.

Then Hank's smile faded and he said, "No, we're not even. You jumped in the black hole to get me out. There's no way I could make that even."

Enos put a big hand on Hank's shoulder. "I've known a lot of brave men in my time, but what you've done the past few days is as brave as anything I've ever seen. We're even, Hank, believe me. Let's see how the gals are doing."

Deedee and Meredith were doing fine.

"They're both asleep," the nurse said.

"I'd like to just see for myself," Enos told her. "If you don't mind. We won't disturb them."

Meredith was sleeping on her back, her long red hair spilling around her face and across her pillow. As Enos stood beside her bed, he felt a tug on his heartstrings. She was the most wonderful person he'd ever met. And he'd almost lost her before he even got to know her well.

Deedee was sitting in a recliner at the foot of her mother's bed, also sleeping peacefully. Enos smiled as he gazed at her. He had a feeling she had grown up a whole lot the past few days. He also suspected that she and her mother would have a better relationship now. He prayed it would be so. And he hoped he would be able to be a part of their lives as well.

As he and Hank left the room a minute later, Enos turned to Hank. "You know, my life will never be the same."

Hank smiled at the big officer. "Neither will mine, sir."

# EPILOGUE

**Three months later**

Meredith left the courtroom and found Deedee waiting for her in the lobby, excitedly waving an envelope.

"Look what I got," the girl said as she hurried to her mother.

"Looks like a letter," Meredith said, smiling. "Who's it from?"

"Hank." Deedee beamed. "He wrote to tell me he's read the Book of Mormon, and he says it seems like it's true. He said he couldn't imagine anyone making it up."

"That's great, sweetie," Meredith said. "We can certainly be grateful for what Hank did for you. It's good that you can do something to repay him, and sending him that Book of Mormon was a great idea. Who knows where reading it might lead him."

"You know, Mom, I still can't believe he risked his life for me. I wonder what made him do that."

"He's just a very good, decent person," Meredith said. "And I, for one, am grateful that there are still people like him in the world."

"I am too," Deedee said. "I'll never forget him. I may never see him again, but I'll always remember him. He helped me see how important you are, and what a big mistake I'd made."

Meredith felt her eyes begin to moisten, so she said, "We have a surprise planned for tonight."

"Oh, what?" Deedee asked.

"Enos has invited us out to his place for dinner," Meredith said.

"Wow, that's great. What time are we going?" Deedee asked as they left the courthouse and stepped outside.

"In just a few minutes."

Deedee looked at her watch. "Isn't it a little early for dinner?" she asked.

"I'm going to do the cooking," Meredith told her daughter.

Deedee gave her mother a sly look. "Is he wanting you to get used to his kitchen?" she asked.

"That could be part of it, I suppose," Meredith said, her face turning just a little red. "After dinner, we're going to go for a ride again."

Deedee looked very intently at her mother, then said with intensity, "I really think Enos is great, Mom."

Meredith put an arm around her daughter's shoulders and whispered into her ear, "Would you like to know a secret?" she asked.

"Sure," Deedee said.

"I think he's great too," Meredith said. "But don't you dare tell him. That's my job, and I intend to get it done real soon."

"I think he really cares for you too," Deedee said.

"Oh, you don't know that," Meredith chided.

Deedee grinned. "Oh yes, I do. I can see it in his eyes when he looks at you—and I'll bet it won't be long until he tells you."

"I hope you're right," Meredith said. "I surely hope you're right."

# ABOUT THE AUTHOR

Clair M. Poulson spent many years in his native Duchesne County as a highway patrolman and deputy sheriff. He completed his law enforcement career with eight years as Duchesne County Sheriff. During that time, he served on numerous boards and committees, including serving as president of the Utah Sheriff's Association and as a member of a national advisory board to the FBI.

For the past thirteen years Clair has served as a justice court judge in Duchesne County, and currently represents the justice court judges of the state as a member of Utah's Judicial Council.

Church service and family have always been priorities for Clair. He has served in a variety of stake and ward callings, and he and his wife, Ruth, an accomplished piano teacher, have five children and nine grandchildren. Clair also does a little farming, his main interest being horses. Both Clair and his wife currently help their oldest son run *the* grocery store in Duchesne.

Clair has always been an avid reader, but his interest in creating fiction began many years ago when he would tell bedtime stories to his small children. They would beg for just one more "make-up story" before going to sleep. Now he enjoys opportunities to make up stories for his grandchildren. *Runaway* is Clair's tenth published novel.

# Excerpt From

# WHISPERINGS

"Please, Daddy . . . It's dark down here . . . Please don't leave . . . The light, Daddy. Turn on the light!" Jessie awoke wet with perspiration. She embraced the moist feather pillow.

Sleep was a distant illusion.

Exasperated at the thought of another sleepless night, Jessie pulled herself out of bed and began her nightly ritual. She headed for the bathroom sink. She knew her effort to wash away the haunting dream with a few splashes of cold water would surely fail, so she then donned her favorite flannel robe, set off toward the kitchen and poured a cup of warm chamomile tea. In her younger days, something stronger—probably Jack Daniels—would have occupied the well-used mug. Having relinquished that vice, her taste buds had since found their way to herbal teas.

After carrying the tea down the almost nonexistent hallway to her study, she placed the cup on the edge of the desk. She slipped into the soft leather of her favorite chair, pulling her knees to her chest. A brightly colored, crocheted afghan carefully concealed any patch of skin still exposed to the cool night air.

Wrapping her cold fingers around the warm mug, she slowly began to sip. She drew in a deep breath and calmly allowed her eyelids to close. The little girl locked in the dark, musty basement inched her way back. Jessie's eyes flew wide open as her head jerked. The splashing tea descended to its usual spot on the table as she rummaged through the neatly stacked papers.

Reviewing the day's client profiles had become a necessary predawn diversion. While she'd often chided her associates for working too late at the office, she had recently acquired the same habit. Only the environment was different.

Blaring music jolted Jessie's head from the back of the chair. She had somehow managed a nap. Annoyed at the clamor of the alarm clock in the next room, she couldn't help but wonder what idiot had invented such a ridiculous way of awakening someone. Moving reluctantly, she reached the clock on the nightstand by her bed.

In the quiet, Jessie sat staring, contemplating the soft, inviting space that awaited just beneath those covers. Slithering into the cool sheets, she lay for several minutes. When her mind drifted to the image of the scared little girl, she quickly rose and stumbled, half-asleep, toward the shower. Her eyes were not yet capable of suitable focus. The light of the sun, inching its way through the bedroom curtains, offered no additional motivation to see clearly. She had envisioned a long, therapeutic shower, the soothing massage of the hot liquid cascading down her back. Within minutes, however, reality emerged and the warmth dissipated. The cold water began its usual interruption, forcing an early end.

Today would be the first time in four years she would arrive to the office late, but most likely, no one would say a word. It was, after all, common practice for partners to be late.

She glanced through her apartment. Any quest for cleanliness would have to be put on hold. The bed would go unmade, and clutter would linger until evening. She threw on her favorite teal knit suit, which fit snugly around her slender waist. Her long, naturally dark auburn hair would normally be braided, coiled, and pinned up into a more sophisticated look. Today, however, it was pulled back with a black barrette.

Choosing to speed at a minimal excess of five miles over the limit ensured Jessie's late arrival. A mere fifteen-minute tardiness was more acceptable than the prominent delay a speeding ticket would have created.

Pulling in next to Susan Steed's car, Jessie sighed. She knew Susan would be the one client to comment on her late arrival. Time-conscious Susan—as the office personnel referred to her—usually arrived fifteen minutes early, hoping for more time in therapy.

To avoid a confrontation in the lobby, Jessie slipped in through the back entrance. No revolving door, no digital keyless entry, and no welcoming committee. Just an ordinary key lock with a simple sign above the door that read *Stone, Welch, Arnold, Winston & Associates. Psychologists. Please use front entrance.*

Jessie had barely opened her office door when the receptionist's voice came over the intercom, "Susan Steed has been waiting."

"I'm on my way." Jessie didn't care for the newest receptionist. Tendra was the niece of the founding partner, Elliott, and made sure everyone knew it. At eighteen, her grades had barely allowed her to graduate from high school. Tendra's explanation for the purpose of schooling was to educate oneself on the "who's who" of society. She was petite, barely five feet tall, and had shoulder-length, curly, vibrant red hair. Jessie often felt the urge to ask if her bloodlines coincided with Little Orphan Annie's. Tendra packed a constant air of false sweetness. After thirty seconds of conversation with her, anyone endowed with even minor intelligence grew nauseated.

Jessie set her open briefcase neatly on the corner of the desk, leaving her access to the client files she had taken with her the night before.

Jessie's office was small in comparison to those of the other partners. She wasn't one to want to impress clients with expensive furniture, art, or knickknacks. The limited space sported a basic oak desk, a filing case, a coat rack, bookshelves, a couch, and a comfortable, high-back chair for clients. Her license to practice and a picture of a local mountain scene graced her walls. She was comfortable here.

Taking a deep, calming breath, she walked out to meet Susan. Meeting clients in the lobby often helped them feel more at ease. However, Susan, who was already walking toward Jessie, didn't care much for courtesy, protocol, or anything else that wasn't originally *her* idea. She pushed past Jessie and slumped into her usual position on the gray fabric couch in the corner. Jessie had barely closed the door before Susan started in on the frustrations that currently littered her life's path.

Jessie positioned herself behind her oaken barricade, retrieved Susan's folder, and laid it neatly on the desk. As Susan's voice droned on, Jessie moved to her briefcase and removed the files, placing them in the pile before her. She leaned back in her chair and placed her hands on the armrests. The hum of Susan's voice began to have its usual effect. Entirely void of any and all excitement, Jessie's eyes became dull and glassy. She lost herself in thoughts of the morning's nightmare.

"Jessie!" sobbed Susan. "Are you listening to me?"

Jessie blinked her eyes rapidly and turned her attention directly to Susan's unfriendly stare. "What? Oh . . . I'm sorry. Please go on."

"Go on? I've repeated my question twice now. Aren't you listening?"

"Of course I'm listening, Susan."

"Then what did I just ask?"

"Well, . . . you . . . ah . . ."

"Oh, what's the use! First you're late—"

*There it is*, Jessie thought silently.

"And then you don't even listen to me. What am I paying you for, anyway?" In one fluid motion, Susan was gone.

Jessie softly closed Susan's file, wishing that her frustrations could close with the same ease. *These nightmares are invading too much of my sleep. I can't seem to concentrate. I'm focusing on the wrong things. You'd think seven years as a therapist would supply me with a greater ability to hide my anxiety and stress from the outside world! I'll have to call Susan in a couple hours and apologize. I'll blame my behavior on the flu or P.M.S.*

Opening the file drawer to her right, Jessie put Susan's folder away and pulled out one marked *Karen Edwards*. Karen would most likely come in swearing this was the week she and the kids would leave home. How many times would she keep saying this until . . .

A slight shadow darkened the file, interrupting Jessie's thoughts. "Oh, hello, Elliott," she said, trying to appear calm. "I didn't hear you come in."

"Not surprised. Seems par for the course lately," rasped Elliott. Standing at just five feet nine inches, Elliott Stone had the ability to make even the tallest of partners and associates feel inferior. Approaching fifty, he was distinguished in appearance. Slivers of gray glistened throughout his dark hair as well as his neatly trimmed mustache and goatee. His eyes, though seemingly undistinguished in color or size, had a piercing quality. He always dressed impeccably and commanded instant respect. He took his work seriously, often being the first in and the last to leave, which made for an endless client waiting list.

"What? What's par for the course?" Jessie asked, silently chastising herself for not using the last few minutes to gain a more professional composure after Susan's abrupt departure.

Elliott rested on a small space on the side of her desk, his hands on his knees. "Oh, . . . not hearing, not listening, not understanding. At least that's the impression I get from your clients, not to mention the staff and everyone else with whom we are mutually acquainted."

"Listen, if you're talking about what just happened with Susan Steed, well, . . . that's just . . . I'm not feeling quite . . ." She searched for words, her face twisting in thought.

Elliott stood and quietly closed her office door. "It's not just this client," he said as he pushed the high-back chair closer and sat. His eyes closed momentarily as he leaned forward and searched for the empathy that he must surely apply. "Jess, I have someone I'd like you to meet. It's time you worked through things."

Jessie's pulse quickened. She felt a rush of blood soar to her head and a sharp pain pierce her chest. If she didn't know better, she would swear sweat was dripping from her entire body.

"I don't follow, Elliott."

"We both know the signs, Jess. I've tried to figure out what's going on inside that head of yours, but you push me away."

"Who am I meeting?" Jessie snapped, her calm veneer beginning to crack.

Elliott opened the door and motioned for his friend. Jessie rose cautiously. Feeling cornered, she leaned against the bookshelves behind her desk, slowly folding her arms across her chest, again sensing the perspiration build.

"Jessica Winston, meet Ryan Blake," Elliott said, watching her intently.

Jessie stared blankly. Her mouth felt heavy, as though it were filled with sand. She knew that name.

"This is by far the calmest response I've received yet. It's nice to meet you, Dr. Winston," Ryan said, extending his hand.

Jessie drew in a slow, deep breath, ignored Ryan's hand, and turned to face Elliott. "I would like to speak with you privately."

\* \* \*

Ryan's six-foot-tall frame was unaccustomed to being shoved out a door, especially by a woman. However unbelievable, the door slammed, barely clearing his nose. He was one of Denver's most renowned therapists. During Ryan's college years, a near-photographic memory had established his reputation as a walking encyclopedia of psychology. If he didn't know the answer to a problem, there most likely wasn't one. Aside from that, his riveting blue eyes, black, wavy hair that fell to just above his shoulders, and skin tanned dark by the sun caused almost every female head to turn for a second look. Some simply stared. Ryan adjourned to the lobby and pretended to be engrossed in a magazine.

Ryan's practice had begun during his midtwenties. His client list contained not only the names of normal, everyday people, but also well-known therapists searching for their own path back to reality. After twelve years of practicing, however, he decided he had had enough. His deceased wife's inheritance, as well as his own bank account, had allowed him to put psychology behind him.

It had been a month since Ryan and Elliott first communicated about Jessie. Following a week of daily conversation, Ryan was forced to put his early retirement on hold. After all, he owed Elliott. But sitting in a lobby waiting for a client to agree to talk with him—on someone else's terms—was a first for him, too. Clients used to come to *his* office. If he hadn't owed Elliott so much, he'd be in his comfortable leather chair, in front of his big-screen TV, sipping a seltzer.

\* \* \*

"Elliott, what is going on?" Jessie barked furiously. "You have no right—"

"Dr. Blake is a friend, Jess," Elliott cut in. "I trust him. I've asked him to spend some time with you, to help you deal with your childhood issues. Nothing else is to be on your agenda, with the possible exception of eating and sleeping."

"Are you crazy? You can't *force* someone into therapy. Besides, he isn't 'Dr. Blake' anymore, if my memory serves me right. I'm certainly not going anywhere with anybody! I can't afford to leave my clients for a week! Not to mention whatever *he's* charging. And besides, doesn't he have enough to handle with his harem of fifteen wives?" she spat angrily, pointing toward the door.

"Jess, Mormons don't do that anymore. You're intelligent enough to know that. And your clients will be fine. I'll have Tendra reschedule all your appointments."

Jessie was more than angry now. It wasn't unreasonable for Elliott to be concerned, but for Little Orphan Annie to be brought into the know—*that* was crossing the line.

"And since his license has expired, technically you're just going off with someone who can offer help. There isn't any fee. I've taken care of everything. And you *are* going through with this. I plan to see you in my office first thing in the morning, a week from Monday. That'll give you ten days to pull it together."

Jessie exploded, "Ten days! You and I both know that is totally unrealistic. We've been over this. I'm doing the best I can. You can't *tell* someone they have ten days to pull it together. He's a *man,* Elliott! What were you thinking when you called him? And what happens if I choose not to do this? Huh?" With each sentence, her hands flailed wildly through the air.

Elliott made no reply as he left the office. Jessie turned around and glared out the window, anger and frustration set firmly upon her face.

After several moments, she turned and found Ryan in her office, gazing at her. The look on her face could peel wallpaper. "This is still *my* office, *Mr.* Blake. It's obvious you're without manners or you would have knocked."

"It's Ryan. I did knock—three times. I figured you were a little preoccupied and didn't hear me," he replied casually.

Jessie regained her composure. After all, this man wasn't at fault, she told herself; it was Elliott. "I'm sorry, Mr. Blake. I'm a little on edge. Look, there's been a misunderstanding. Elliott hadn't cleared this with me before he sent for you. And, well, your services aren't needed. If you stop by Elliott's office on your way out, I'm sure you'll be well compensated for your trouble." Jessie motioned toward the door.

Responding to her dismissive gesture, Ryan threw the smile he was famous for. "Elliott said you usually leave around five-thirty on Fridays. I'll be back then to pick you up."

His grin gave Jessie the leverage she needed to be rude again. "I'm surprised you find this so amusing, Mr. Blake. Personally, I find this whole ordeal quite ludicrous. We shouldn't even be having this conversation. I won't be going anywhere with you at five-thirty."

Ryan's countenance withered as the door slammed in front of his 250-pound frame—again.